A RUSTON FESTIVAL BOOK

Mardi Gras MEET CUTE

BY JESSICA BOOTH

This is a work of fiction. Any names or characters, businesses or places, events or incidents, are fictitious. Any resemblance to actual persons, living or dead, or actual events is purely coincidental.

First edition: October 2025

Identifiers: ISBN 979-8-9870116-8-3 (trade paperback)

Other Books
by Jessica Booth

A Match Made in Autumn

A Picture Perfect Summer

The Spite Before Christmas

The Race to Midnight (novella)

Dear Reader:

This book containst themes of parental verbal and physical abuse toward an adult child, as well as conversations about discrimination against women in both relationships and in the workplace. There are conversations about sobriety and past alochol abuse. It also contains open door sex scenes between consenting adults.

While this book is a rolicking good time with a HEA, I urge you to first and foremost protect your mental health.

Happy reading!

XOXO, Jessica

For Kirsten:
This book wouldn't exist without you.
Thanks for believing in this story,
and pushing me to grow.

JESSICA BOOTH

JESSICA BOOTH

Prelude

LAUREN

January 5, Epiphany Eve

If anyone knows about cutting it close to a deadline, it's me.

My red Jimmy Choo slingbacks clack on the worn tile of the grocery store floor. It's nearly 10 p.m. and there's barely anyone else here so close to closing time. A couple of people in scrubs browse the aisles while shelf stockers work with earbuds in. Not much competition.

Surely they have at least one left.

I round the aisle to the bakery section, my gaze snagging on the flickering fluorescent light that makes the deserted space feel just a little bit creepy. Someone should fix that.

I scan the display tables. Cupcakes. Cookies. Birthday cakes.

And then I spy it. There's one left. A sigh whooshes from my lips.

It's been a rough day. Late breaking news meant a long day at the office. We had to change out the front page story, and it's my job as editor-in-chief to sign off on the final copy and images. It's a role I take seriously, especially since my intense work ethic and attention to detail are what propelled me into the top spot at the local paper before age forty.

But that also means I didn't leave work until after our local bakery was closed. And missing that particular deadline means I didn't get a chance to pick up one of their king cakes. That's a problem because tomorrow is Epiphany, the official beginning of the Mardi Gras season. And you can't start Mardi Gras without a king cake.

The frosted cinnamon cake, baked in a circle and decorated with purple, gold, and green sprinkles with a plastic baby tucked inside, was my sole responsibility for dinner with my sister and her family tomorrow. And I've had to work during so many of those family dinner invitations lately that I can't let Leslie down.

I'm still thinking about missing out on family things, oblivious to anything but pastry acquisition, when I reach for the last king cake box. At the exact same time, another hand lands on it.

It startles me, and I chastise myself for not paying better attention to my surroundings. I glance up, thinking a grocery store employee might be picking it up for the evening.

Whiskey-colored eyes dancing with humor look back at me. The owner of those eyes grins, his face crinkling with the motion, a hint of crow's feet making an appearance at the corners. He's handsome, ruggedly so, with his long brown hair pulled into a bun on top of his head and scruff dusting his sharp jawline. But the way he's dressed makes me think he just rolled out of bed. His flannel PJ pants and Nirvana t-shirt give me flashbacks to my college days. But who am I to judge? After all it *is* nighttime. Pajamas feel appropriate, more so than my pencil skirt and heels.

"Attention shoppers," an automated voice says over the store speakers. We both glance up, as if searching for the disembodied voice amid the store's rafters. "The store will be closing in five minutes. Please choose your final selections and make your way to the register to complete your purchase."

I glance to where both our hands still sit atop the king cake box.

I've been called a bitch countless times in my life, as many competent and confident women are, especially those who have leadership positions and firm boundaries. But I'm not a disagreeable person. I just know what I want.

And right now, I want this king cake.

I open my mouth to tell this handsome stranger that I got here first and I really need this cake, already preparing my reasons why. But before I can speak, he removes his hand and takes a step back. He lifts both hands in surrender.

"Take it. It's all yours," he says in a vaguely familiar deep, rumbling voice.

I hesitate, drawn in by his words, by the tone of his voice. It sends a shiver through my body, tapping into a long buried something that I'd all but forgotten. And that something makes me study his features just a bit longer. Wide eyes, mischievous smile, tall frame. I'm staring, I realize.

But so is he.

I take an involuntary step toward him and he moves in my direction at the same time.

I open my mouth to speak, to say who knows what, when a grocery store clerk walks up to us.

"We're about to close the bakery down," he says kindly. Then he walks back behind the bakery counter. The spell binding me to this stranger evaporates.

I tear my gaze from him and look down at the white box in my hands with Mardi Gras clip art all over it. I know I should be polite and tell him that he can have the cake if he wants it, but I'm desperate enough to accept his chivalry. So, I pick up the box and nod once in thanks. His smile widens as he tucks his hands into his pockets and shrugs.

I turn and walk toward the register, heels clicking as I go. When I reach the cashier, I glance back over my shoulder, but the stranger is gone. And with him goes that odd physical tug that felt like a hook behind my sternum. Weird.

When I tap my card, I tell the cashier to have a good night, then head outside to my car. And as I turn the engine, I'm surprised to find that, for once, my brain hasn't slipped into the running lists of work tasks that cycle endlessly in my head.

Instead, my thoughts linger on those brown eyes and the pull to that stranger who surrendered the last king cake. I glance to where it sits in my passenger seat and smile. Not a bad way to end a night. Not bad at all.

Interlude

PEACH 103.1

Epiphany, January 6

This is Beau Baxter and you are listening to Peach 103.1. Tonight on the show, we're talking about missed connections—those times when you encounter someone for a brief moment, perhaps just a minute of their life, and then you go your separate ways. Moments when you felt a connection, perhaps even a romantic one, with a stranger.

Log onto the Peach 103.1 app and share some of your missed connections. Here are a few that listeners have submitted this evening.

Dan from Farmerville says, "You were walking your gray pit bull around the park with your headphones on, wearing a pink sleeveless shirt. I was sitting on a park bench on my lunch break. We made eye contact when you passed me. I felt the air crackle between us."

Well, good luck to you there Dan. May your Lady Love walk her dog across your path again.

Fran from Choudrant says, "You were installing a new roof on my neighbor's house. When the sun was at its highest, you took your shirt off and crawled down the ladder. You didn't have anything to drink, so I went inside and got you water. You said, 'Thank you, pretty lady.' Mr. Roofer, if you come back to work on that roof again, please knock on my door."

Well Fran, I hope things don't stay up in the air with you for long!

Last one before we go to commercial break.

Max from Ruston says, "You walked into the bakery section of the grocery store wearing red heels and a black skirt. It was late at night and there was only one king cake left. We both wanted it. But I wanted you to be happy more than I wanted that cake. I hope we run into each other again, and maybe next time we can share a slice of king cake."

Well, there you are folks. Keep using that app and let us know about your missed connections. Who knows, that other person might just be listening tonight.

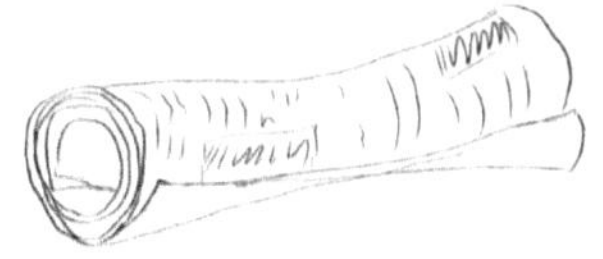

Interlude

THE RUSTON DAILY LEADER

January 6

Ruston to Welcome First Mardi Gras Krewe and Parade

By Lauren Landau, Editor in Chief

Ruston enters North Louisiana's most-festivals-per-capita scene once again with its very own Mardi Gras krewe and parade. While the Mardi Gras season thrives in the lower half of our state, especially New Orleans, other nearby North Louisiana cities, like Shreveport and Monroe, have their own krewes and parades. These events will include a ball to induct members of the local community as royalty, and, of course, a parade.

"We're thrilled that the mayor approved the Chamber of Commerce's proposal to found a Mardi Gras krewe for our great city," said the krewe's board president, Gladys Beaumont. "We hope bringing this Louisiana tradition to Ruston will draw tourists, stimulate the local economy, and get the good times rolling."

"This is a great opportunity for the community to come together," said Amelia Hebert, Vice President of the Chamber of Commerce. "We are incorporating community fundraisers and events into the lead-up to the parade, so everyone can participate and help strengthen our city."

Mark your calendars for the krewe ball on Saturday, February 22. The parade will roll on Sunday, March 2. And the whole season will conclude with Fat Tuesday on March 4. More details on this year's theme will be announced in the coming weeks.

Chapter 1

LAUREN

January 7

"Are you sure you have the right person?" I ask, phone clutched to my ear. I turn to look out my office window, my slicked-back blonde ponytail swinging over my shoulder.

"Lauren, you're perfect for this," Gladys Beaumont says. "Ruston is finally establishing its own Mardi Gras krewe and we need a royal court. You're important in the community and have poise and grace. You're exactly who we want as our first Krewe of Persici Queen."

Rarely am I speechless. I tap my stiletto against the faux wood floor in my office, my gaze sliding over to my computer where emails continue to flood my inbox. I need to make the final call on tomorrow's front page story. I don't have time for this.

"Ms. Beaumont," I say, trying to keep my tone even. "I really don't have time with all of my work responsibilities. And you can certainly find someone younger."

"Lauren, you are young!" she exclaims. And I suppose my forty years do seem young to her seventy. "And you work too much," she continues. "Every time I see you, you're doing an interview, or meeting with one of your reporters. This will be fun. And besides, it's a great story for the paper."

"Or a conflict of interest," I mutter.

"Nonsense. No one in Ruston cares a lick about all that. Besides, our steering committee already met and voted. You were the winner. No one else even came close. So, you see, you've got to do it."

I close my eyes and rub my fingers over them. I have to handle this delicately. Gladys Beaumont owns the biggest funeral home in town and they are one of the newspaper's best advertisers. I already know that if she insists on me participating, I won't have much of a choice. She's a nice woman with a good heart who gives to local charities. But, more importantly, Gladys is the true queen of Ruston and pissing her off is the equivalent of social suicide.

I sigh. I've lost this battle and we both know it.

"So, you'll do it then?" Gladys asks, delighted.

"I'll do it," I agree, the pointed tip of my shoe tapping more quickly on the floor. "Just email me the schedule and I'll be at the parade."

"Oh dear, that's only a small part of being the Mardi Gras queen, you know that," she chuckles. "First we have the ball, where we'll introduce you to the court. We've already got the event in the works. It's going to be a delight. My partnership with the local flower business means it will be a sight to behold. And we've hired one of the paper's former photographers to document the night. You remember Katie."

My brain is still stuck on "ball." Visions of myself laced into a ridiculous dress with sequins for days while I stumble around the dance floor parades through my head. "Oh," I stutter.

"Don't worry, dear, you'll be perfect. I'll have our secretary email you the shop where you'll go for your dress fitting. Our inaugural theme is 'Birds of a Feather,' all plumage and finery."

Bedazzled flamingos dance through my mind and I start to feel lightheaded. I know Mardi Gras well enough to know that there is nothing low-key about the clothes required for balls and parades. I run my sweat-slicked palm over my charcoal-colored pencil skirt, my red shoe tap, tap, tapping.

"Yes, well, that sounds fine," I swallow, desperate to end this call before I'm told that I'll have to give a performance in front of every wealthy woman in the Delta. "I really have to get back to work, but I'll touch base with you soon."

"Lovely, dear. We'll be in touch with information about the fundraiser, dance lessons, costume fittings, and ball rehearsal. Have a wonderful day!"

She ends the call and I allow myself ten seconds to process what I've just been roped into, the extensive list she just rattled off. The amount of time that I'll have to be away from my desk to make it all happen, and the subsequent late hours I'll need to work to make up for it.

My stomach gurgles, nerves churning with feelings of being overwhelmed to make anxiety gumbo. Taking on this additional role is going to be hell. My brain starts doing mental gymnastics to find a way to back out, but I think I'm stuck.

Gladys Beaumont wants me there. Wants me to have a starring role in Ruston's first Mardi Gras parade. Managed to get a whole committee to vote me in. A committee likely composed of people who support the newspaper. So unless I'm in a hospital bed for the next six months, I guess I'm doing this thing.

A small voice, one I thought lost to time, perks up in the back of my mind at the words "dance lessons." I danced in high school and it was one of my one true joys, my escape from the hard knocks of teen angst. I had forgotten about that version of Lauren, that hopeful, ambitious soul who used to dream of jetéing across a stage in a tutu or shuffling around in my tap shoes.

I smile to myself at the memory. But then my computer screen catches my eye and that bowl of anxiety soup in my stomach bubbles once more.

With a deep breath, I pull up my email and get back to work.

Chapter 2

MAX

January 7

I watch as the end of Nirvana's "Smells Like Teen Spirit" winds down on my computer screen, then slide my headphones into place and lean into the microphone.

"And that's it for tonight, folks. This is Beau Baxter, signing off. Have a great evening, and remember to tell your mom you love her."

I cut to commercial, then queue up the programming that runs overnight at the radio station. Mentally, I'm already home on my couch with my scruff of a miniature Schnauzer, Magnolia aka Mags, curled up on my lap and last night's pizza warmed up for dinner.

Just as I stand to leave, my phone buzzes. I unearth it from my pocket to see that my grandmother is calling. I wonder what it is this time. Perhaps she found a "respectable" job for me with another one of her colleagues, or Dad's hounding her again with lectures on how I'm overdue to get married and buy a real house.

I love my grandmother. Truly. She may not agree with my career choice as a radio DJ, but she's always been there for me, even when I made reckless decisions in the past. Way more than my parents ever were, which is why I always take her calls.

Maybe she just wants me to pick up her groceries. At 8 p.m. On a Thursday.

"Hey, Grandma," I say, answering the call. I snag my keys and metal water bottle covered in stickers from the National Parks. Then I walk down the radio station hallway, waving at the lean night crew as I leave work and head out to the parking lot.

"Max, my darling grandson!" she exclaims. "How was your show tonight?"

I hesitate. She rarely asks me about my job. And I can't help but wonder if she's angling for something from me. "About the same as usual," I hedge.

"Good, good. So, I'm calling, dear, because I need you to do something for me."

I silently congratulate myself on being right. She wants something.

"Need me to pick up your groceries?"

"No, dear, nothing like that. I need you to come to an event. Or, a couple of events, actually."

"Grandma, I already told you, I don't want to work for one of your friends. Finance just isn't my thing, and I don't think I'd last out on an oil rig."

"While I would love it if you finally agreed to one of my networking meetings," she sighs, "that's not what this is. This is more of a . . . party."

I fumble with my keys as I unlock my decade-old silver Toyota Tacoma—another thing my grandmother thinks I should upgrade. "Uh huh. Something tells me this isn't the kind of party I would normally go to," I say, thinking about the 90s tribute band I saw last night.

"It's better," she chirps.

I climb into my truck and crank it up. Reaching into the console, I unearth a ponytail holder and quickly wrestle my long dark hair into a respectable bun. "Somehow I doubt that."

"It is. Because I'm in charge of it and I need you there. It's the ball for our first ever Mardi Gras krewe. We need to have a full house. And I'd like you to be there as my guest."

I sink back into the seat, truck still in park, and wait for the next shoe to drop. "What's this really about, Grandma? You can have any guest there you want. Why me?"

She hesitates, something she almost never does. "Well, the thing is, our steering committee this year wants members of the local media to be on the royal court. And, likely because you're my grandson, you were nominated," she pauses. "And then unanimously voted for."

My mouth quirks in a grin. "For what, Grandma? Prom king?"

"Almost! Mardi Gras King."

I cackle, deep and echoing inside the small, dark cab of my truck. "You want me to be the king of your highfalutin royal ball?'"

"Oh, now, don't say it like that," she chastises, but then I hear her laugh, soft and wispy, over the phone. "And I must say, I know I'm biased, but you will be the most handsome man there."

"Grandma, you know I can't ever tell you no. When is it? What do I need to do?"

"I knew I could count on you," she says.

I jot down the information on the upcoming events on a grocery store receipt unearthed from my glove box. Then I tell my grandma goodnight and end the call. The whole drive home, I imagine myself in a sparkly suit dancing the night away with half the town's single women.

This won't be so bad. Not at all.

Chapter 3

LAUREN

As I walk into the spacious community center hall, I note the tall ceilings arching above me and the large windows letting in the January sun. My heels click on the lacquered wooden floor as I step around oversized stacks of large cardboard boxes and look around.

There's not much in here yet. I see the stage where the band will set up and a few folding chairs. I try to imagine how this space will be transformed for a sparkling Mardi Gras "Birds of a Feather" ball.

I'm the first one here, early for once. I tuck my earbuds into my ears and decide to enjoy the rare few minutes I have to myself. I hit play on my audiobook, the rumbling tones of the male narrator declaring his love to his female love interest over pancakes making me smile.

Back in my reporting days, I always liked to take my time getting a feel for the space and the environment so I could paint the story. I collected any background tidbits, jotted down details that made a story come to life. And while I'm more an editor than a reporter now, years spent climbing the journalism ladder aren't quickly forgotten.

I walk around the space, allowing myself these few moments to get lost in my audiobook. I imagine the fantasy of the perfect happily ever after with a man written by a woman. This is the only kind of romance I allow myself to indulge in. My real life ones have never come close to the ones in my books. Plus, I can start and stop these fictional romances whenever I want. Just as things start to get spicy in my audiobook, I hear the building's door open and bump the wall. I spin around.

"Oh, hello, dear," a cheery voice calls.

I reach for my earbuds and pop them back into their case. Gladys enters from the back door, along with three others. The steering committee. They must be.

I recognize Amelia Hebert, the wife of Rhett, one of my reporters, and wonder if he had anything to do with my placement on this court. I decide to ask him a few pointed questions the next time I see him. But Amelia smiles broadly and waves to me. Next to her is an older man, probably in his early sixties. William Fisher, the head of the community bank. And finally, Dorothy Willis, Gladys's best friend and head of the Junior League.

Well, no backing out now.

"Lauren dear, we're so glad you agreed to be our first queen," Gladys says. And I truly believe she's delighted. Maybe this won't be so bad.

She introduces me to the rest of the committee, and Amelia steps in to give me a hug. She explains that they have invited members of the local media to participate in the royal court this year, and I wonder if Amelia has roped her husband into being one of the krewe captains.

I follow them around the space, listening distractedly as Gladys and Amelia discuss how everything will be set up for the ball. We pause as we get to the front door, next to the towering stack of cardboard boxes.

"Part of being queen means having your very own special beads for the parade," Gladys says, motioning to the boxes. "Normally, royalty funds their own throws, but in our inaugural year we've gotten a town grant to get this going. So, I've taken the liberty of picking out some for you. As the queen, you'll be our royal peacock, and all your throws—the cups, doubloons, beads—will have peacocks on them."

The reporter and fact checker in me wants to speak up and tell her that the male peacocks are the ones with all the beautiful feathers, but saying that in front of her steering committee probably wouldn't be well received, so I just nod.

Gladys reaches past me to the open box on the top of the stack and fishes out a teal-colored set of Mardi Gras beads, with a gorgeous, full-colored peacock pendant at the end of it. She hands it to me. I study the piece, noting the way the gold on the beak shimmers. It is lovely, if a bit gauche.

"And this," she says, reaching into another box, "is your mask."

She holds up a mask that would certainly offend the peacock it's supposed to represent. The feathers on it are huge, extending out a foot past the end of the mask in all directions.

"Go ahead, try it on," she insists. I glance at the four faces staring at me with bright smiles. Though I swear Amelia is verging into giggles.

Hesitantly, I reach for the monstrosity and slide it onto my face.

It's heavy. And itchy. And I can barely see out of it. I reach up to try to adjust it so I can see through the eye holes and drop the beads I'm holding in the process. They clatter loudly to the wooden floor, the sound echoing as they bounce. Embarrassed, I reach down to try to scoop them back up, apologizing. But the bird mask blocks my vision, and I can't see anything.

Perched on my heels, I fumble around, feeling for the damn things.

"I'll grab them," Amelia says.

I step back to get out of the way and my shoe heel lands on something small, round, and hard. I try to straighten, but my pencil skirt holds my knees hostage and my gigantic bird mask obstructs my vision. All attempts to right myself fail as my heel snags what must surely be the missing Mardi Gras beads. I slide, and like a windblown yard flamingo, my arms pinwheel.

I hear cries from my audience and a couple of, "hang on, I'll help!" before I collide with the stack of boxes.

At first, with my face pressed up against a box, I think they've saved me. This could have been much worse. *This is fine*, I tell myself.

But then, it's not fine. Not at all. Because the boxes give, tipping over like a stack of bricks, and my balance takes me with them.

In one big crash, I fall with them, my peacock mask flying backward, finally allowing my field of vision to re-emerge. So I see it as it all goes to shit. Strands of beads tumble out of boxes in an explosion of teals and magentas. The doubloons spin away, the oversized coins like wheels on the run. And I go with them, slipping and sliding as the round beads of plastic suddenly become the vehicles of my destruction.

I sidestep the tumbling boxes, fumbling and slide across the floor, swearing and stumbling, unable to stop my forward momentum. I'm going to break something—my arm, my leg, my face—if I can't stop myself. And then it's too late. Gravity is winning. I'm going down. I close my eyes and brace for impact, preparing for my body to hit the floor.

And then I come to an abrupt stop as I plow into something solid . . . not the floor. No, it's too soft, too vertical, too tall. And it cradles me? My whole body locks up.

"Well, I do love it when a beautiful woman falls right into my lap," a warm male voice rumbles beneath my ear.

I hesitate, then slowly, so slowly, lift my gaze to a chin covered in a cropped, dark beard. I pull back and try to stand, my ankle nearly crumpling on my broken shoe's heel.

"Whoa there. Easy now," he says, his tattooed arms coming up to hold my forearms and steady me. "You okay there, birdie?"

I lift an eyebrow at that. Birdie? Is he referencing the peacock mask that started this mess? Oh, I know he did not just make fun of me after the embarrassment I just experienced.

"Fine." My words come out more clipped than I intend.

"Well, look who's here just in time," says Gladys as she delicately steps around the debris-laden floor. "Your king has arrived just in time to catch you."

She sounds way too fucking delighted.

I shove down my embarrassment and turn to study my would-be rescuer. My stomach flips. He looks instantly familiar and my thoughts crawl through every wrinkle of my brain as I place him. He's handsome in a rugged, likes to spend weekends in a tent, kind of way. Strong jaw dusted with beard scruff. Familiar dark eyes glinting with hints of gold. Long, dark hair tied back in a bun with a few strands slipping loose. Wearing… sweats?

Handsome. Way too damn handsome. And he smells all woodsy, like he spent the afternoon hiking through a pine forest. It all clicks into place and my stomach feels like it's being tugged right through my bellybutton. The grocery store. The last king cake. Our lingering stare and that moment of nothing that held the potential for *something*.

And now, here we are, staring at each other again. Suddenly, where his arms brace my forearms to steady me seem to burn. I yank them away.

"Well, this isn't how I planned to introduce you," Gladys says, looking between the two of us, smile widening. "But this will do. Lauren, meet our Mardi Gras King. This is my grandson, Max Beaumont."

Chapter 4

MAX

I know who she is, of course I do. The woman from the grocery store. Lauren, as my grandmother helpfully told me before I got here. And I can't stop staring at her—again. Something about her has latched onto me and I can't seem to shake it. She's gorgeous—her blonde hair, blue eyes, and long legs are my personal brand of catnip. But there's something more. Interesting doesn't feel like a strong enough word. Captivating.

My grin widens. This gig my grandma signed me up for just keeps getting better.

I lean in, close to her ear so only she can hear me. "Nice to meet you, Lauren. Officially."

Her scent wafts around me, peppermint and coffee. My heart pounds a little harder. I glance down. No wedding ring. Perfect. It's been nearly six months since my last date. No one's caught my interest. Lauren Landau, however, has my full attention.

She nods her head, professional, despite her impressive skate over Mardi Gras beads in a pencil skirt and a now abandoned bird mask. "Nice to meet you, Max."

"Now, where were we? Should we continue our tour of the space?" my grandmother asks, trying, and failing, not to glance at the beads scattered across the floor. It's a look I've seen from her a thousand times over the years. One that says, *I don't know quite what to do with this situation, but I'm going to power my way through it anyway.* The same one she used when Dad would berate me for not wanting to join the family business.

"You go on ahead," I say to Lauren and my grandmother. "I'll start cleaning this up." I glance at the mess. Beads, doubloons, and cups have rolled everywhere, under tables and stacked chairs. This is going to take a long time. But I'm trying to show my grandmother that I can be a gentleman.

And maybe impress Lauren. Just a little.

"I made this mess. I'll help clean it up too," Lauren says.

"You have a broken shoe," I say, glancing down at the one in question. She stands unevenly, one heel decidedly missing. "There's no way you can help pick up in those."

She hesitates for only a moment, then leans down and removes both of her shoes, revealing perfectly painted, candy apple red toenails. It's oddly distracting. Oh God, am I a foot man? No. Never once in my life has that thought crossed my mind. But right now, fuck. And now I'm staring. And it's getting awkward. I wrench my gaze to Lauren's face. She's got her chin jutted out, ready to fight if it comes down to it.

The challenge on her face ignites a fire deep in my gut. And man, do I love a challenge.

I smirk. She raises an eyebrow.

"And you're going to be able to help clean up in that skirt?" I challenge.

In response she bends at the knees and scoops up a handful of beads, then walks over to a toppled over cardboard box, straightens it, and tosses the beads inside. Then she turns back to look at me and crosses her arms.

The way she just moved, the challenge? I groan internally. That really did something for me. That fire inside me grows hotter. I cross my arms, mirroring her pose, refusing to show her just how much she's getting under my skin. I flex my hands where they're tucked in close to my chest, trying to ease some of my building desire. I like the chase. And I can already tell that Lauren will put me through my paces.

My grandmother clears her throat. The young woman next to her tries to cover her laugh with a cough.

I reach down and scoop up two handfuls of beaded necklaces, then march over to where Lauren stands. I reach past her, brushing her arm, as I dump them in the box. In answer, she squats and begins to fill her arms with so many strands of beads that I briefly wonder if she'll be able to stand back up. But I shouldn't have questioned her. She rises like she's holding nothing more than a pillow full of feathers, and dumps them into the box.

Like the caveman I am, I imitate her, making sure to scoop up even more, my arms spilling over with glinting shades of purple, gold, and green.

And then she shuffle-runs with her legs constricted in her skirt, her bare feet slapping across the tile floor as she squats and lifts more, then hurries over to an empty box and to unload her haul.

It's on.

In a blink, the two of us are darting across the floor, scooping up piles of beaded necklaces, cups, and doubloons and emptying them into boxes like toddlers promised a treat for whoever cleans the most.

And it's *fun*.

For the next fifteen minutes, I let myself get lost in the competition. Reaching down to pick up everything I can get my hands on, watching Lauren shuffle across the floor in that tight-fitting skirt. Getting distracted by it in the most delicious way. I keep hoping to catch her staring at me, but she seems to be wholly focused on our spontaneous competition.

The floor is nearly clean. I spy one more handful of beads and grab it, then dash to the open box. Lauren is closing in on it at the same time. The desire to win this absurd competition courses through my blood. I sprint, aiming to pass her and drop my final collection into the box. But Lauren seems to have the same idea.

And as we both reach for the box, our arms collide, the beads she's holding inadvertently slapping my bare wrist. We drop the last of them in the box and turn to look at each other. Her chest is heaving, her cheeks flushed. She's wild and beautiful, and in the right situation, those lips might be intensely kissable.

I realize I'm breathing hard too, and a bead of sweat trickles down my cheek and into my beard. I lift my arm and brush it away, Lauren's gaze following the movement. Her eyes linger on my forearm. I flex it. Just enough to keep her attention on me. Her gaze snaps to mine, her sea-blue eyes flaring. In annoyance or desire, I'm not sure. But I'm willing to find out.

"Well," my grandmother's voice cuts through the tension between us. "That's one way to take care of a problem. I appreciate your dedication to your new roles, and your supreme focus. Now that that's out of the way, shall we finish our tour?"

"I'm Amelia, by the way," the brown-haired young woman next to my grandmother says, stepping forward and extending her hand. I take it, noting the glinting diamond ring on her left hand. It's habit to check, one I can't seem to shake even now. "I'm on the board of the new krewe with Gladys and represent the Chamber of Commerce," she says, laughter dancing in her eyes.

I meet the rest of the group, then obediently listen as my grandmother gives us the lay of the land, noting where things will be set up for the ball. Lauren does the same, pointedly ignoring me, though I swear I can feel the air crackle between us. I try to catch her eye several times, but fail. She's too busy staring fixedly at every spot my grandmother points to, acting like the area where the band will play is the most interesting thing in the whole damn world.

As our walkthrough draws to a close, my grandmother hands us each a piece of paper with a list of events we're expected to attend. Dinners, rehearsals, costume fittings, a fundraiser, dance lessons, the ball, a float loading party. And, of course, the Mardi Gras parade.

"This all looks great," I say, trying to lean into the charm that has served me well most of my life.

My grandmother smiles at me indulgently. "I'm so glad to have both of you as part of this very first event for our city. Amelia will send you both an email with information on next weekend's fundraiser. I look forward to seeing you there."

She gives me a hug and shakes Lauren's hand, then turns to leave. Lauren walks over to scoop up her shoes, then trails after her. I hurry to catch up.

"Hey, Lauren," I call out. She pauses, but doesn't turn around. I walk to stand in front of her.

"Since we're going to be the star couple of the event," I begin. She frowns. "I thought it might be nice to get to know each other a bit. Make things easier, more fun. Would you like to go to dinner Friday night?"

She starts to respond, then stops. "Sorry, I can't. I have to work." Then she walks past me and out the door. She doesn't even glimpse over her shoulder on her way out.

It's been a while since I've been totally and completely rejected like this. And damn if I don't love the challenge. I will always respect what a woman tells me. If she says no, then she means no. And I won't push Lauren now because I know she means it.

But I plan to win her over, to show her I'm a good person. So when I ask again, her answer will be different.

Chapter 5

LAUREN

I don't know what got into me. Why the hell was I running around that damn community center hall bare-footed, in a pencil skirt, scooping up beads like I was in an elementary school relay race? I haven't behaved like that since, well, elementary school.

But something about Max ignites my competitive side. The part that inspired me to chase down the stories that ultimately landed me raises and career promotions. The ones that propelled me to become editor-in-chief by the time I was thirty-four.

It didn't hurt that today my competitor was handsome as sin and totally not the kind of man who usually catches my eye. He made me feel . . . rebellious. And I liked it.

Not that I'd ever admit that to anyone, especially not him. Men like him, with cocky attitudes and come hither stares, are used to girls falling for their charms. But not this girl. I've been burned one too many times to fall back into another relationship that leaves me heartbroken and alone.

With that internal pep talk completed, I decide to head back to work. It's pushing dinner time, but I want to sign off on a few more stories before I call it a night. We have a small staff, and we all have to wear multiple hats. When one of us is out on vacation, that means I pick up extra duties. And this week we have two people out of the office.

My cell phone rings. I look down to see that my little sister is facetiming me. I'm still sitting in my parked car at the community center hall, so I answer it.

My family already gives me hell for working too much. I know it's because they miss me, but it still hurts. No need to give Leslie another reason. I hold my phone back so my face fills the screen as the video feed comes to life.

"Aunt Lar Lar!" my niece cheers. Blonde ringlets tumble into her eyes and bounce off her cherub cheeks. I smile. At six years old, Hazel is all joyful exuberance and tantrums. I'm relieved to see that, right now, the smiles are turned on. "Guess what we did at school today?"

My sister leans into the frame. "Hey, Lauren. Mind entertaining her for a minute while I run upstairs to change Asher's diaper?" She looks harried, but happy. Leslie has always loved children and rolls with the needs of her three little chaos monsters with the grace of a queen. Usually anyway. Her messy bun and dark circles under her eyes indicate she's had a rough day.

"Yeah, of course," I answer.

Hazel leaps into a story about how she and her friend, Ginger, made up a dance to "Shake It Off," then puts the phone down to show me. I can only see the top of her bouncing curls from the angle of the phone, but it's more than enough. It's adorable. And loud. I don't know how my sister manages it, but I'm glad she does. She single-handedly got my parents off my back about settling down and starting a family, neither of which I have any interest in doing. My work fulfills everything I need in life. Almost. And what it doesn't, my sister, my nieces and nephew, and my cat take care of just fine.

The phone jostles and my sister appears on the screen, toddler Asher tucked onto her hip, pacifier in his mouth. He snuggles in close to his mom.

"Thanks for your help, Lauren. Hazel's shown me that dance at least three times today already and I just needed a moment to take care of this guy," she says, nodding into Asher's dark curls.

She glances at the screen and squints at me. "Gotta say, Lar, surprised you're not at work."

The jab lands, but I pretend it doesn't. "I'm not always at work."

Leslie sighs, but lets me win. "So where are you, then? Out on a date?" she teases.

I scoff. "Hardly. I've kind of gotten pulled into helping with this new Mardi Gras krewe thing in town."

"Oh right, I saw a post about it on Instagram," she says.

"Not in the paper?" I tease.

"I love your work, Lar, but anytime I pick up a piece of paper, Asher rips it from my hands and shreds it up so much that it would be best suited as bird cage liner. Much easier to doomscroll social media for a few minutes during nap time. It is what it is."

"I know, Leslie. I do. I was just teasing."

Asher reaches up and tangles his chubby little fingers in a strand of his mom's hair that's fallen from its bun, rubbing his thumb over it. Leslie immediately moves to disentangle his hand, already squinting and preparing for him to yank it. "So, what are you doing with the Mardi Gras stuff? Working on a story?"

I had hoped she wouldn't ask. I'm still not sure how I feel about my role as Mardi Gras Queen, especially since Gladys is treating it like I'm Miss Louisiana and need to do a tour circuit. "Oh, nothing too big," I hedge. "Gladys Beaumont asked me to participate and you know how much her family's business supports the paper."

"Pshhh. You do her a favor by putting her ads in next to the obits." I cackle. Leslie has never been one to hold back her thoughts. She continues. "And participate, huh? Did she get you to agree to ride on a float in the parade?"

She doesn't know the half of it.

"Mayyyyybe."

"Our festive Lauren, leading a Mardi Gras parade on her very own float," she jokes.

"It's not that funny," I say petulantly.

"Oh I think it's great," Leslie says. "It will be good for you to get out there, live a little. See the sun a bit. Being under fluorescents all the time can't be good for your brain."

"It's not like I live some cloistered life in a hermitage, Leslie. And it's not like I'm quitting my job to do this," I protest.

"Lauren, don't you see though? You don't have to hold it all together all the time. Get out there. Enjoy this. Your staff is small, sure, but they are great and Rhett has been on staff so long he could run the paper for you while you're out. It's okay to take some time off every once in a while."

It's a speech I've heard a thousand times, one that plagues me with guilt. Guilt for even considering taking time off. And guilt for wanting to. I run a tight ship. My whole staff depends on me. Sure, maybe part of it's because I have trouble letting go of control over certain tasks, but I want them to be perfect.

"I'll think about it," I finally say.

"Mama!" Hazel yells in the background. "I spilled my juice!"

"I've got to go, Lar. But don't be a stranger, okay? Come over for dinner on Sunday. Tell us all about this float you'll be riding on. Love you."

"Love you too," I say and end the call.

I sit there for a few minutes processing the last couple of hours. The visit to the community center hall. Tumbling over the strands of beads like a newborn deer. Max. Those warm brown eyes and tattooed forearms. His invitation to dinner. My sister telling me to live a little. I slam my eyes closed and rub my temples.

And, just for a moment, I allow myself to picture it: putting down the workload, always making it to family dinners. Going on a date. Embracing those tattooed arms. A kiss. I shake my head. Following that path is a distraction. One I can't and won't do. Work needs me. It's the one thing I can control in my life, the thing no one can take from me.

I start my car and turn on my romance audiobook, one where she's slaying dragons and being worshipped by a fae lord who dotes on her. And then I drive to the office.

Chapter 6

MAX

Red, circular welts line my wrist where Lauren inadvertently slapped me with a strand of beads in her haste to dump them in the box ahead of me. I grin, masochistically loving that she left her mark on me. I flex my hand watching the phoenix tattoo on my left forearm bend its wings with the motion.

"You're going to behave, right?" my grandma says, stepping up behind me and sliding her hand over my arm.

We're both standing right outside the community center hall, everyone else already gone for the evening. I turn and hug her, finally giving my favorite person the greeting she deserves. She hugs me in return and then pulls back.

"Of course I am, Grandma. I told you I'd do this Mardi Gras thing, and I'll do it right. You should never doubt me," I wink. "And I know why the steering committee picked me. They want to make you happy."

She laughs dryly. "Yes, well, that's true. But I supported their nomination because I knew you'd do a great job charming this city as their first Mardi Gras King."

"But why Lauren as queen? She seems so, I don't know, anti-Carnivale."

Grandma sighs, sliding her hands into her pockets. "That's why I nominated her. I like her. A lot. The two of us work together on the funeral home ads. She's a good editor. She knows who to talk to and when. And, every once and a while, I catch a glimpse of her wicked humor. I just thought, why not? I bet she'd have fun if she was pushed to do it. Besides, she could have said no if she wanted to."

"Like anyone can tell *you* no."

She slaps me good-naturedly on the arm. "That's not true," she laughs.

"Oh, yes it is and we both know it."

"Be nice to her," Grandma says.

"I'm always nice," I push back.

"She's a smart woman. She'll be a great asset to this krewe. But I want her to have fun with it too. And if there's one person who always knows how to have fun, it's you," she says.

"I did try to invite her to dinner."

"After that little cleaning stunt you two pulled? Not the time, Max. Let her get to know you over these events. Show her that you're fun to hang out with."

"Grandma. Are you matchmaking?"

"Why, whatever do you mean?" she says with faux innocence.

Little does she know that she doesn't have to meddle in this particular case. I'm attracted to Lauren, and the way she just challenged me ignited the thrill of the chase. I'm already all in on trying to win Lauren over.

"What's the next event you signed us up for?"

"The fundraiser for the Boys and Girls Club this weekend. I've got you both sashes and crowns. You'll just need to show up and read some books to the kids. Nice and easy."

"Well then, consider your king ready and willing."

I head home to fix a quick dinner and let my dog out before my evening shift at the radio station. As soon as I open the door, my small, wire-haired miniature Schnauzer rescue starts rapidfire barking and howling.

"Hey, hey. Come here, Mags. It's okay, girl." I reach down and scoop up the little menace, trying to contain her wind-up toy movements as she paints my beard in licks, her whole body wiggling with excitement.

After she's had her fill of me, I set her down and she scurries off to the food bowl, knowing that's where I'm heading next. Not for the first time, I wish I could take her with me to the studio. But she's just so… loud.

I feed her, then take her out to do her business. Once we're both back inside, I head to the fridge and pull out leftover red beans and rice. I dump it all on a paper plate and put it in the microwave. I've always liked my bachelor life. No one to tell me what I have to do, where I should be. It's peaceful, if sometimes lonely. But I've always managed to find a woman to fill the loneliness in short bursts of time throughout the years. Not long term, I'm not even sure I want that, but here and there it helps.

I remove the steaming plate at the microwave's beep. I make my way to the kitchen table and pull out my phone, propping it up against my aluminum water bottle so I can look at it while I eat.

I google "Lauren Landau Ruston" and hit enter. My browser immediately populates with article after article written by her. There are newspaper awards, photos of her with the mayor, a photo of her with our hometown viral celebrity, Margie Murphy. I keep scrolling, hoping to find her social media profile, something where I can see her having fun and find out what she enjoys in her down time.

But there's nothing.

Another challenge. I can handle that. I'll just have to ask her when I see her at the fundraiser this weekend. It will give me a conversation starter. I'll find out what she likes.

I'm still thinking about Lauren as I head to my bedroom to take a quick shower. I nearly trip over my hiking boots in the hallway after last weekend's trip to explore the trails in western Mississippi. I should really put those away. And the abandoned backpack that's still sitting there too.

"What do you say, Mags? Up for another trip in a few weeks?" She wags her whole little furry, gray body in response. I love my solo hikes with Mags out in the woods. For a small dog, she has no problem keeping up with me, and when she needs a break she rides on top of my backpack like a pro.

Out in the woods no one can get to me or look down at me with disappointment. They can't make me feel small. Out in the woods, I can just be myself.

Leaving the hiking supplies where they are for now, I strip my clothes off and get into the steaming shower. And as I scrub my shoulder length hair, I think of Lauren, of the way her ass looked in that tight skirt, how her red lips quirked in challenge, and of what I'll do to win her over.

Chapter 7

LAUREN

January 13

The Mardi Gras season changes every year based on when Easter happens to fall. And, this year, it's really only about eight weeks. When I agreed to be Ruston's first ever krewe queen, that's how I rationalized it. Eight weeks is easy, especially since we were a couple days into the season already when Gladys asked me to join.

Yet, as I read through the email listing my events to attend over the next seven weeks, I'm not sure how I'm going to squeeze it all in, especially with work demands.

I think about what my sister said about asking my long-term employees to step in and take on additional responsibilities over the next month or so. Guilt twists my gut. Letting go of the control, asking others to take on some of these time-demanding tasks, especially when we're short-staffed, feels wrong.

I read through the events again. There's no way I can do all this without help.

I pick up my office phone and dial Rhett's extension. He's my best reporter and can handle anything I throw at him. Even this.

"Hey, boss," he says on answer. I smile at the endearment everyone in the newsroom calls me. It's one born of respect and being in the news trenches together for so many years.

"Rhett, can you come to my office? It's nothing bad," I add hastily.

A moment later he's at the door, knocking on the frame, shy smile on his face. "Everything okay?" he asks.

And it's a legitimate question. Most summons like this one are to prepare for a fast-moving or difficult story that's landed on my desk.

"Everything's fine. Well mostly. I—" I pause, take a breath. "I need some help."

Rhett steps into my office, face falling into concern. He sweeps a hand back through his auburn hair. "What is it, Lauren? Are you okay?"

God, he probably thinks I have a terminal illness.

"Yes, I'm fine. It's nothing serious. I have been asked to participate in this new Mardi Gras krewe, which is, unexpectedly, going to require a lot of my time. And I need some . . . assistance in running the newsroom while I'm out." I twist my hands together, agitated and strangely embarrassed. I hate asking for help.

Rhett's smile breaks across his handsome face. "Well, why didn't you just say so? We've been begging you to take some time away from the office in forever, boss. Just tell me what you need me to do and when. I've got you. We all do."

And so I do. I outline the days I'll be off, the basic duties I need him to cover, what decisions I will still need to make. It's a lot, but seeing it all written out like this and knowing what Rhett is capable of, it suddenly feels less heavy.

"Got it," Rhett nods. "I'll pull in some of the others for a couple of these things. But we can handle it. You go enjoy your time as queen."

I freeze. "Where did you hear that?"

"Hear what?"

"That I'm the krewe queen?"

Rhett laughs, an honest to goodness belly laugh that I rarely hear from my shyest employee. "Boss, my wife, Amelia, is on the steering committee. She was at the walkthrough with you a couple of days ago, remember?"

My cheeks heat. I hadn't remembered. Or maybe I had just conveniently forgotten. Especially after my humiliating surf across the floor on Mardi Gras beads.

"Oh, that's right. I guess she told you about it after we met at the community center?"

Rhett sucks his lips in to keep from laughing again. "She may have mentioned it."

I watch him try to hold in the laugh, and the attempt causes a giggle to bubble up in my own throat. It bursts from me, surprising us both. Rhett lets loose and soon the two of us are laughing until tears track down our faces.

"Did you really run barefoot through that room picking up Mardi Gras beads in some kind of twisted competition with Beau Baxter?"

"Well I certainly acted like an idiot cleaning up those beads, but no radio DJ in sight. Just Gladys Beaumont's grandson, Max."

"Lauren," Rhett hedges. "Beau is Max's DJ alias. Beau, as in Beaumont."

"Oh. *Oh*."

I've heard of the local DJ, of course I have. Anyone who listens to Peach 103.1 is familiar with the man's deep voice and offbeat humor. And I did think he sounded familiar, but I never put two and two together.

"Well, I guess they're asking local media to participate this year. Makes sense. Do you know him at all?" I ask.

Rhett shrugs. "Just in passing. He graduated a couple years ahead of me at Louisiana Tech. He was big into the party scene, and that was never my thing. But we took a couple of broadcasting classes together. He was always the life of the party while I mostly tried to fade into the background."

Two years ahead of Rhett in college. That would likely put him at around thirty-three. Seven years younger than me. I chastise myself for being even remotely taken in by Max's charm. I clear my throat. "Yes, well. I would appreciate you not sharing that whole queen thing with the staff. At least not yet. I'm sure it will come out soon enough," I say, imagining the whole team throwing a big celebration that I'm not quite ready to embrace.

"Okay, no problem. But, just so you know, Amelia did mention a press release going out next week. And aren't you doing public appearances? I don't think it will stay under wraps for long. Plus, we are a newspaper." He smirks. "But they won't hear it from me."

I sigh. He's right. It's only a matter of time before my queenly debut becomes a matter of local public discourse. And with a local DJ at my side, there's no doubt that will be sooner rather than later.

Chapter 8

LAUREN

January 16

When I pull up to the high school football field, I'm surprised to see how packed it is already. It's January in Louisiana, so the weather is anyone's guess, but we lucked out with sunshine and fifty degree weather. A perfect day for an outdoor fundraiser.

I spot bounce houses and food vendors as I walk around. The sound of laughter echoes across the space, children running across the grass, bubble wands sliding through the air. And the sweet smell of cotton candy dances on the breeze. I told Leslie about the event, so I'll likely see my nieces and nephew at some point today.

This is good. This whole queen thing is allowing me to have more family time already. And Rhett is holding down the newsroom today. Nothing to worry about.

"There you are," Gladys calls out. I turn to see her walking across the field in a purple shirt that says "Krewe of Persici." She's got some sparkly items in her arms, and I fear I already know what she has in store for me.

"So wonderful to see you, dear," she says. "Here's your sash and your crown. I'm glad to see you wore sensible shoes today. You're going to need them." She glances down at my purple Vans.

She hands over a violet t-shirt matching her own, as well as my royal accessories. I walk over to the stadium restrooms for a quick change and emerge holding my crown. I can't quite bear the embarrassment of wearing it on my head. Perhaps it would help if Max were here with me, but I don't see him anywhere. If he managed to get out of this, I'm going to be furious. Just because his grandmother is in charge doesn't mean he should get special treatment.

Gladys sees me when I re-emerge. She escorts me to a booth sponsored by the library and introduces me to the branch manager. I'm going to be reading at their outdoor story time today with my crown on, Gladys makes sure to clarify. I thank her, then walk to the book table to choose my selection.

I glance around, waiting to see Max arrive. Surely I'm not doing this solo, right? But why do I even want him here? I've climbed the career ladder all on my own. Reading to kids while wearing a crown is nothing in comparison to that.

"Aunt Lar Lar!" a little voice yells. I turn to see Hazel darting for me across the field, blonde curls bouncing and purple sweatshirt sliding off her shoulder. My heart lifts instantly. I bend down just as she gets to me, the smell of butterscotch clinging to her from what was surely a dropped lollipop. With my family here, it's easy to drop my professional mask and relax. I'm hit from the other side by my eight-year-old niece, Leona.

"Hey girls, I'm so glad you came."

"What story are you going to read?" Leona asks.

"Here, come help me pick one out," I say, taking each of them by the hand. I spy Leslie out of the corner of my eye chasing eighteen-month-old Asher across the field. I'm glad to be able to support my sister in this small way.

When we reach the book table, the girls ooh and ahh over the selections. There's a brief argument before they finally agree to let me "eenie meany miney moe" it, and land on *Where the Wild Things Are.* Hazel cheers. Leona stomps her foot, but leaves it at that. I glance at my watch. My story time is due to start in five minutes and a small crowd of children has started to gather around the chair set up for me.

"Aunt Lar Lar! Put on your crown!" Hazel says. And how can I possibly say no to that? I lift the crown I draped over my arm and place it on my head. Hazel and Leona both tell me how beautiful I look.

"I hope everyone is having a good time supporting the Boys and Girls Club," a deep voice calls over the speaker system. My heart speeds up, recognizing it as Max's immediately. "We're out here raising money for a great cause. Every donation and purchase you make today helps the children of our city grow and learn. We have a great lineup of activities for you, and one is getting ready to start right now."

My blood freezes in my veins. Surely he's not going to . . . "Our very own Krewe of Persici Queen Lauren is at the library booth, and she's about to read a book for storytime. And believe me, friends, our beautiful queen is not someone you want to miss. In the meantime, if you have music requests, come on over to our booth at the Peach 101.3 and make your request. I'm your DJ, Beau Baxter."

My body is doing that weird hot/cold thing. I'm not sure what's going on. How I feel about anything: the attention, the public callout, the fact that Max is Beau. I mean, Rhett told me that, but it's just now registering that the voice I listen to on my drive home in the evenings, the deep, sexy one that reminds me of the male audiobook narrators I adore, is Max. And did he just call me beautiful? What a ridiculous flirt.

But I don't have time to think on it for long as a rush of children stampedes in my direction. I sit in the reading chair, each of my nieces at my side, while other kids find a place on the grass to sit.

I pick up *Where the Wild Things* Are and take a deep breath, allowing all my years as a professional journalist to boost my confidence. I'm just reading to a bunch of kids. While wearing a sparkly crown. No big deal.

And it is a lot of children—at least a hundred if I had to guess.

"Yay, Aunt Lar Lar!" Hazel cheers. I smile at her. I'm going to treat all these kids like they're my nieces, I decide.

The longer I read, the more into it I get. And when I shout "Let the wild rumpus start," the kids love it. They clap and roar like the wild things in the book. And by the time I finish, I'm grinning. This was different. Fun even.

Kids flood around me in their rush to get to the library table and pick up a book to take home with them. I watch as my nieces join the crowd of children, then glance up, looking for Leslie.

Instead I see warm brown eyes, full lips tipped up in a smile. He wears a sparkly crown with his long hair tied in a knot in the center of it. His arms are folded across his chest, tattoos rippling as he flexes his hands. Handsome doesn't even begin to describe Max Beaumont. Devastating. Distracting. Trouble. And in a crown, no less. Like he just stepped out of one of my romantasy audiobooks about tatted fae lords.

I do not need to let my thoughts go there, but my cheeks heat just the same.

He lifts a hand and gives me a little finger wave. I raise my hand and do the same without thinking. Then quickly drop my hand and look down at it. No, he doesn't get to turn me into a blushing girl. I look back at him, purse my lips and raise an eyebrow. He lifts one in return, then walks toward me.

Max is also wearing a purple krewe t-shirt, no jacket despite the cold. The glitter on his sash glints and sparkles as he moves.

"Hey, birdie," he says just loud enough for me to hear him.

"That's not my name."

He tucks his hands into his jeans pockets and shrugs. "You looked good with that bird mask on last week. It's a compliment."

"Hardly," I laugh. "I could barely see out of that thing. I don't know how Gladys expects me to wear it at the ball and dance in it."

His chuckle is deep and rumbling. Part of me wants to lean my head against his chest and feel it purr through my body. I clench my hands. Why am I so lured in by this man? From the moment I first laid eyes on him in that grocery store, my body has betrayed me every time I'm near him.

"And what's your designated bird?" I ask.

He bows his head. Is that a blush? He peeks up through his lashes at me. Yep. Devastating.

He sighs. "It's truly awful."

"Can't be worse than a male peacock," I prompt.

He laughs. "Oh, it can and it is. It's a good thing I love my grandmother."

I fold my arms and wait. He mumbles something.

"I'm sorry, I didn't quite hear that," I say, leaning in closer to him. He smells like cedar, sweat, and maybe laundry detergent? God, it smells delicious.

"A pelican," he grumbles out.

"As in the state bird of Louisiana?"

"Yes," he murmurs.

A laugh rips out of me. The image of him wearing some kind of huge, gaping, pouched beak is the funniest thing I've imagined in a very long time.

"It's not that funny," he tries, but I can hear the laughter in his voice.

My laughter grows louder, and I realize that for the second time in two days, I'm laughing with my full body. It's been so long and it feels amazing. And it's all because of this crazy Mardi Gras invitation.

I swipe the tears from my eyes and look at Max. His grin is wide, his teeth seeming to glow in the sunlight, one eye tooth slightly crooked.

"So," he says, stepping closer to me.

I melt at his proximity, just a little. A little piece of me is beginning to regret turning Max down the other night. Yes, I've been burned by men many times, but Max doesn't seem to be like any of those losers. He's comfortable with himself, not trying to pretend like he's something he's not.

If he asks me to dinner again, I don't know if I'll be able to refuse him a second time. And that is a terrible, no good, very bad idea. I barely make enough time for myself, and I'd be a terrible date. Still, I lean in closer to him, like he's a magnet I can't pull away from.

"You seemed to have fun today," he says.

"It wasn't bad," I concede.

"I liked your book choice," he smirks.

"And why's that? You relate to the wild things?"

"Were you not paying attention to the story, birdie? Max isn't just any wild thing. He's the king of all the wild things. I rather think it's fitting since I am King Max, at least for Mardi Gras."

"Why am I not surprised that you relate so well to a boy who wears comfortable pajamas and bosses others around?" I tease.

"Maybe I should invest in one of those onesies he wears in the book. Those things do look comfortable."

I can't help but smile at the image.

"Want to walk around with me for a bit? Let the good people see their king and queen?" he says playfully.

I relax. This is what I'm supposed to do. A clear direction. Just two people doing their designated roles as krewe king and queen. I nod.

He reaches toward my face and I pause. His hand moves up and he straightens my crown, then lightly brushes my cheek as it trails back down. My heart thrums in my ears.

"Can't have the queen walking around with a crooked crown," he murmurs. His deep voice tugs at my stomach. Lower.

He extends his arm and I loop mine through his at the invitation. The heat of his forearm presses into mine, despite the cardigan I've donned to chase off the cool air. This feels intimate, despite the public setting. I almost wish I had slipped my cardigan off before this, so I could feel my skin press into his. I simultaneously love and hate the thought. My fingers flex on his forearm. He moves slightly closer to me, but neither of us acknowledge the casual—and not so casual—touches, as we greet everyone we walk past, pretending like this silent, confusing conversation isn't happening at all.

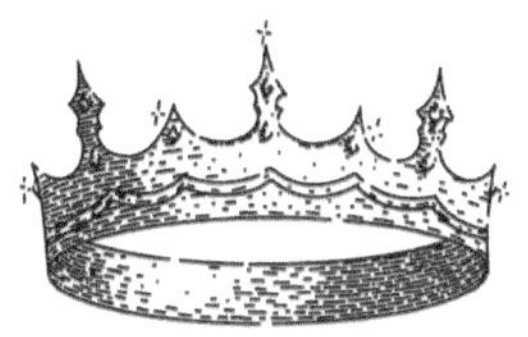

Chapter 9

MAX

Lauren's arm presses into mine. Her leg brushes against me periodically as we walk. I have my charm dialed up, greeting people as we pass, being the Mardi Gras king my grandmother asked me to be. The man I often am when I'm out partying. The confident one. The one who lets nothing get to him.

Focusing on that keeps me distracted from having Lauren so near. That and the small talk I engage in with everyone who walks by us. Lauren does the same, greeting everyone professionally, her smile pressing into dimpled cheeks.

But I can't help but feel satisfied that the smile I see on her face now can't compare to the one she showed me when she laughed about me having to embody a pelican theme for Mardi Gras. God, the way her face lit up ignited something in my chest. Something that probes me to keep flirting with her. To figure her out. What makes her tick? What will make that smile come back? I don't want to scare her away, so I bide my time.

But damn, I hate having to be patient.

"How'd you manage to get out of reading books to the kids with me?" Lauren leans in and asks as we continue to walk.

"I didn't get out of anything. Our other DJ called in sick and I had to step in until another replacement showed up. I would have much rather been by your side reading."

"And roaring with the kids, no doubt," she grins.

"Don't pretend like you weren't joining in on their fun. I did manage to get over there in time to watch you read the last few pages. You seemed to rather like being part of the wild rumpus," I tease.

She turns and smirks at me, but doesn't deny it.

"Besides, that was good practice for you. I'm sure the Mardi Gras ball will be full of wild things dancing and roaring," I continue.

"And then you really will get to be King Max. Your dreams are coming true."

"Even better, because I'll have a stunning queen by my side," I say, testing the waters with her.

"Do you flatter all the girls like this?" she asks, cheeks beginning to glow.

"No, I save the best of my charm for queens."

She stumbles just a bit and I hold onto her arm, helping steady her. "You okay?"

"Fine," she says. "Just embarrassed."

"For someone who likes to wear fancy shoes, you sure do seem to keep stumbling every time I'm around you."

"Maybe you have bad karma," she says.

"Or maybe it's my magnetism."

She chuckles. "Oh, to have your confidence, Max Beaumont."

As we walk, an idea takes shape in my mind. I wonder if Lauren would be open to doing something else with me. Not a date, per se, but something fun. Something that would make her smile. Something that would say, "hey look, there are other people here with us and this is definitely not a date." Even though I want it to be.

She pauses our walk to bend down and greet a kid who runs up to her and asks her about her crown. Her blue eyes light up with her joyful smile. Her expression turns to surprised delight when the child hugs her. My eyes trail down her back to where her jeans hug her ass. I swallow and force myself to look away. Not the time and not the place, especially with my grandmother keeping a critical eye on every move we make.

Something knocks into my legs and wraps its arms around me. I startle, looking down to see a little girl, who is probably in kindergarten, with blonde curls and a huge grin.

"Well, hi there," I say to her.

"Hi, Mr. King Man," she replies.

Lauren turns to look at us, smile growing wider. "I see you've met my niece."

"And what's your name, then?" I ask her.

"Hazel!" she cheers, then lets go of me and dives for her aunt.

"Thanks for slowing her down," a woman says as she walks up to us with a toddler perched on her hip and another little girl trailing her.

"No problem," I say, my smile dialed up to a ten. If that little girl is Lauren's niece, then this must be . . .

"Hi, I'm Leslie, Lauren's sister," she says and nods to me.

"Max. Nice to meet you."

She eyes me from head to toe, then turns to her sister and wiggles her eyebrows. Excellent. I might just have an ally in Leslie. And Lauren seems to have warmed to me today, talking more, being playful. Now's the time, I decide.

"So Lauren, I was hoping we could hang out a little bit in the spirit of getting to know each other before all these Mardi Gras events."

Her shoulders slump and disappointment tugs at my stomach.

"Dinner might be impossible," she says a bit reluctantly. "I'm already missing more work than I'd like to in order to be part of the Mardi Gras krewe," she says. She glances around like she wants to bolt, but this time she's pinned in place by a small child and can't escape through a door, so I try again.

"Doesn't have to be dinner. Just somewhere we can hang out and chat a little."

She hesitates, turns to look at Leslie, who nods at her encouragingly. Lauren narrows her eyes. "What did you have in mind?"

I smirk. "Well, after getting a glimpse of how competitive you are, I thought you might be up for some bowling."

She starts to say no. I can see the syllable forming on her lips.

"How do you feel about multiple competitors?" Leslie asks me. "I love bowling." I knew she'd make a great partner in crime. We both turn to look at Lauren.

"You want to go bowling?" she asks her sister.

"Sis, I want to do anything that will give me a night off from all this chaos," she says, flicking her chin to where her daughters now tussle in the grass. "I love them, but this mama could use a break."

I watch as a silent conversation passes between the two of them, one of those that only siblings can completely understand. The kind I used to have with my younger brother, Charlie.

"I'll bring someone too," I add. Maybe that will make Lauren feel a little more at ease.

She relents. "Fine, but it will have to be a time when I'm not short-staffed and under deadline pressure. Like on a Sunday afternoon."

"Tomorrow sounds perfect," Leslie says.

I nod. "My day off. Meet you both at Peach Tree Lanes around two?"

"Let me double check with my husband and make sure we don't have anything scheduled, but that should be fine," Leslie says.

We both turn to look at Lauren. She rolls her eyes and smiles. "Fine. I know when I'm being ganged up on. You two win this time. Bowling tomorrow it is. But," she hesitates looking at me. Her direct stare makes my stomach flip.

"First we better get back to walking and waving. Gladys is staring so hard at the back of your head right now that your hair might catch on fire from the laser beams shooting from her eyes."

I spin around, just in time to see my grandmother terribly pretend that she was never looking at me. I chuckle.

"Right then. Where were we?" I ask, extending my arm to Lauren. And when she takes it, my soul seems to settle like a cat curling up in a sunbeam.

Chapter 10

LAUREN

January 19

I still can't believe I let Leslie's insistence that I need to have more fun wriggle into my brain and motivate me to show up at a bowling alley of all things. Because it was definitely my sister, and not the delightfully wicked smirk that played across Max Beaumont's mouth when he asked me to go bowling with him. And it certainly wasn't him taunting my competitive nature. Nope. Not at all.

It doesn't help that since yesterday, I haven't been able to stop thinking about the way Max and I linked arms, the way he flirted with me. It's been a while since a man has looked at me like I hung the moon and stars. And while I'm still reluctant to jump into anything romantic, I can't help but indulge in the warm, glowy way his attention made me feel.

Walking into the bowling alley is like stepping back in time. The wooden lanes, neon shapes on the walls, and, let's face it, the shoes, all look like they have existed here in a time capsule since the 1980s. The stale smell of popcorn and spilled soda makes me feel a little nostalgic.

I walk up to the counter to get a lane for the four of us, though it occurs to me now that Max never said who his plus one would be. Something twinges in my gut that I refuse to acknowledge—because it couldn't be jealousy.

"Hey, sis!" I turn to see Leslie walk through the door. I realize that I'm not used to seeing her without a child clinging to her body. She looks great, relaxed in a way I haven't seen in years. Her blonde hair, the same color as mine, is styled and down, though I note the ponytail holder around her wrist. I really should try to do stuff with my sister sans kids more often.

"I already got our lane," I say. "We're down at eleven."

"Is Max here already?" she asks.

"Not yet."

We walk down to our lane and put our things down, then go to pick out our bowling balls.

"Hey there, birdie!" a familiar voice calls. And damn, the man really does have an amazing voice. It's no wonder he ended up in radio. He'd be a great romance audiobook narrator too, my brain helpfully suggests. My cheeks heat just thinking about the things he'd be saying in that kind of job.

I turn, holding a fluorescent pink ball in my hands.

"Good choice," Max says. He steps past me to the ball rack to select his own. His arm brushes against mine, skin to skin, and it sends a shiver down my spine. He steps back holding a lime green bowling ball. And I wonder if that light touch was on purpose.

"I guess I better pick mine then," a female voice says from behind Max. A beautiful woman with jet black hair, full lips and brown eyes moves past him. My stomach immediately forms into a tornado.

After all Max's flirting I really thought . . . what? I have no right to think anything. Max asked me to dinner and I said no. So what if he kept our arms linked and flirted a bit at the fundraiser? That was all part of being Mardi Gras king and queen. I don't need anyone but me, I remind myself for the millionth time.

"I'm Lauren," I say, extending my hand. It comes off more stiff than I intended.

"Janessa," she says with a smile, perfect teeth on full display.

"I'm Leslie," my sister offers.

"Great, now that we all know each other, let's get our shoes and get this game started," Max says.

I reach for my bag and pull out a pair of shiny white bowling shoes.

"Didn't know you bowled enough to own your own pair of bowling shoes there, birdie. Am I about to get my ass handed to me?" Max asks.

I look down at my shoes. "No. Nothing like that. It's just that the thought of wearing a pair of shoes hundreds of people have worn before me . . ." I cringe and have to stifle my gag reflex.

"No worries. Just as long as you don't mind the rest of us renting shoes," he says. He winks and walks over to the shoe counter.

When he gets back, he sits down next to Janessa and the two of them change into their bowling footwear. They joke and she gives him a gentle shove. A clawed talon of jealousy twists into my heart. I wish I'd never agreed to this evening. Never let Leslie talk me into going bowling with him.

Leslie steps over to the board and puts all of our names in. I'm up first and I haven't bowled since high school. My palms are slick as I reach for the hot pink ball waiting for me on the rack. I pause to swipe my hands down my shirt, then pick up the ball. My tongue darts out, wetting my lips. I glance at Max to see that he's watching me intently.

I turn and walk up to the lane. I square my shoulders, trying to logic my way through this. If I toss the ball straight on, it will knock down the pins. Easy. I slide my fingers into the ball and line myself up. I swing my arm back and then forward, releasing the ball.

It thunks onto the lane and begins to slowly roll—straight into the gutter. Well, fuck.

"It's okay, Lauren," my sister chirps. "That was your warm-up roll. You got this."

When my ball re-emerges from the chute, I reach for it. But I'm even more agitated and determined to get this right. I pick up the ball, square my shoulders, and launch it down the lane. It skirts the edge of the gutter as it rolls. I cross my fingers on both hands and whisper, "Come on, come on. Get those pins!"

And it does. Or at least it gets one pin on the far right side. My shoulders slump.

A heavy hand lands on my back. "Chin up, birdie. Not every competition involves picking up beads. This just may not be your game." Max's voice is taunting. I simultaneously hate and love it. "Now step back and watch a pro at work."

I don't know what comes over me, but when he says those words, I stick my tongue out at him like a child. He laughs and shakes his head. I return to my seat and cross my arms. Max squares up, swings his arm back, then moves it forward, his right leg crossing behind him like some kind of ESPN pro. And dammit if that ball doesn't sail right down the center of the lane and knock every single pin down.

"Woo hoo! Way to go, Max!" Janessa cheers. He turns to her and gives her a fist bump. I'm going to throat punch them both.

He turns around and winks at me. Both my eyebrows raise and my jaw locks.

Leslie hops up next. She takes down four pins with her first roll and the other six on her second.

"A spare! Nice!" Janessa says.

Does Janessa really have to be so nice? She stands and saunters over to the ball rack. She's probably in her early thirties and looks like she's into Crossfit. Of course. Janessa makes her selection and moves to the lane. She swings it back, forward, and releases. Gutter ball. I relax, just a little. But on her second roll she knocks down every single pin.

My subsequent bowls aren't much better. When my ball manages to stay in the lane, it knocks one or two pins over. Max is clearly the best of our group, his score far ahead of all of ours, but Leslie is holding her own.

"Max, why don't you show Lauren how to throw the ball so she's not crossing her arm over her body so much?" Janessa says on my next turn.

I frown. "I don't need help."

Max sighs. "Asking for help isn't the worst thing, you know." Then he stands and walks over, positioning himself behind me. "Is this okay?" The sound of his deep voice rumbling against my ear makes desire pull low in my abdomen. I want to lean into him and shove him away simultaneously. But my body seems to make the decision before my brain can catch up.

All my protests evaporate. "Um, yeah. Sure."

His calloused hand slides down the back of my left arm, and goosebumps trail along in its wake.

"Lift your left arm like this. Let it help you support the ball. Good, now raise your right while holding the ball. And square your shoulders." His right hand finds mine, cupping the back of my hand to help me hold the ball. His hand lingers there and then he leans forward, the front of his body pressing into my back. I push back microscopically, my body luxuriating in the feel of him so close to me.

With him holding me like this, his piney smell mixes with the lavender laundry detergent scent on his clothes and fills my senses. And I imagine turning in his arms and pressing my face into his firm chest. I'm very glad he can't see my face right now, because I know, beyond a shadow of a doubt, that it's as red as a boiled crawfish. He turns his head so that his lips nearly brush my ear. Is he doing this on purpose? Trying to unnerve me? My pulse thrums.

"That's good," he says, his breaths warm against my ear. "The reason your ball is dropping into the gutter is because you're moving your bowling arm across your body as you throw it. Try angling your body like this," he says, moving his left hand down to lightly shift my hip forward. I swallow, my body lighting up at the feel of his hand there. "Perfect. Now, swing your arm back, and as you go to release, point your thumb at that front pin."

"Should I hook my foot back like you?" I try to say it like a joke, but my voice comes out hoarse.

He chuckles. "Don't worry about that fancy stuff. Eye on the prize. You have to do the basics first to get what you want." And I wonder now if we're just talking about bowling.

"I'll walk you through it." He takes a step back, leaving his left hand lightly on my hip. Now, swing back, step, thumb forward, release.

I follow his directions and the ball shoots straight down the center of the lane, knocking down nine pins.

"Way to go!" Janessa cheers. It startles me. I forgot we were here with other people. God, he's here with another woman.

"Thanks," I mumble, pulling away from his touch and retreating to my seat next to Leslie.

"Where you going, birdie? You're up again," Max says. And I swear his voice has dropped an octave.

"Oh, right." This time I bowl on my own and manage to knock down the one remaining pin for a spare.

"See Max, I don't care what anyone says about you, you're a good teacher," Janessa laughs, slapping him lightly.

I look away from them. Leslie catches my eye knowingly.

"So Janessa, how do you and Max know each other?" my sister probes. I'm not sure if I love her or hate her for the question.

"He didn't tell you?" she scoffs. "Max, are you really that embarrassed by me?" I shift uncomfortably. They must have been together for a long time then.

"This idiot is my cousin," Janessa says. "My mom and his dad are siblings. We were born in the same year, same week! So we were always thrown together at every family function. Our families were close, so they practically raised us like twins."

"I'm the prettier twin though," Max says immediately.

Janessa cackles. "Oh, you wish, Maxie."

My whole body unclenches, my nerves unspooling from my stomach into my limbs. My sister discreetly bumps my shoulder in silent acknowledgment that she knew exactly what I was worried about.

"I have to agree with Janessa. She's got you beat in both looks and attitude," I say.

"Oh, I like her," Janessa says, standing up and walking over to sit on my other side. She gives me a quick side hug. "You and I are going to be good friends, I just know it."

Friends. That's not a word I've thought of in a long time. Too busy working. Too busy squeezing every ounce of my non-existent free time into my parents, sister, nieces, and nephew. But I like the idea. And, now that the fog of jealousy has cleared from my mind, I realize I like Janessa.

"I'd like that," I say.

After that, the whole dynamic of the game shifts. With a little bit of instruction and the tightness of my shoulders gone, I begin to knock over pins every time I bowl. I even manage to get a couple of strikes on my own. We all cheer for each other, giggling as Janessa squats and swings the ball between her legs and then releases for a strike, executing a perfect granny bowl.

As our game winds down, Max's bowling skills seem to get better and better. And when he bowls three strikes in a row, an animation pops up on our score screen. And I laugh so hard I nearly can't breathe. Max turns to look at me one brow raised.

I gasp out, "Sorry, I just think it's so funny. You call me birdie, but you're clearly the turkey." He bellows out a laugh too and soon all four of us are cackling and teasing each other.

As we wrap up our game and pack up our things, Janessa gives me a hug and tells me she can't wait to hang out again. Leslie does the same, telling me she needs to hurry home to the kids.

Max lingers next to me. The sexual tension from when he helped me learn how to bowl earlier is back. And suddenly I'm remembering the heat of his body pressed into mine. The way his hands trailed down my arms and touched my hip. I wonder if he's thinking about the same thing as he stuffs his hands into his pockets.

He clears his throat. "I'm glad you joined us for bowling today."

"You know what? I am too."

"Even if you lost?" He smirks.

I frown. "Hey, I didn't do that terribly."

"You just needed a little help," he says, his voice charged with suggestion.

My voice lowers, and the flirtiness surprises me. "Janessa's right. You're not a bad teacher."

"I wanted to get to know you a little better, but I feel like we barely got to talk today. Too much bowling and laughing. Maybe we could try again? To meet up and get to know each other a bit, I mean?"

I consider. Today wasn't a date. Not with Janessa and Leslie here. It didn't feel like one. He wasn't fussing over me or buying me food. Wasn't cuddled up next to me. We had a moment when he was teaching me, but that's all it was. Some forced proximity, some touching. Anyone would get flustered in that situation. No, I don't think Max is asking me out, even if I might actually, secretly, want it deep down.

"Sure, what did you have in mind?" I reply.

His shoulders relax. "Want to go with me to take my dog to the dog park one day this week? We can work around your schedule. Maybe go on your lunch break? I work evening shifts, so mornings or lunch time are best for me."

"Yeah, that sounds nice."

"Great, here," he says, handing me his phone with the contacts screen open. "Add your phone number so I can send you the details."

My heart flutters as I type my contact into his phone and hand it back. He types something for a second, and then my phone buzzes in my pocket. I lift it to see a text from an unknown number.

"Hi birdie," is all it says.

"I'll be in touch," he says. Then he steps in and gives me a hug. I return it. It's friendly and doesn't linger, but I still feel the ghost of his touch against my arms as I walk away.

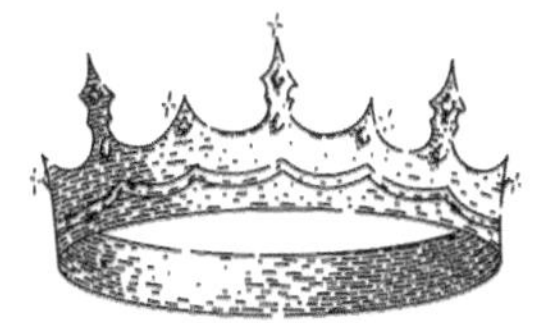

Chapter 11

MAX

January 20

I can still feel Lauren's forearms flexing beneath mine as she lifted the bowling ball. Still smell her peppermint shampoo and feel the way her hair tickled my nose as I leaned in close to her. Desire clenches in my gut, and for the hundredth time I'm both surprised and grateful I got her to agree to go to the dog park with me later this week.

But first, I have to go to work. I like working evenings at the station. I have to cover the drive home, which is a lot of commercials and traffic updates, but after that, it's smooth sailing.

I settle into the radio booth and pick up the well-worn headphones. I slide them over my ears, their noise cancellation blocking out anything and everything that's not playing on Peach 103.1. I ease the microphone down and look at the commercial line up, then start prepping my evening playlist. There are a few songs we have to play, but it's more lax as we push into the later hours.

More music means more down time for me. And while I typically spend that time reading or playing a game on my phone, tonight I can't stop thinking about Lauren. It's been a long time since I was this hung up on a woman.

During the next stretch of songs, I reach for my phone and pull up the messaging app. Should I text her? Or will it chase her away? Damn, I can't remember the last time I didn't confidently forge ahead to pursue exactly who I wanted, how I wanted.

Irritated with myself, I type out a text and hit send before I can think better of it.

Max: Recovered from getting scorched at bowling yet?

I stare at the screen waiting for a response. I'm about to put my phone down when I see those three tell-tale dots letting me know she's typing. I can't help the grin that spreads across my face.

Lauren: Scorched, huh? Your ego must be gigantic tonight.
Max: Not just tonight *smirk face emoji*
Lauren: Well that's obvious.

There she is. I love it when she pushes back.

Max: What are you up to tonight?
Lauren: Is this seriously a "U up?" text?

My heart thumps a little faster, desire tugs low in my groin just thinking about the implications of that. I'd show up at her door, knock and listen as her heels clicked along the kitchen floor. Because she'd definitely have them on. The red ones. And she'd be wearing an oversized t-shirt that hangs off one of her shoulders. Maybe one of mine . . . I blink, realizing that it's time to cut to commercial break.

Thank goodness I've done this job for so long. I switch to autopilot mode, giving a quick rundown of the music that just played and leading into the few nighttime commercials. The ad for Ruston's first Mardi Gras parade plays, and it feels like a sign from the universe. Like texting with Lauren and listening about these events we're doing together means something big.

My phone buzzes and I'm already grinning. Until I see who it's from.

Mom: Max, we miss having you at the house. Please come to dinner next weekend. Or we'll meet you somewhere. Your choice. Please honey.

The desire that was fizzing in my stomach sours instantly. What my mother means, what she's not saying, is that I need to talk to my father. I need to listen again as he tells me what a failure I am, while he berates me for not joining the family business like my perfect younger brother. Pretend to be interested while he asks me when I'm going to grow up.

I pull my gaze away from the text and back to the station feed on my screen. The commercials wrap up and I give my welcome back spiel and talk about what's about to play, then feed in the music.

My phone lights up.

Lauren: It was just a joke, Max.

And I realize that I never responded to her. Shit. My thoughts are so confused and I've lost all my confident bluster from earlier.

Max: I know, sorry. At work. Still want to go with me to the dog park tomorrow? My grandma mentioned something to me about the upcoming ball, and I thought it might be good to talk about it in person.

Lauren: Yeah, sure. I can do that. How do you feel about mornings?

I wince and rub the back of my head. My shift goes until 11 p.m., and then I usually go home and stay up way too late catching up on shows I missed or doomscrolling on my phone.

Max: How early are we talking?

Lauren: 7?

Ouch. But she is giving me the time of day. Literally. And I do need to talk to her. That wasn't a lie.

Max: Sure. I can manage. Mags will be thrilled. Tomorrow?
Lauren: Tomorrow.

And just like that, I'm excited again. I get to see Lauren tomorrow.

Chapter 12

LAUREN

January 21

It's 6:45 a.m. in January. And even in Louisiana, that means it's pretty chilly outside. That hasn't deterred the handful of people already at the park, dogs jogging dutifully beside them. I pull my beanie hat down a little lower, squishing my ponytail against my neck. My fingers tap against my leggings as I look around, searching for a familiar bun.

I check my watch again. 6:52. My brain keeps jumping to today's workload. Reminding me of the day's schedule, headlines to approve, stories we started yesterday. My mind is on a neverending press loop that's impossible to turn off.

Yip, yip. I look down to see a small ball of wild gray fur zoom past me.

"Mags, get back here, girl."

My stomach warms at the sound of that rich voice. I turn. Max is in dark gray sweatpants and a navy hoodie with the Peach 103 logo printed across the chest. He's got the hood pulled up over his head, his hands shoved into the front pocket. He smiles when he notices me looking at him.

"Hey, birdie," he says warmly, jumping around a little bit to warm up. "Up for a walk?"

The little ball of zoomie fur returns, hopping up on her back legs and howl-barking at her dad. Max leans down and clicks the leash into her purple harness.

"Lauren, this is Magnolia, Mags for short. Mags, Lauren."

"Mags and Max, huh? What a perfect duo."

I lean down and rub the top of her head, and Mags's whole backside wiggles in response. "Nice to meet you, Mags." When I stand, she takes off ahead of us, eager to pull Max along the path.

As we begin our walk, I trace circles on my leggings, trying to figure out what to say. Bowling was fun, albeit a bit tense. Texting with him last night was exciting. Though when I flirted back he seemed to shut down, and I don't know what to do with that. Maybe it's just another sign that I need to stop any romantic thoughts now, a little watch out from the universe that Max Beaumont is no good for me.

"So," we both say at the same time, then laugh awkwardly.

"No, you first, I insist," Max says.

"What did you want to talk about? Something for the ball?"

Max smirks and looks ahead of us, pulling his lips in as if he's trying to stifle a smile. "Grandma called me and told me that she's very worried I'm going to embarrass her at the Mardi Gras ball, and would like me to take dance lessons." He glances at me, waiting for a response.

"Well, Gladys is a perceptive lady. No doubt she's probably right." A little thrill runs through me at the thought. Dance lessons like the ones I loved in high school and college. Maybe Max will ask me to come as his partner. The two of us pressed together like we were at the bowling alley. I shiver.

A laugh rumbles out of Max. "But the thing is, birdie, that the dance she wants me to do for the ball is fancy. Waltzes. Stuff like that. Do you know how to waltz?"

I start tracing circles on my leggings again. He already knows the answer and I can see where this is going.

"I've danced some before and I can just follow your lead," I reply.

"Nope. I don't think that's going to cut it. Do you really want to make your Mardi Gras queen debut being dragged around the dancefloor by an ogre like me?"

I balk. He has me and he knows it. "You'd hardly be dragging me. I'll be moving right along with you."

"And when I go to dip you and you fight me and hit the ground?"

"Don't try to dip me and we won't have a problem."

"Plus, I think Grandma has a very specific dance she wants us to learn. One she saw at a New Orleans Mardi Gras ball. She wants this first Ruston ball to be the ideal start to all the krewe traditions to come. And this dance, she insists, is part of it. So unless you want generations to imitate the way you'll be stepping on my toes, it's probably best that we do these dance lessons together."

He's still watching me. I can feel it. I turn to look at him as we walk side by side, loving and hating the challenge in his face I see there.

"I have a full time job, Max," I try.

"And so do I." His tone shifts from friendly to combative.

"I know you do," I push. "I never said you didn't."

"I heard what you implied. You think being a radio DJ isn't a real job? I put in forty hours a week, just like you."

And wow, have I hit a nerve. One I didn't even know was there. I stop walking. He keeps going for a few more steps before realizing I'm not with him and turning around to come back to me. Mags follows him.

"Max, I never said you didn't have a full time job. Where is this coming from?"

His jaw clenches and he looks down at Mags, then back to me. I watch as he seems to force his shoulders to relax. He closes his eyes for a beat. Reopens them, looks at me.

"I'm sorry. You're right. You never said that. It's a prejudice I've heard my whole career. But that's not your fault."

I study his face, the way his eyes squint, how his hands continue to flex. I reach out and place my hand on top of his. He glances down to where our skin touches.

I soften. "Max," I say, looking him in the eyes. "I'm an advocate for all communications professionals, and that includes radio. I admire what you do. You have to know how to hit all the right beats on the fly, and that's impressive. I didn't mean anything about you or your work when I said that. I'm sorry if it came off that way."

Max stares at me intently, glancing to my lips, then back up to my eyes. Finally he nods. "Okay."

And dammit, I sort of hate that he doesn't call me birdie.

"Besides, I work way more than forty hours a week," I say with chuckle.

But he doesn't laugh. "You shouldn't have to do that," he says instead.

I raise an eyebrow. "I have a small staff and need to control everything that leaves our office. It's part of the editor gig, or at least the way I've set it up. I'm the person who makes sure that every single thing on that page is correct. I do final headline checks, make sure the right stories are coming in. Make the call to pivot when news changes. It's more than a forty hour a week job." I shrug.

I turn and start walking again, embarrassed at having to defend myself. I've always been proud of my work, and that look he's giving me, like he feels sorry for me, rankles.

"Lauren, wait," Max says, hurrying to catch up to me. He lightly grabs my arm to turn me to face him. "I didn't mean anything by that. Honestly. I've just seen first hand, from my dad, what working all day every day has done to him. How his career is the only thing that matters in his life. But he isn't you."

"Everyone thinks I work too much," I say, looking down at my red Hokas. I glance back up to his warm brown eyes. "But I've worked hard to get to where I'm at. I'm proud of myself. Happy with my job."

"I know that. Everyone who looks at you knows that," Max says. "How could they not? You kick serious ass as the editor of that newspaper. I'm just trying to say that it's good to have fun too. To not let life soar past you. We only get one shot at this life, and I've found that it's a lot better when I stop trying to make everyone else happy, and work on making myself happy."

"Who says I'm not happy?" I ask, insecurity coloring my words.

"Lauren, you have to know I don't mean that." And dammit, I do know. I really do. But before I can speak, he continues. "Let me start over. You're awesome at your job. No one doubts that. But if you ever want to take a break, try something fun like, I don't know, going for a hike in a national park, or hell, going to a football game and tailgating, I'm here. I'd love to have fun with you."

I imagine the scenarios he mentioned: trekking through pine trees, spying rabbits hopping across the path. Snuggling up next to him at a Louisiana Tech football game in winter, holding hands. I blink, and I'm back at the park staring at Max.

"I believe you," I say. "I guess I just have my own insecurities I need to come to terms with."

I plaster on a smile, but inside my heart is bruised, because Max is repeating the same thing my family has said to me for years. *Why don't you ever come visit, Lauren? Why don't you date, Lauren? Why don't you have friends, Lauren? That job isn't worth it, Lauren.*

He studies my face and nods. We silently agree to let the subject drop. We start walking again, following Mags along the path.

"What's your favorite ice cream flavor?" Max asks.

"That's random."

He shrugs. "Part of this meetup is to get to know each other better. So what's your favorite ice cream?"

This is safer ground. I relax. "Strawberry. You?"

"Pralines and cream. Any pets?"

I smile. "I have a gray cat named Lola. She's a piece of work, but I love her. My turn. Dream vacation?"

He lights up. "Hiking to Everest Base Camp."

"Not all the way up the mountain?"

"No thanks. I don't want to die. Just want to see Nepal and some yaks," he says.

I giggle. "Doesn't sound like much of a vacation. I think I'd like to go somewhere tropical. All inclusive. Good seafood. No noise. Somewhere like St. Lucia."

"That sounds nice too," he agrees. "Favorite type of food?"

"Tex Mex. Give me chips and salsa and a margarita and I'll be your best friend forever."

"Noted," he says, his words warm.

We finish the trail loop, throwing questions back and forth to each other the rest of the time. And, I have to admit, this and the bowling were a good idea. Already I feel more comfortable about going to the Mardi Gras ball knowing Max will be there with me.

When we reach the parking lot, I'm surprised to find myself disappointed, wishing for another loop and round of questions with Max. I glance at my watch. 7:45. I wince. I'm normally at work no later than 8:30. I need to get home, change, and hurry to the office.

"Before you go, wait just a second. I got you something." He hurries over to his car and lets Mags hop onto the back seat, then reaches over to his passenger seat and pulls out a styrofoam takeout container. "This made me think of you," he says, handing it over.

I open the lid cautiously. As soon as I realize what's inside, I laugh. It's a perfectly cut slice of king cake with purple and green sprinkles on top. I glance at its side and can see a thick layer of cream cheese and . . . "Is that the baby?"

"You know what that means," Max says wickedly. "You have to buy the next king cake. Guess that means we'll be doing this again."

The silliness and thoughtfulness of the gesture does something funny to my heart. "I guess so."

He steps over to me and gives me a hug. It's not overly long, not crossing the friend zone. But it feels good.

"I'll text you the details of the dance lesson options. Try to figure out something that fits both our schedules," he says. "Have a good day at work."

"You too," I say. And then we both turn and get in our cars, but as I drive home, my smile doesn't leave my face.

Chapter 13

MAX

January 23

I hustle into the dance studio ten minutes late. I can already imagine Lauren's scowl after waiting on me for at least twenty minutes. But when I enter the studio there's only one woman there, and she's not Lauren.

"Oh, hello. You must be Max," she greets in a lilting voice. "I'm Amara. I'm your dance instructor. I was beginning to wonder if this lesson was canceled." She says it lightly, but I'm embarrassed all the same. I really need to do better about being on time. But I am surprised Lauren isn't here yet.

"Sorry about that," I say. "Must be a crazy day for all of us. I'll make sure it doesn't happen again. I'm going to check on my dance partner real quick and then I'll be ready."

She nods and I hurry over to a chair in the corner to deposit my bag. I swipe open the screen of my phone, expecting to see something from Lauren—maybe a text that she's running late. But there's nothing.

I type out a quick text and send it to her, then pause waiting for a response. I wait some more. Amara clears her throat and I drop the phone. "Sorry," I mumble.

I join her on the studio floor. "Not sure where my partner is tonight. But I'm ready." I try to pay attention as she explains the steps of a waltz, but I can barely listen. My mind is trapped in a pattern of worried thoughts. Lauren is never this late. She wouldn't just stand me up, right? Was she in an accident? Is she okay?

"Now then," Amara says, approaching me. "Extend your arm like this. Yes, good." She then proceeds to lead me in a box step. Or at least she tries, but I end up stepping all over her feet. I can see her frustration, though she tries to hide it under politeness.

We go on like this for a solid fifteen minutes. Her instructing, me trying and failing, too distracted and worried about Lauren to be fully present for this dance lesson. Amara huffs and all but throws up her hands in defeat. "Let's take a ten minute break."

I nod and hurry over to my phone. Still no response from Lauren. My stomach tightens into a knot. I swipe to call her before I can think twice about it. Her phone rings and rings. I'm just about to hang up when she answers.

"Hello?" She sounds irritated, and I momentarily wonder if I dialed the wrong number.

"Lauren?"

"Yes, what is it?" She sounds distracted and not at all like herself.

Now I'm mad. How dare she talk to me like this after she agreed to be here.

"I won't keep you long," I snap. "I was just calling to make sure you were okay since you didn't show up for dance lessons."

A pause. "Oh shit. I'm so sorry, Max." She forgot. An anchor sinks in my stomach, dragging my feelings with it. She forgot about dance lessons. About me.

"It would really help if you were here," I try to steady my voice, not at all ready to forgive and forget. Not when she's had me worried for the past half hour and she forgot about me.

"I know. I'm sorry. We had a story break late in the day and I completely lost track of time. I didn't realize what time it was," she says. There is guilt in her voice and it softens me, just a little.

"You can't control the news. I get that. But are you still coming? The instructor is ready to toss me out the window and I could use some backup."

"Max, I'm sorry. I can't. Not tonight. This story is big, everyone else has gone home, and I have to be here to put the paper to bed."

Right. She already said that. I guess I just thought that we planned this together. That our plans, that I might be more important than her work. But that's not fair. She barely knows me. She doesn't owe me anything. Of course her job comes first. Even at 7:30 p.m., more than two hours after she should have been off work.

"Yeah, of course," I agree, letting it all sink in. "I'll just take notes for next time."

"Thank you, Max. I am sorry about this. Text me later. We'll reschedule." She hangs up.

"Ready?" Amara asks.

And what else can I do? I nod, take a quick sip of water, and go back to the studio floor.

I'm so glad it's my night off work. All I want to do is go home and ice my poor feet. I am good at many things, but waltzing is not one of them. And I'm not sure Amara wants me to come back again. God, I wish Lauren was there with me tonight. We could have laughed it all off together. Bantered when we both messed up. Tonight felt . . . lonely.

I missed having Lauren with me tonight, especially after we were vulnerable with each other at the park the other day. I thought digging into those feelings together meant something—even if it wasn't exactly romantic. But I remember what she said that day too, about how strongly she feels about personally making sure everything in the newspaper is impeccable. And now she's at work alone to make sure it gets done.

An idea forms in my head as I drive home. I turn the wheel and head to the local Mexican restaurant. I place a quick to-go order, making sure to get an extra helping of chips and salsa, and their amazing chicken tacos. Then I head for the newspaper office.

When I get there, I notice that a lone light shines from the corner office through the blinds. I go to the front door and knock, unsure if anyone will answer. Nothing. I knock again. Still nothing. I reach for my phone and call Lauren. It rings twice and then she picks up.

"I'm sorry, Max. Really I am," she says on answer.

"I know and it's okay. Are you still at work?"

A heavy sigh. "Yeah. It's going to be a long night."

"Come to the front door?"

"Of work?"

"As long as you're still at the office, then yes."

I hear a shuffle, then the click of heels. And then I see her when she turns the corner in the dark hallway to approach the glass-front door. Her fair hair has been twisted up into a messy bun on top of her head, strands sticking out in every direction. There's a red pen tucked behind her ear and she's wearing glasses. I never thought I had a thing for hot librarians, but Lauren just single-handedly changed my mind.

She unlocks the door. "Max? What are you doing here?" Her glasses magnify her eyes, making her look a bit owlish and utterly bewildered. It's adorable.

I hold up the paper bags. "Dinner. I remember a certain someone telling me she'd sell her soul for chips and salsa."

"Gimme," she says immediately, reaching for the bags. I laugh and hand them over. "Come in. I'm sure you're starving too."

I don't even hesitate, following her into the dark building. She navigates through a few cubicles and a hallway until she reaches the small corner office. Her office.

I look around as we enter, noting the piles of newspapers, notepads, and scattered pens. I spot a framed photo of a grey cat on her desk next to another of her nieces and nephew. The walls hold a couple of framed Blue Dog art prints, as well as several rows of awards.

I take a seat in one of the chairs across from her desk. She opts to sit in the other seat next to me instead of across the desk. And that small gesture, more than anything, shows me that she's glad I'm here. We open the bags and the smell of chili pepper and guacamole fills the room. Lauren groans as she unwraps a taco and takes a bite.

"Amazing. You're a saint, Max Beaumont."

"Can't say anyone has ever called me that before, but I'll take it. Max Beaumont: Patron Saint of Tacos."

"I'd pray to him," she says with a laugh. But I like the sound of that a little too much. I reach for my own taco and try to hide the heated look I know is crossing my face.

"Are you the only one up here?" I ask between bites.

She shrugs. "Yep. That's not unusual though."

"Why don't you have help?"

"All that's left to do in order to wrap tomorrow's issue is for me to tweak the breaking article. I'm almost there. Then I'll send it to our production people and they will send it to press from their home computers."

"You can't do this from home?" I ask, taking another bite.

"I could," she allows. "But home is sacred to me. I don't like to bring work there if I don't have to. It's one of the few sane spaces in my life. Best to stay here until it's done."

"But is it safe? You being here alone like this?" A surge of protectiveness flares in me. I don't like her up here alone. Not at all. "What if someone tries to break in?"

"I just ignore it if anyone knocks at the door. Besides we have cameras and I have a phone. I can call for help if I need to."

"You're very chill about all this."

She shrugs. "I'm used to it. Thanks for dinner, by the way. This was thoughtful of you." She dips a chip in salsa and pops it into her mouth.

"I'm thoughtful," I insist.

"You are," she agrees. "It just hides behind all that bravado."

"It's not bravado if it's true."

"Keep telling yourself that."

"Besides. I missed you tonight. Our instructor, Amara, made me feel like an idiot. Had to come check on you to make sure you didn't just ditch me." I try to make it a joke, but it comes out a little too seriously.

Even though I'm having fun with Lauren right now, my feelings are still hurt that she didn't call and let me know she couldn't make it to dance lessons tonight. My dad's voice resonates, unwanted, through my head, telling me I shouldn't get emotional. But I quickly shove him away. He doesn't get to have a place inside my head anymore. Lauren, however—

"Max. I didn't mean to stand you up. That was shitty. I should have called. I'm terrible about getting wrapped up in my work and blocking everything else out. It's not just you. I do it to my family too. It's, well, I need to get better at it. I'm sorry."

My heart softens. And, even though it shouldn't make me feel better, hearing that it's not just me she's done this to somehow helps. And I can tell how much she regrets losing track of time.

"Can we try again for dance lessons in a couple of days?" I offer as an olive branch. "Amara had a spot open up, but I'm not going alone. I'd rather just wing it at the ball and do the macarena than face down that solo humiliation again."

She laughs. "Your grandmother would murder you if you pulled that stunt."

"True. But Amara might murder me if I keep trying to waltz with her."

Lauren reaches over and places a hand over mine. "I'll be there. I promise. I can get someone up here to be back up." She pauses, a smile flickering at the corner of her lips. "And I'll bring my steel-toed boots for dancing, just to be safe."

I chuckle. "You got it, birdie."

Interlude

THE RUSTON DAILY LEADER

January 24

Old Fashions, New Purpose

By Rhett Hebert

Get ready to be dazzled! The outfits you'll see at this year's Mardi Gras ball and parade are inspired by a long and prestigious history. Influenced by European royalty, the debutante style gowns often feature bespoke beadwork, intricate sequin patterns, and sky-high collars.

While each dressmaker has their own style, the distinctive gowns and suits at Mardi Gras events don't happen overnight.

Traditionally, dressmakers work with krewe royalty and the year's theme to make one-of-a-kind garments that wouldn't be out of place in a museum.

"I spent my young adult years in New Orleans apprenticing under a well-known dressmaker there. Even though I later moved to Ruston, I still get called for consultation on Mardi Gras garments," said Rhonda Jenkins, owner of Grand Garments on Central Avenue in Ruston. "It's a real treat to be able to lead the gown making for our very own Mardi Gras royalty this year."

Gladys Beaumont, who serves as the director the Mardi Gras

krewe's steering committee, helped guide the clothing designs for this year's event. "We wanted to choose a theme to make a real statement our first year," Beaumont said. "After some brainstorming and a vote, the theme 'Birds of a Feather' was chosen. We urge all who are buying tickets for the ball to keep the theme in mind when choosing your outfits."

Beaumont also said that there will be bird-themed throws at the parade, as well as special feathered souvenirs for all who attend the ball.

The Krewe of Persici ball will be held at the Community Center Hall on February 16. Get your tickets now as the event is projected to sell out.

Chapter 14

LAUREN

January 24

I stare at the hot sauce packets still sitting on my desk. No one's ever done anything like that for me—brought me food at work. Especially not a man, even one who is just a friend.

My cheeks heat thinking about the way Max appeared at the front of the office building holding up a takeout bag in his sweatpants and hoodie, all casual and snuggly looking. And I wonder, not for the first time, if I should keep him in the friend zone or try to take a step toward something more.

I sigh and scoop the extra packets into my desk drawer. I haven't wanted a relationship in years after always being disappointed by the men I've dated. None of them have ever understood me, or tried to understand my passion for work. But, then again, none of them have made me want to take breaks from work either. Not like Max does.

I'm even grudgingly looking forward to our dance lesson tomorrow.

My desk phone rings. The name "Beaumont" pops up on the screen. I grin.

"Well hello there Mr. Pelican," my voice comes out throaty and playful. Seductive even.

"Not how I'm usually greeted," a female voice laughs. "But I guess this means my grandson told you what his bird is for the krewe."

Gladys. Shit. I blush from head to toe.

"Oh my goodness, I'm so sorry Gladys. I saw the last name and just thought—"

"That I was my grandson? No worries, dear. I'm glad you two are getting to know each other better. Especially because I've arranged a costume fitting for you both this afternoon. Can you be there at four? I know it's a bit early, but Max has to be at work at six."

I think about Max showing up last night at my office, on his night off. The way he made time for me when he didn't have to. Of all the overtime I put in nearly every day. "Yes," I say before I can think better of it. "I'll be there."

"Wonderful, dear. See you this afternoon."

When I head out of the office at 3:30, I swear an uncanny silence settles over the newsroom.

"Everything okay, Lauren?" Rhett asks, standing up to look over his cube wall. I hear the sincerity in his voice and realize that the only times I've ever left early before were for the births of my nieces and nephew and the one time I had an appendix emergency that left me in the hospital for a couple of days.

"Just Mardi Gras business," I say. "You've got things handled the rest of the day?"

He grins. "We've got you covered, boss. Go on and have a good time. Don't worry."

And, for perhaps the first time ever, I shrug off my guilt and walk out of the office the door early.

The peacock bird mask from that night at the Community Center Hall should have prepared me. But, it did not. Nothing could have prepared me for this sequined, bedazzled, feathered monstrosity that has the audacity to be called a dress. I have to work hard to keep the grimace off my face.

"That dress must weigh twenty pounds," I mutter.

"Thirty!" the dressmaker proclaims like it's a badge of honor. And for her, I suppose it is. "It will take a couple of people to get you into this. But that's what we're here for. And then we'll have you stand out here while we tuck and pin it so it fits you perfectly." Her round glasses magnify her eyes to almost anime character size. And both in age and appearance, she's a dead ringer for Edna from The Incredibles. She brushes her black bangs away from her eyes and plants a hand on her hip.

"Now then, dear, if you'll just come back behind this screen here—" She's cut off by the shop's front door chime.

We both turn as Max walks in, hair tied back in a messy bun, a backpack slung over one shoulder. He's wearing a black Smashing Pumpkins t-shirt with a tan flannel over it and worn jeans. He's trimmed his beard back so that it's cropped close to his face. His casual look is the opposite to my fitted skirt and blouse.

"Hey, Ms. Rhonda," he says waving to the dressmaker. Then he turns to look at me and cracks a grin. "Hey, Lauren."

I swallow.

"Yes, yes," Rhonda says. "You're next, Max. Lauren, if you would?" She points to the clothes screen where I'm to change. I walk behind it. "Go ahead and strip down to your bra and panties, dear, then I'll go get my assistant and we'll help you get into your dress."

I hear a choking sound come from somewhere in Max's direction and smile to myself, thrilled to have that effect on him. Dutifully, I strip down to my underwear. "Ready!" I call out.

Rhonda and her young assistant, Kennedy, appear holding the massive dress between them.

"We're going to squat down and you're going to step into the dress," Rhonda instructs. "We will stand and pull it up with us, then zip you into it."

I follow their directions, mentally preparing for the itch and scratch of the sequins. But when the dress lands on my shoulders, it's surprisingly comfortable. It's been lined with a soft fabric that protects me from all its showy elements. Kennedy steps behind me, working the zipper.

"Perfect, perfect," Rhonda says. "Now, come out here and step on the dress platform. Kennedy will start pinning you while we get Mr. Beaumont dressed."

I step from behind the barrier and the room lights up as the sunlight from the windows hits my gown's sequins, light scattering to paint a blue and purple kaleidoscope across the room.

I look at Max to get a read on him, fully prepared to see him trying to stifle a laugh. But he's not. He's staring, sure, but he's not laughing. Something much hotter simmers in his gaze as he looks at me. He bites his bottom lip and runs a hand over his messy bun. I glance down and notice my cleavage above the wide neckline. My cheeks heat.

"Mr. Beaumont, we have your suit over here, if you would," Rhonda says.

He takes a step forward just as Kennedy steps behind me and pulls in the back of my dress so that it fits me tightly, making my breasts peek out even more. I reach up to cover myself but Kennedy says, "Please don't move. It's important for you to stand just like this while I pin your dress."

And so, like a damsel in distress, I leave my heaving bosom on full display. Heat creeps up my chest, but I hold my head high, trying to pretend like my boobs are not on full display and surrounded by sequins like a couple of prized crown jewels.

"Can I get a little more coverage on my cleavage?" I whisper to Kennedy.

"Yes, we'll add that in the alterations," she replies, never moving her eyes from where she pins my dress.

Max has to pass me to get back to the clothing screen. As he reaches me, he pauses, slowly looking me up and down. His gaze snags with mine and he mouths one word: "Stunning." Then he walks behind the partition.

Kennedy continues to pin my dress while I hold still and obsess over what Max just said to me.

"Here are your pants and shirt, dear," Rhonda says. "Your jacket and bowtie are out here waiting for you."

Seems Max doesn't need a team to get him into his clothes.

"You do look stunning, you know," Kennedy says quietly. "Look." She turns me to face a floor length mirror.

I gasp. Yes, the dress is gaudy, peacock blue, and feathered. But the off the shoulder look fits my body in all the right places. It makes me look like it belongs in Vogue, which causes me to preen like, well, like a peacock.

"Told you," Kennedy whispers, her cheeks dimpling.

I study myself in the mirror, noting the way the dress sparkles and the attention that was paid to each detail. A sequined pattern that mirrors peacock feathers has been sewn into the dress. It's truly a work of art.

When I glance back up to the mirror, I see another face behind me. I turn to see Max in a pair of charcoal gray pants and cream-colored button-up shirt. He wears a cream-colored, sequined coat and golden bowtie. Our eyes hold each other's in the mirror. I've never seen him in anything other than casual jeans or pajama pants. Seeing him like this, in a expertly tailored, albeit gaudy, suit, takes my breath away.

I turn slowly to look at him. We take each other in. "Well now you're truly a birdie," he says, one side of his mouth ticking up in a smirk.

"I was expecting more . . . pouches for a pelican," I say.

His smirk transforms into a grin. "I think this is audacious enough. Besides, I want to make my peacock queen proud."

My grin matches his, both of us studying the other intently.

I imagine us in our bedazzled outfits walking arm in arm in the Community Center Hall turned ballroom, the event lights reflecting off our combined sparkles as we take to the dance floor together. The way he will be my king at the event. It's a beautiful fantasy that makes the little girl still nestled down in my soul squeal in delight. Literally dressing up to go to the ball and dancing with a king—of a sort. Oh yes, little girl Lauren wouldn't believe her luck at this turn of events. The thought is enough to shove any of my lingering grumpy thoughts about participating as Mardi Gras royalty out the window completely.

Chapter 15

MAX

As Rhonda flits around me, pinning my coat, I can't take my eyes off Lauren. She's always so buttoned up, business-ready. And I love that about her. But that dress? My God. My gaze trails along the lines of her collar bones, down to her bare shoulders. I want to run my lips along them, to bite at where those delicate bones emerge.

I should stop staring. This is probably getting awkward for everyone else in the room. But I can't tear my gaze away from her.

Rhonda steps in front of me. She's tiny, but demanding, and pulls me forward to inspect the length of the coat. "Good, good," she murmurs. "This will be ready for you in a couple of weeks, plenty of time before the ball." Which is in three weeks. "Go change and leave this on the hangers behind the dressing screen."

I duck my head, trying not to be captivated by Lauren. She wants to maintain a friendship, I remind myself. *But she was staring at me too*, my subconscious chimes in. And her gaze was far more heated than that of just a friend.

I take my glittering coat off and hang it up. Then take the button-up and bowtie off, hanging them too. I kick off the shiny, black dress shoes and slide them against the wall. I start to undo my pants when something crashes out in the shop, followed by a screech.

I don't even think, I just move. I run from behind the barrier and see Lauren on the floor, practically drowning in fabric. I hustle over to her and kneel beside where she's laid out on the floor. Kennedy is on one side of her, asking if she's okay. I scan her face. She looks out of it, her eyes wide and blank.

"Lauren, look at me. Are you okay?" I demand. I want—no, *need*—to fix whatever is wrong with her.

"Probably just got overheated in the tight, heavy dress," Kennedy murmurs. "Happens with our brides all the time."

Rhonda hurries over with a cool rag and presses it to Lauren's forehead. She hands another to Kennedy who presses it to her neck. In a moment, Lauren's gaze comes into focus again. It finds me immediately. Her brows furrow.

"Where am I?" she mumbles. "Am I dreaming?"

"I should call 911," I say immediately.

"No need for all that," Rhonda brushes me off. "There you are, dear. Just lay here and we'll get you some water." Kennedy stands and goes off to retrieve the drink.

Lauren lifts her hand and lightly touches my chest, which I realize is bare. Her finger trails over the twists and curves of the tattoo on my pec. Her touch is light, but it electrifies me, shooting desire through my entire body. Which it should not be doing when she just passed out and is still laying on the floor. I shift and reach up to place a hand over hers where it touches my chest.

"Hey there, birdie. You're okay." My voice is low, hoarse.

She blinks, her eyes fluttering. "Oh," she says dreamily. Her eyes narrow. "Oh!" She tries to pull her hand away, cheeks flaming. Their beet red color stands out in stark contrast to her blonde hair. And I love it. Love it so much I want to bend down and press a kiss to the apples of her cheeks. I hold her hand against my heart, and I know she can feel it beating wildly beneath her palm.

I reach down with my other hand and push her hair back from

where it's trapped in the cool rag on her forehead. "It's okay. Just a little too much heat."

Kennedy comes back with a bottle of water. "Can you sit up?" Rhonda asks. "We'll help you."

I drop Lauren's hand and reach forward to help ease Lauren into a sitting position.

"It's okay, dear. You just passed out. Happens to our brides occasionally too. Here, drink this." Rhonda hands Lauren the water bottle and she sips at it.

Her eyes are wild, scared I realize. Without stopping to think about it, I move to sit behind her and give her a solid surface to lean against. My bare chest presses into her back and those damn dress sequins are sandwiched between us. They scratch my skin, but I ignore them.

"You don't have to do that," Lauren whispers.

"I want to." I can't stop the words, and I wouldn't even if I could. I want to help her, to hold and comfort her.

"Probably best to get you out of this dress," Rhonda says. She reaches between us and pulls down the zipper. Lauren inhales deeply. I can't stop staring at the lines of her beige bra revealed beneath the dress's fabric.

"That's better," Lauren says. "Maybe don't alter the dress quite so tight," she laughs, then leans back into me. I close my eyes, savoring this moment, knowing that seeing a hint of her bra will likely never happen again.

"Ready to stand?" Rhonda asks. Lauren nods. "Slowly now."

Together we help her up. Then Rhonda and Kennedy walk with her behind the dressing screen. A few minutes later she emerges, dressed in her work clothes. Her pony tail is slightly mussed, but she's no worse for wear.

I'm so busy looking her over to make sure she's okay, that it takes me a second to realize she's staring at my bare chest. I glance down, then back up at her and smirk. I run my hand across my pecs, flexing them a bit so she'll keep looking. My hand trails across my chest, and

I'm very glad that I've kept up my gym routine.

Lauren suddenly looks away at Kennedy, who's smirking. "Right," Lauren says. "See you both in a couple of weeks." Then she hurriedly walks past me and through the front door, the chime sounding with her exit.

I turn away from the door and look back to Rhonda and Kennedy, both of them grinning widely.

Chapter 16

MAX

January 25

Amara stares at me warily. No doubt she's remembering our first disastrous dance lesson. And who could blame her? I glance at her feet and see that she's wearing tennis shoes instead of those heeled dance shoes she had on last time. I wince, knowing I'm the reason she changed her footwear.

"Let's get started?" she asks pointedly.

I glance to the studio's door one more time, my stomach sinking. I'm beginning to wonder if Lauren is bailing on me again. Am I a fool chasing her at every turn?

I nod, walking over to Amara. I assume the waltz stance she taught me last time. She steps up to hold my hand and I take her arm. "One, two, three," she instructs softly, then we begin to move. It's not quite as difficult as last time, my body finding the steps more easily.

Just as I'm starting to get into the flow of it, the studio door chimes and I halt mid-dance step, causing Amara to whisper curses under her breath. Lauren steps through the door, her normally neat ponytail tousled by the wind. I'm so relieved it feels like a giant concrete gargoyle just toppled off my shoulders. I can't stop staring at her.

Amara clears her throat. Right.

"Lauren, this is Amara," I say as I walk toward where she still stands at the door. I turn to our dance instructor. "Amara, this is Lauren, my dance partner."

"The one who skipped our last session?" And yeah, she's definitely salty.

"I'm so sorry about that, Amara," Lauren says before I can respond. "It was rude of me not to call and let you know I wouldn't be here last time. I got caught up in a work emergency. Which is why I'm late today, as well. Demanding job. Again, my apologies."

Amara relaxes and nods. "Right then. Put your stuff down over there, then join us on the dance floor. I see that you've worn heels, which is perfect. You'll need them."

Lauren hustles to oblige Amara. Our dance instructor has to be nearly a decade younger than me, but manages to command us both like a general. Lauren steps to the middle of the floor and Amara proceeds to show her how to hold her arms, then walks her through the basic box step. To my utter surprise, Lauren moves with Amara like she's been dancing her whole life.

"That was very good," Amara says, a hint of a smile crossing her lips.

"Thank you," Lauren acknowledges. "I did dance a long time ago, but the muscle memory is still there."

"That's good, because he'll need all the help he can get," she says, side-eyeing me. "And you'll need to watch your toes. Now, together."

I walk to Lauren, taking one of her hands in mine, my other hand lightly resting on her shoulder blade. She places her arm on top of mine. Her touch, even in this formal setting, still heats my blood.

"Good," Amara says, adjusting our arms by a few degrees. "Now box steps. One, two, three."

I'm hyper aware of every place that Lauren and I touch. I'm distracted by her scent, her nearness. My mind immediately flies back to the way she rested against my chest at the dressmaker's shop yesterday. I'm so lost in my growing obsession with her, that when Lauren tries to move in our box step, I stumble.

"Try again," Amara says.

Lauren leans in and whispers, "So I guess I'm winning this competition round, just like the bead cleanup, huh? I'm clearly the better dancer."

My grin snaps into place. And suddenly, I'm laser focused on getting this dance right. "Not so fast there, birdie."

"One, two, three," Amara says as she claps out a beat.

And I move, focusing on my feet. It works. Sort of. "Quit staring at your feet, Maxwell," Amara snaps. "Look up. Hold your posture. It's much easier that way."

Lauren giggles. Amara walks over to a speaker and fumbles with it, then soft instrumental music with that three-count beat plays. Amara calls out the beat and we move again. Better this time.

We make two complete box steps before I step on Lauren's toes and she winces. "You may be better at bowling, but you're definitely losing this round, Maxwell," she says.

"You're awfully cocky tonight for someone who passed out just from wearing a dress yesterday."

"You try wearing a dress that weighs as much as a kindergartner cinched tight around your chest in a hot room and see how long you last."

"You doubt me?" I scoff.

"Absolutely I do," she says.

And then I step on her toes. She winces. Shit. I was doing so well, too.

"Again!" Amara shouts, and we start moving. The more we practice the basic box step, the easier it becomes. I'm thinking less and letting my body move in the practiced motion. My cautious stumbling steps transform into smooth, gliding movements.

I'm not supposed to look at Lauren directly, so instead I focus on her ear, noting the way it comes to the slightest of points at the tip, the way her honey-colored hair wisps around it. I like looking at this part of her too, especially because I can look at her without openly staring. I watch her pulse thrum in her neck just below her ear. Fantasize about leaning in and pressing my lips to it, feeling that flutter just beneath my lips. Allowing my tongue to slip out and taste the salt of her skin.

"Good!" Amara snaps and we halt.

My gaze snags with Lauren's. A wide grin spreads across her face, one born of pure, unadulterated joy. She loves this, I realize. And happiness looks good on her. Her cheeks are flushed with the exercise, her eyes alight.

"See, I told you I could do it," I whisper to her impishly.

"Now, time for spin turns and whisks," Amara says.

My face falls in horror. "There's *more*?"

Amara looks at me like I just asked if gravity is real. "Yes, of course there's more. Did you really think you were just going to move in a square for your royal dance?"

Lauren giggles, then slaps a hand over her mouth. But her eyes crinkle in delight. And I realize that I'd take a hundred dance lessons to see that smile on Lauren's face every night.

Determined, I walk up to Lauren and extend my arms. She steps into me and we begin again.

Chapter 17

LAUREN

February 1

After our dance lesson, Max asked me to dinner, and this time, my answer was an immediate yes. The way he reacted when I agreed, like I just woke him up on Christmas morning, boosted my self confidence to the ceiling.

But it takes us nearly a week to find a time we can both go to dinner. I've had to cancel because someone called out sick. Twice. I'm surprised Max still wants to try, especially given how I was treated by other men in similar circumstances, but he's persistent.

I drive to meet him at the restaurant straight from work. We agreed that we'd have dinner first, then practice our waltz afterwards. Max borrowed his grandmother's key to the Community Center Hall, so we'll go there to get a feel for how we dance together on that floor. I'm already exhausted from struggling to sleep last night and the long work day, but I'm determined not to bail on him again.

I pull up to the restaurant and park. It's a seafood place. No fancy dress code, but not exactly a diner either. Something nice. I pull down my car visor, open the mirror, quickly fix my hair, and swipe on some lip gloss. That will have to do. I close it and get out of my car, grabbing my small purse. I walk into the restaurant and try to glance past the hostess stand to see if Max is already here.

"May I help you, ma'am?" the hostess greets me.

"Yes, I'm meeting someone. I'm not sure if he's here yet?"

"What's the name?"

"Max Beaumont."

"Ah yes, right this way," she says, plastering on a smile.

I follow her through the low-lit space, noting the dark wooden walls and forest green seating. It's cozy and elegant. I'm still not sure if this is a "get to know your Mardi Gras royalty friend" dinner, or a date. But I'm going into it with an expectation for friendship and an openness to more. Maybe.

The hostess stops at a table and says, "Here you are."

I frown. We've stopped at a table with two couples already seated. One couple appears to be in their sixties, the other closer to Max's age. "Oh, no. This isn't the right table. I'm just meeting one other person," I say politely.

"Oh, I thought you said Beaumont?" the hostess asks, clearly confused.

"I did. Max Beaumont," I reply quietly, trying to keep from disturbing this group's dinner. "Neither one of these men is Max."

She fidgets, glancing at the table then back to me. Finally she leans in to whisper, "Ma'am, the older gentleman is Maxwell Beaumont. That's the only reservation here under that name."

Have I entered the Twilight Zone? What is happening here?

"Can we help you with something, ma'am?" the alleged Maxwell Beaumont asks.

"I'm sorry. There is just a mixup. I'm supposed to be meeting someone here for dinner, and it appears you both have the same name." I try to smile and fail. Is this some elaborate joke? Did I actually work too hard and fall asleep at my desk and am stuck in a nightmare?

"Is that right?" the other Max says, leaning back in his chair with a smirk. He turns to face the hostess. "Why don't you see if you have a reservation for Beau Baxter?"

She lights up immediately. "We do."

"And here he is," a deep voice, one that rumbles across the radio waves most nights a week, says from behind me.

"Well, isn't this a surprise?" the other Max says.

"Dad," Max says tightly. "Mom. Charles, Alicia, hope you're having a nice evening."

Max slides a hand to the small of my back and I turn to look at him. His face is tight, lines etched around the corners of his eyes and mouth. His humor and cocky attitude are completely gone.

"And I thought you said you couldn't join us for dinner this week," the older woman says. "What a nice surprise."

Did Max rope me into having dinner with his family? I start to ask him, but he answers before I can say anything. "Ah well, that remains true, Mom. As you can see, I already have plans tonight." His hand moves from the small of my back to rest on my hip.

"I see," his dad says gruffly. And I don't like the look that darkens his face. Not one bit. "Well, son, aren't you going to introduce us to the woman you've snubbed your family to spend time with?"

His grip around me tightens. A beat passes. "Lauren, this is my family. Family, this is Lauren. We won't take up any more of your time. Have a nice evening." His voice is calm, too calm. But I have learned enough about how his dad treats him about his job to recognize the fury bubbling beneath his words.

Max turns us and begins to walk off. As we leave, I hear his dad mutter, "Another slut after our money."

I freeze, ice shooting through my veins like knives. Memories of similar slurs from previous boyfriends start running on a loop through my consciousness. Max, his arm still wrapped around my lower back, tugs me forward. I follow him, unsure of what else to do. Part of me wants to bolt, leave the restaurant and never look back. A bigger part of me wants to grab the largest pitcher of ice water I can find and dump it right on top of old Mr. Beaumont's shiny, balding head. I'd laugh maniacally as ice cubes slid into his undies and down his ass crack.

We halt in front of a small table for two. Our hostess waits for us as Max moves to pull my chair back for me. I sit and watch as he rounds the table to take his own seat.

Silence falls between us. My head is spinning with questions. After his money? Is that man insane? Is that what Max thinks about me? Max is a radio station DJ, for goodness sake. And Gladys owns a funeral home, but I doubt her career means that money-chasing women are after her grandson. I yank myself out of my thought spiral to study Max.

He's staring down at the white table cloth, face still tight. If that comment made me start to go off the rails, then what must Max be thinking? There's a reason he must skip dinner with his family. After that little interaction it seems obvious why he avoids them, but there's a more immediate issue. "Max, are you okay?"

His head snaps up, and I realize that he's not sad, he's furious. "I'm doing everything in my power not to go over there and punch my father in front of some of the biggest gossips in Ruston. He should not have said that about you. I'm sorry he did, Lauren. That's not what this is with you and me, not who you are. I know that." His jaw clenches as he grinds his teeth. His hair is brushed back into a low bun, so I can see every plane of his face. See the way the anger and frustration ripple over it.

"Do you want to talk about it? About your family, I mean?"

He stares at me, a look of pain crossing over his face.

"What can I start you with to drink this evening?" a young man asks as he walks to our table.

I glance at the offerings, noting the wine selection. I could use some liquid courage tonight. "A glass of your house red, please."

"Coke for me, extra ice," Max replies.

Our waiter walks off to get them started.

"I should have asked if alcohol was okay," I say, already feeling like I've misstepped.

"You don't have to ask me anything. Get whatever you want," he hesitates, as if trying to find the right words, or maybe just searching for courage. "I've been sober for three years now. Lauren, don't look at me like that. It's fine, I promise. It's something I'm open about and I'm at a place with it that when others drink a glass of wine or two around me, it doesn't bother me. Plus," he says, the first signs of joy hinting at his eyes. "I'll be your designated driver if you need one. So enjoy it."

We both look over the menus for a moment, and when our server returns, we place our orders. Shrimp and grits for Max and crab cakes for me.

I start to wonder if I should bring up his family again when Max answers the question for me.

"It's complicated," he says. "My family, I mean."

Chapter 18

MAX

This was supposed to be a fun evening with Lauren. We worked hard to find a time that was okay for both of us. And somehow, in a terrible twist of fate, my family just had to be here tonight. Sure, I knew Dad visited this place from time to time, but I wanted to take Lauren somewhere nice. To avoid any confusion with my namesake, I made the reservation under my radio alias.

And it bit me in the ass. Of course it did.

I sigh and lean back in my chair. Lauren is concerned, her upset response to what my dad said earlier washed away. God, she's too good for me.

"How complicated?" she asks.

I rub my hand along the back of my neck, trying to calm the rising tide of anger, embarrassment, and frustration.

"You sure you want to hear this? I feel like we're just now really getting to know each other," I deflect.

"Max, it's up to you. Share whatever you're comfortable sharing. But I want to know more about you. Share your mental load. Be a good friend."

There's that damn word again. Friend.

But she wants to know about me. After all this time of trying to get her attention, she's fully locked in. And it's genuine.

I take a deep breath. Exhale. "I'm a disappointment. To all of them. Dad's grandfather started an investment business that expanded into an empire over the generations. Dad sold off most of it for a fortune, but retained a list of high-profit clients. He expected me, as his oldest son, to step into the role after him. He primed me for it my whole life. My brother too. The Beaumont Legacy. And, in order to do that, he had a plan for me. MBA. Well-connected wife. All the societal things expected of me."

"Ah," Lauren says. "But you didn't do those things?"

"I tried at first. But, God, I hated my finance courses. Failed every last one of them. Spent my college days trying to please my father and never quite living up to his expectations. I tried to talk to him about it, but he wouldn't hear it. And then, when I was twenty, it came to a head over my birthday dinner. I stormed out. Told him I was done. Charles could run the business. Dad threatened my inheritance. I didn't give a single fuck."

I grab my Coke and take a swig. Lauren waits patiently for me to continue. She's leaning forward, chin resting on her hands. Her full attention is on me.

"I switched my major to communications. Stopped showing up for the dates he demanded I go on with his clients' daughters. Started earning my reputation as a party boy." I pause to see Lauren's reaction to that revelation.

But she just lifts an eyebrow. "Go on."

I sigh. "I spent way too much time drinking my way through college and going to frat parties. It's a miracle I managed to graduate. And the only reason I did was because one of my communications professors took mercy on me and forced me into the school radio station booth to make up for my failing grade in his class. Turns out I was pretty damn good at it."

"What did your dad think of your major change?"

"Because we weren't talking, it took a while before he learned what happened. But when he finally found out, he hated it, of course. Threw a big fit. Tried to get the school to kick me out. That only made me more determined. Long story short, I graduated and got a job at the radio station. Started part-time and now have a full-time gig. The pay isn't great, but it makes me happy. Plus," I say, leaning in conspiratorially, "they let me wear pajama pants to work."

Lauren rolls her eyes and chuckles. "I guess you are pretty good at your job."

"Lauren Landau, do you listen to my radio show?" Her whole face heats and all of my anger whooshes out of me. It's replaced by something like pride. I sit up a little straighter. "You do!" I drop my voice into my lower, more formal radio tone. "Listeners, tonight we have a special guest. One might even call her a fan of Beau Baxter."

She kicks me under the table. "Stop," she laughs. But I notice the color on her cheeks has cooled. "I catch your show on my evening drive home from the office. Your voice is . . . comforting. And you're funny. Of course I listen."

Well, hot damn. My face cracks open in a grin and all thoughts of my past wash down the drain. I want to stand up and beat my chest like Tarzan. Lauren likes my voice. She thinks I'm funny.

Our server arrives with our food, placing our plates in front of each of us. We dig in, the tension in the air nearly gone.

"What's your favorite part of my show?" I ask, eager for her to compliment me again.

She considers. "I like the call-in trivia questions. I always guess and get a lot of them right. All those years of journalism research, I suppose. What's your favorite part of your show?"

"The music. At night they're a lot more lax about what songs have to be played. I dig into the vault for my favorites. Nirvana, Smashing Pumpkins, Stone Temple Pilots. It's fun."

"I'm proud of you for doing what you love," she says genuinely. "I know how you got there wasn't exactly pleasant. But you're doing what makes you happy and you kicked the alcohol habit. Fuck what your dad says. You're amazing."

"Lauren. Did you just say fuck?"

"That's what you took out of my little motivational speech?"

"Fuck yeah, I did."

We both laugh. And as we wrap up our dinner, the server brings out one giant piece of king cake with two forks and sets it between us. "On the house," he says. "Big fan of your show, Beau."

I thank him, and, as our eyes meet over the Mardi Gras dessert that keeps bringing us together, we smile and reach for our forks.

Chapter 19

LAUREN

Max tried to pay for dinner, but after the comment his dad made about me only wanting his money, I refused. I support myself just fine. I know Max doesn't think I'm a golddigger, but if details about our dinner find their way to his family, I want it to be known loud and clear that I took care of myself.

I stuck to one glass of wine, and after a big dinner and dessert, the alcohol buzz has faded. Part of me is tired and pining for the soft comfort of my bed. But a bigger part of me is looking forward to our post-dinner dance practice.

Max seemed chipper about it, but then again, maybe that's just the caffeine from the three Cokes he had at dinner.

As I drive over to the Community Center Hall, tailing behind Max, I'm a little jittery with a mix of excitement and nerves.

I still need to sit with how Mr. Beaumont's comment made me feel and what it triggered. And, I'm about to be dancing alone with Max. Sure, it's a formal dance with a distinct amount of space between us, but the last time we practiced waltzing, we bumped into each other constantly. Not to mention the way it felt to clasp hands, arms touching.

I turn my music up a little louder.

We both turn into the Community Center's lot, parking in the spots closest to the front door. Early February is cool, though not unbearably so. Still, when I step out of my car, I tug my jacket in a little closer. Max gets out of his truck and I follow him to the front door, keys jangling as he sorts through them. He finds the one he's looking for and twists it in the lock.

The door opens to the dark, cavernous space. What felt industrial during the day now feels a little spooky at night. I shiver. I can see the outlines of boxes stacked against the wall and remember what happened with them last time I was here. What a mess.

Max steps inside and feels along the wall for the light switch. I hear him slapping and shuffling, then suddenly all the lights flicker on. I have to blink a couple times as my eyes adjust. Not so spooky in the light. I cross to the middle of the floor and look around, slowly turning as I study the empty space. The chime of a Bluetooth speaker turning on sounds, and I glance over to see Max tinkering with his phone.

Norah Jones's "Come Away With Me" drifts through the speaker, her voice like the comforting purr of a cat.

"I googled songs that you can waltz to," Max says with a shrug. "Turns out there are whole playlists of them, so I picked one."

"Great planning on your part."

"Why thank you, my queen. Shall we?" he asks, overdoing it on the charm. He walks to me and extends his arms.

I step into him, find our waltz stance, and we start moving. It's clumsy at first and we mess up several times. But we don't give up. I start counting the beat out loud as we find our rhythm, then slowly drop the count as our bodies fall into the movements. Both of us are focused on getting this right, and definitely not where our hands touch, or how our bodies accidentally bump into each other.

Norah Jones fades into "Perfect" by Ed Sheeran. And the whole atmosphere shifts as Ed belts out one of the most romantic songs out there. I start to make a joke about it, but freeze when I realize that Max is staring at me with… is that longing? My heart stutters in my chest. We keep moving, but I barely register it. We seem to float, and I swear I can hear each beat of my own heart as it falls in line with the three-count.

I stare at Max, knowing neither of us is supposed to be looking at each other while we waltz and unable to stop myself all the same. His hand slides down my shoulder to my hip until it lands on my waist. My hand finds his shoulder. I let go of his other hand, bringing it to his chest. I can feel his heartbeat beneath my palm, and I'm reminded of how I touched his bare chest just like this at the dress shop. I glance at my hand, marveling at it resting there over his button-up shirt.

We've moved closer to one another and his beard tickles as it brushes against my temple. It's intoxicating and I allow myself to lean into it, just a little bit. He does the same, and then our heads are resting against each other as we sway, jaw to temple.

Fire ignites in my abdomen, searing into my core. I can't remember the last time I felt desire like this. It's the kind that makes me want to throw caution to the wind and ignore all my responsibilities. To fall into bed with Max Beaumont and pretend like the rest of the world doesn't exist.

The thought shakes me out of my trance. I'm not going to throw my work responsibilities away for anyone, especially not for something that would likely only be a quick fling. Another slut after our money. I lean away from him, our bodies still moving together.

"Why did your dad say that about me?" I ask. Max halts, his body losing the motion of our dance and making me stumble. But I continue. I need to know. "Why would he think I'm some kind of golddigger?"

My voice has chilled with all the memories of past boyfriends, of always being seen as the perfect accessory to their careers, never being taken seriously in my own right.

Max sighs. "Because that's happened to me in the past. And my dad tries to use it as leverage to get me to date who he wants me to date. Women who come from their own wealthy families. Women who, in his mind, would be the kind of financial match he wants for me. But Lauren, you have to know I don't think that about you."

I drop my arms, raising them across my chest to rub at the tops of my arms. It creates a much needed barrier between us. "I don't think you do," I allow. "But that's not the first time someone has said something like that to me. And it's just, I don't know, gross. I've worked hard in my career to get where I'm at. Some might say too hard. But I'm proud of myself and I won't be seen as some accessory to a wealthy man."

"Hey, hey," Max says, gently resting his hands on my shoulders. "Look at me, birdie."

I look up into his soulful brown eyes and around his face at his tangled strands of hair that have escaped their bun.

"Do I seriously look like the kind of guy who wants some little trophy wife?"

I eye him, then slowly shake my head. "But your dad—"

"Is an asshole," he finishes. "And I've done my best to go no contact with him. Besides, what radio DJ lives that kind of life?" He smirks.

"But your dad would talk about me. Other people would talk."

"Lauren, so many people in this town know you. And I can't think of a single person who would ever put you and golddigger in the same sentence."

"Besides your dad."

"He doesn't count. He thinks everyone is after his money. That's why he's so damn miserable and lonely."

"Does he think that about your mom?" I wince. I shouldn't have asked that. "I'm sorry—"

Max shrugs. "They met before our family really made their money. And she's stuck with him despite his shitty attitude. My younger brother, Charles, is doing the family business thing. They don't need me. And I don't need them or their money."

"And Gladys?" I ask.

"Thinks my dad is a moron. She raised him in a middle class household. She came from humble means. And when I started pushing back against my dad, she was there for me every time. Let me stay at her house. Cooked breakfast for me. She still tries to help my dad and I get along, but I think my dad is beyond saving."

"I'm sorry, Max. That really sucks."

He shrugs. "It's not about me. This is about you. I want to spend time with you, Lauren. I enjoy talking to you, dancing with you. And it makes me furious that my dad is trying to push away yet another person I enjoy spending time with."

"I'm not going anywhere. I just don't want to ever feel like someone's accessory."

"Have I ever made you feel that way?" he asks, concerned.

"No," I admit. "And I don't want your money."

"Well, that's a relief, especially since my dad cut me off," he jokes.

"Max, that's terrible."

"It is what it is. It's fine. I don't need the money. Working at the radio station gets the job done. It pays for my place, allows me to take care of Mags. Gives me the chance to take a vacation here and there. I'm happy. What else do I need?"

I study his face, noting his earnestness. I believe him. "Okay."

"Okay what?" he asks.

"Okay, let's keep hanging out. And not let the bastards get us down."

He extends his right pinky. "Pinky promise?"

I lock mine with his. "Pinky promise."

Chapter 20

MAX

February 5

As the Mardi Gras ball creeps closer, my grandma uses her connections to convince my boss to invite Lauren onto my show to talk about the Mardi Gras events. Tickets are on sale and they have goals to meet to make sure that this event happens again next year.

I'm not sure how I feel about it. My radio booth is my safe space. It's where I spend hours every week, headphones over my ears, playing music out into the void, taking the occasional phone call. I get to hide behind my radio voice and persona. My booth is a little messy, a little cluttered. What will Lauren think when she sees it? Will she think less of me? I should probably throw away that half-eaten bag of Nerds Gummy Clusters.

I do radio interviews all the time. But those are over the phone while I'm tucked away in my flannel pants and t-shirts in a soundproof room.

But, surprisingly, Lauren agreed to this interview. And there's no way I'm going to be the one to back down.

This will be our hard launch into being krewe king and queen. Anyone who hasn't heard about us yet is about to. Because after the radio interview, Lauren agreed to print a story in the newspaper about the krewe and royalty. I think Lauren might be, quite literally, trying to stick it to the man, a.k.a. my dad. Try to make her feel like shit? She's going to show the world what a queen she is.

I get to my booth early the day of the interview and start picking up a bit. I wipe down the table and keyboard. I arrange my Hobbit Lego set so it sits nicely at the back of the desk. I even dust the small, framed photo of Mags that sits in my space. I leave the trinkets of other DJs who share this space on their shift alone. That will have to do.

I've been in her office, I remind myself. This is no different.

I read through the questions I wrote down for the interview. This isn't my usual style. I much prefer to wing it, doing a little research beforehand and tossing out questions as part of a conversation. But I'm so damn nervous that once Lauren is in my space, her pepperminty smell distracting me, I'll forget everything and just stare blankly at her.

When the clock hits six, I start my evening programming. Lauren will be here at seven. I do my usual spiel, giving traffic and weather updates and play a few songs. Then it's time for my teaser.

"Good evening, Ruston. Beau Baxter hanging out with you tonight here on Peach 101.3. We'll have a special guest in the studio with us tonight. Lauren Landau, the editor-in-chief of your Ruston Daily Leader and this year's Mardi Gras queen, will be on the show at seven to talk all things Carnivale. Now for your weather."

I continue with my usual routine.

At 6:50, movement outside my interior studio window catches my eye. I turn to see Lauren watching me. She waves. My stomach flips and I wave back. I point to the door and wave for her to come in. She opens it and walks through, closing it behind her. I hold a finger over my lips, motioning for her to stay quiet.

"And that was 'Don't Want to Miss a Thing' by Aerosmith, still a rock ballad for the ages. After the break, we'll have Lauren Landau in the studio with us. So don't turn that dial. This is Peach 103.1." I hit a button and let the commercials roll, then slide my headphones down around my neck and turn to look at Lauren.

Her gaze is moving around my work space, noting the sound cushioning panels on the walls, phone, and computer monitors.

"Your office is much cooler than mine," she whispers.

"Thanks," I say with a smile. "Come sit down and let's get you settled. It's simple. You just put the headphones on and move the mic to right about here. Make sure you speak directly into it, but you don't need to put your mouth on it."

"No making out with the mic, got it."

Do not think about making out, I silently chide myself. But her humor helps make things feel normal between us. "Good listening, birdie. Now, we'll keep this simple. I'll manage the lead in, then start the conversation. Just be your delightful self. No swear words. Use full sentences."

"So, don't be a toddler."

"Or a teenager," I agree with a smile.

I turn to my screen, watching the countdown.

"Welcome back to Peach 103.1. I'm Beau Baxter, and tonight we have Lauren Landau in the studio with us. This year's Mardi Gras queen is here to talk about the upcoming events and give you a taste of what's to come. Lauren, welcome to the show tonight."

"Thanks for having me, Beau."

It's weird hearing her call me that. But it will help me stay focused, be professional. "Ruston's first Mardi Gras queen. Congratulations. How did you get elevated to royalty?"

"Thank you. The new krewe has a steering committee. They nominate locals and vote. This year, they wanted media professionals to hold the royalty positions. It turns out my position as editor at *The Ruston Daily Leader* made me the perfect candidate."

"And they are quite lucky to have you." I pause, realizing I haven't explicitly told my audience that I'm this year's Mardi Gras king. And I didn't communicate this to Lauren. I'll try to steer the conversation away from that, I decide.

"Talk to us a little bit about this ball coming up."

"Everyone's invited," she says, sounding like a real queen. "The theme is Birds of a Feather, and we are asking the community to buy a ticket and dress the part. There will be dancing, special themed souvenirs, and a chance to see Mardi Gras culture first hand."

"Have you been to the parades in New Orleans? Do you expect the Ruston parade to mirror those?"

"Yes, but it's been a while. Our parade is going to be more in line with other Northern Louisiana parades. Think family-friendly. We want everyone to be able to enjoy themselves, no matter their age."

"Talk to me about the krewe royalty's outfits. Rumor has it that they are something quite special." My voice dips into humor.

"Well you're right about that, Beau. The costumes will be a surprise, but I can guarantee they will take your breath away. Might make you pass right out when you lay eyes on them."

Oh, she's *playing* with me. On my own show no less. "Is that right? Well now, that is something to look forward to. That sounds like it might be difficult to dance in."

She chuckles. "I have a knack for dancing, as it turns out. My king though, he might have a little trouble." She winks. Okay, so maybe my station manager told her to keep my identity quiet. I relax.

"Any tips for getting listeners ready for the ball and parade?"

"Just come in ready to have fun. I was a little nervous when I first agreed to be queen, but every step of this process has shown me that everyone working on the Mardi Gras events has their whole hearts in it. From the steering committee, to the dressmakers, we have a stellar group ensuring all of this comes together into an unforgettable experience."

She's a natural. Her ease behind the mic is making me fall for her just a little bit more. She stepped into my world and sees the good in it.

"Mardi Gras is known for the throws people catch on the route. Any chance you've stumbled upon what's going to be tossed this year?"

Lauren's eyes grow wide and she shakes her head. And I know she's caught my meaning. "Why, yes I have stumbled upon them, Beau. And I can't wait to scoop them up and throw them to the community."

"Just don't throw them too hard. You wouldn't want to fall off the float."

She laughs. "Oh, my dance lessons have given me better balance. I think I'll be just fine."

I notice that my clock is signaling that it's nearly time for a commercial break. "Well, the entire city is excited about these upcoming events. Where can people buy their ball tickets and learn more about the free parade?"

"You can find us at the Krewe of Persici's website."

"Thanks for coming on the show tonight, Lauren."

"Thank you for having me."

"We'll be back after the break. This is Pcach 103.1." I start the commercials and lower my headphones. She does the same.

"Stumbled upon throws? Really, Max? You're never going to let me live that down are you?"

I chuckle, loving that I got under her skin. "The setup was too good. I had to take it."

She shakes her head, but she's smiling. "This is very cool, you know," Lauren says, looking around my office.

"This? My little radio cave? I like it alright."

"I can see why you do. You're great at this."

"Thanks, birdie. That means a lot to me." I glance at the clock. "I'm about to have to go back on. You can sit and listen if you want?"

She hesitates.

"But you don't have to," I say immediately.

"I want to, but I have something to finish at work and—"

"I understand." Because I do. That's who Lauren is. And she still made time to come on the show tonight. Even if it was just to do promotion work for the krewe.

"But maybe tomorrow we could do something? Hang out?" she

asks hesitantly.

"After ball rehearsal?"

"Oh, I forgot. Yes. After rehearsal would be great."

I glance over and see that my timer is up. I slide my headphones on and do my intro, welcoming everyone back to the show and quickly queuing up a song. I look back to talk to Lauren, but she's already standing in the door to the hallway. I wave and she waves back, then she turns and is gone.

Interlude

PEACH 103.1

Beau: Good evening. You're listening to Peach 101.3 and this is Beau Baxter. It's Mardi Gras season and today we're talking about all things Louisiana culture and tradition—from king cakes to parades and everything in between. We have Felicia Smith, history professor at Tulane University, on the show tonight. She's been talking to us about New Orleans history and some of the traditions we still practice today. Good to have you on the show, Felicia.

Felicia: It's good to be here.

Beau: Let's talk about something that's become integral to New Orleans culture: the Second Line. If you've ever been down to the Big Easy, you may have seen parades of people playing jazz music and holding umbrellas as they dance through the streets.

Felicia: I saw one this morning actually. Always a good time.

Beau: Where did Second Lines come from?

Felicia: Well, they have macabre beginnings, as many things do in New Orleans. They are celebrations, yes, but they are also used to honor those who have died. They were started by African Americans as a means of advertising social services in neighborhoods.

They evolved, as so many things do. Now you'll see a Second Line form for a wedding, a funeral, and even at our music festivals. Anyone can hop in and join along.

Beau: Is there ever a First Line?

Felicia: *Laughs* Why, yes. The First Line is the beginning of the parade, so to speak. It's where those being honored lead the way. For weddings, that's the bride and groom. For funerals, the coffin and pallbearers. And that's the group that holds the umbrellas. The band follows behind. And all the celebrants that join are the official Second Line.

Beau: Sounds like a rollickin' good time.

Felicia: You know what they say, laissez les bon temps rouler! Let the good times roll!

Chapter 21

LAUREN

February 6

Did I ask Max out? I think I did. His presence in the radio studio, the way he spoke with such confidence, the deeper timbre of his voice while he was on air. That audiobook narrator tone that does things to my brain . . . and other parts of my body.

I had to get out of there before I did something stupid like pounce onto his lap while he tried to work.

And the teasing. The flirting.

My phone buzzes. A text pops up from an unknown number.

Unknown: Great job on the radio tonight.
Lauren: Who is this?
Unknown: Max didn't give you my number like I told him to, did he? This is Janessa, his cousin. We went bowling together.

I relax. I've had a couple of readers turn to obsessive followers over the years. I can never be too careful.

Lauren: Oh! No, he didn't. But I saved you to my phone now.

Janessa: Great! And I'm serious. You and Maxie have great chemistry. I think the whole town is going to want to come to the ball and parade after that interview.

Lauren: I don't think anyone knows Beau is Max?

Janessa: Meh. Enough people do.

Janessa: Anyway. Two things. One, can we grab coffee sometime? It's hard to make friends as an adult, and I really like you and Leslie. She can come too if she wants.

Janessa: And two. You should probably know that next Saturday is Max's birthday.

The text suddenly reminds me of just how much older I am than Max.

Lauren: Thanks for the heads up. How old will he be?

Janessa: 34.

A six year age gap. Is that cringey? Am I a cougar? I mean that's a reasonable gap right? Men and women date the other way around all the time. And we're not even dating. What am I thinking? And, oh God, I asked him out on his birthday.

Janessa: That doesn't make you a cougar. So don't stress about that.

How did she know—

Janessa: I know that's why you asked his age. But don't worry about it. Max is a great guy and an adult. Have fun at rehearsal tomorrow.

Janessa: And text me a good day for coffee.

Lauren: Thank you. For the intel and the invite.

Janessa: Looking forward to it.

My inbox is flooded with congratulation notices the next day. The word about me being Mardi Gras queen is officially in the public discourse, and everyone I've worked with throughout the years has taken a moment to find me on my almost non-existent social media, email me, or leave a voicemail.

My phone buzzes. I glance at the screen.

Leslie: Well aren't you the hottest thing in town right now.

I roll my eyes.

Lauren: Hardly.

Leslie: I have to admit, that bowling moment with you and Max was some intense sexual tension. But the radio show last night? Whew! I'm fanning myself. And good for you.

The program was so formal. So information based. What am I missing? Yes, conversation with Max was easy. And yes, we had some inside jokes. And perhaps some banter. But chemistry of the romantic variety? Surely not.

I allow my mind to return to the scene of Max in the radio booth, our headphones on, mics live, and smiles dialed up. His deep voice was contained to the booth without any echo thanks to all the sound absorption. Even with a live mic, it was strangely intimate.

And that's when I hear it. The sounds of trumpets echo in the newsroom, playing out a familiar song. Startled, I stand and walk to my office door to see what's happening. Only to find that my entire staff has lined up in the walkway between the short line of cubicles. There are umbrellas, beads, and masks. "The Second Line," a familiar Mardi Gras anthem, booms through a Bluetooth speaker as my staff forms their very own Second Line down to my office.

I'm not sure what to do. Part of me wants to hide under my desk. But, as is happening more and more these days, a bigger part of me wants to join in the fun.

"There's our Mardi Gras queen!" a voice calls out. Everyone cheers.

Rhett steps forward, takes me by the hand, and pulls me into the spontaneous festival through the small office. Never once, in all my years as editor, have we all done something so celebratory together. I watch as my staff laughs, dances, and pumps their umbrellas through the cubicles. And as we finish our circuit, a reporter calls out, "A big cheer for our very own Mardi Gras queen, Lauren Landau!" Everyone thrusts their umbrellas into the air with a shout.

Our line editor wheels out the biggest king cake I've ever seen on one of our paper carts. I'm touched by how much work they put into this on such short notice. I glance at Rhett and he's smiling at me knowingly. Maybe not such short notice then.

He saunters over. "So boss. I know you let the radio station scoop us on your big news. We'll talk about that later. But we are running the story in tomorrow's paper." He smiles and hands me a slice of king cake.

By the time I head out the door for our ball rehearsal, I'm sugared up and . . . not stressed for once. It was a quiet news day and I think the whole office needed to blow off some steam. It was nice to see my coworkers mingling and laughing. Maybe we should form a committee to do more things like today for staff morale.

I plug my phone into my car and zone out to my audiobook. It really is a gift to be able to listen to declarations of love and the intimate details of a couple enjoying each other while going about my daily life. I listen while I drive, getting lost in the details of the story. By the time I make it to the Community Center Hall, the scene in my book is over and I'm feeling a little hot and bothered.

I take a minute to collect myself, pulling down my rearview mirror to make sure I look put together. My cheeks are flushed, so I decide to stand outside in the cool air for a moment before entering the building.

A truck pulls up next to my car and parks. A door slams. "Hey there, birdie." I turn to see Max, mouth quirked up in a half-smile. "Whatcha doin' out here?"

"Just taking a minute before I go into all the chaos."

He leans against my car and folds his arms. Even beneath his jacket I can see the way his arms flex. And the way he stares at me awakens all those warm feelings I was just trying to tamp down. But I don't hate it.

"How was work today?" he asks.

"Pretty chill for once. Fun at the end. Guess my team heard the radio program last night. They threw me a little surprise congratulations party."

"Sounds like your team loves you. Can't say I blame them."

I swallow. What is that supposed to mean?

"Everyone who meets you loves you. And everyone in there tonight will too," he says, nodding at the windows where we can see people mingling as they wait to start the ball rehearsal.

"It was fun. The surprise party at work, I mean. We even danced. Had a little mini-Mardi Gras parade. It's been nice lately, getting out of my comfort zone. Dancing, going on walks, speaking on the radio. I love my job. Wouldn't trade it. But maybe somewhere along the way I forgot that there was more to life than just working my way to the top of my career ladder." I glance down at my feet, surprising myself at my admission.

"You know," Max hedges. "Mags and I like to go hiking. You could come with us if you want. Just a quick weekend trip before the ball and parade. A fun way to get out of here and clear your mind."

"Oh, I don't do tents," I say immediately.

A burst of laughter erupts from Max. "Oh, no doubt. We could find a cabin or something. Plumbing. Running water. Climate control. Do some day hikes and chill at the cabin. Maybe grill. I know that's probably not your usual speed, but—"

"But it sounds like maybe it's the speed I need. I can't remember the last time I took anything resembling a vacation."

"We could make it a two-nighter if you want," he says. I can hear the eagerness in his voice. I like the sound of it, maybe a little too much.

"Think Mags will mind me tagging along on your adventure?"

"Nah. Remember, I told you. Everyone loves you, including Mags."

"Okay," I say, liking the idea more and more.

"Yeah? This weekend?"

My gut reaction is to think of work, to write off the invitation that's just a few days away. I don't do impulsive things. Or I don't anymore. But once, before bad boyfriends and my career dreams, I did. I went to concerts last minute and headed to the beach with my girlfriends. A spark of joy ignites in my chest. I push down the impulse to say no.

"Yes, that should work. Let me arrange back-up at work just in case and make sure Leslie can check on my cat while I'm gone."

"Great. I'm looking forward to it. I'll bring most of the gear, but get a decent pair of hiking shoes," he says, glancing down at my heels.

"I can handle that," I laugh.

"Right then. Well, they're probably wondering where their king and queen are. Shall we?" he asks, extending the crook of his elbow to me.

I take his arm and we head inside.

Groups of people chitchat while the steering committee walks around in a cluster looking at the floor and stage, making notes.

"Hey, Lauren," a familiar voice calls out. It's a voice that warms me to my bones.

"Margie! What are you doing here?" I hustle over to give my friend a hug. Margie Murphy took the town by storm with her viral YouTube channel making peach jams and other foods. Paired with her direct personality, people drive from miles around to see her. Her untamed graying auburn hair floats around her face and she wears a familiar pair of overalls.

"Frank and I got roped into being krewe captains," she says, and she can't hide the smile that spreads across her face.

"When's the wedding?" I ask, as her fiancé walks over to shake my hand.

"Later this spring when the weather warms up," she says.

"I'm Frank," her fiancé says, extending his hand to Max. His graying hair and beard make his green eyes stand out. He's wearing a flannel shirt, which, from all the news coverage I've seen of his insane Christmas decorations, seems to be his usual uniform. Frank moves in next to Margie and slides an arm around her shoulders. They're adorable. That's the kind of love I used to pine for. The kind I almost believed doesn't exist anymore. But these two make me believe again.

"This is Max," I say. He shakes his hand and nods. "Glad to see some friendly faces in here."

"Can't say I'm much of a dancer," Margie says. "But Gladys wants to support Frank's charity for kids who need help with their medical expenses and we couldn't rightly say no to that."

"My grandmother does know how to persuade people," Max chuckles.

"Well I'll be," Margie says. "I didn't realize you were her grandson. Now that you say it, I can see it. She talks about you and your brother all the time. Nice to finally meet you."

Max tenses beside me at the mention of his brother, but he doesn't say anything.

A microphone screeches to life and everyone in the room winces. "Now then everyone, thank you for coming to the ball rehearsal tonight," Gladys says over the mic. "We've got a lot to cover and we don't want to keep you here all night. The ball is in just over a week and, just like a wedding, there's a ceremony to this sort of thing."

Gladys unfolds a piece of paper and straightens her glasses. "First we'll have the welcome reception. That part is easy. Everyone will come in, hit up the bar and mingle. You can join them of course.

After about forty-five minutes, you'll need to head backstage and change into your ornate royal costume. This includes your dresses, suits, back pieces, and masks. Then we'll start the tableau. Lauren, Max, this is your time to shine."

I fidget. Max slides a hand to my lower back to steady me. I lean into it.

"The tableau is, of course, the presentation of the royal court. Max and Lauren, you'll lead this. We'll call your name and you'll process out and take your place at the stage. Our prince and princess will be called next, then the captains."

Everyone moves to the front of the room as Gladys calls out their titles and they take their places. Amelia instructs us where to walk and where to stand, just like a wedding party. Gladys wasn't wrong there.

"Once you're all up here, we'll have a basic waltz so everyone can see those beautiful bird costumes. We really want to make this first tableau fantastic and draw attention to our fundraisers. There will be music, of course. Now, let's walk through it."

Max and I head to the back of the room, taking the front of the line. I lace my arm through his, and his smile warms me, spreading through my chest and giving me the confidence boost I need. When Gladys calls our names, we walk down the middle of the room and move to stand in the center of the small stage. As everyone else is called, we hold our position, making a game of squeezing each other's arms.

"And this is when we'll begin the easy waltz you've all been learning. After that, you'll all take your seats down at the royal table and we'll enjoy dinner. Those back pieces are difficult to wear while eating, so we'll have assistants to help you remove them for a portion of the evening. Everyone with me so far?"

A chorus of affirmative rumbles goes through the room.

"Wonderful. Then we'll open up the dance floor. We have a jazz band coming and they will be playing a mix of popular jazz and Mardi Gras songs, as well as some wedding reception-style favorites."

Max leans over to me. "This really is a lot. Think we'll remember it all?"

"Think Gladys will let us forget?" I whisper back.

He leans closer, his warm breath tickling my ear. "Good point."

"Then, after a while, Amelia will take to the stage and introduce our fundraiser recipients. Max and Lauren, as king and queen, you'll be tasked with dancing with partners in exchange for donations. There will be raffle baskets that Margie and Frank will oversee. The steering committee and other krewe members will collect donations throughout the evening and deposit them in our staging area room."

"Then, when it's time to close it out, we'll have one last royal walk through with some throws for the crowd. That will end the night! And that will be it until the float loading party and parade. Everyone got it?"

Lots of murmurs follow. Amelia walks to the microphone and makes a "gimme" motion with her hands. "Just a few quick follow-up notes. The run of show will be emailed to each of you so you can review it before the ball. We will queue you up that evening and let you know when it's time to do your part. And, finally, keep practicing your waltzes! You'll be on stage in front of everyone."

I squeeze Max's arm at that. He leans over to me. "You have nothing to worry about, birdie. You're light on your feet. I'm the one who needs to worry. Though," he pauses, leaning slightly closer, "when I'm dancing with you, it's easy to stay close and follow along."

Chapter 22

MAX

February 8

I still fully expect Lauren to cancel this hiking weekend. There's no way she's going to leave the newspaper for two and a half days and head out into the woods with me, right? I keep checking the reservation for the tiny house I got for us in Hot Springs, Arkansas. I can still cancel it if I need to. Maybe I should. Maybe this was all a terrible idea and I pushed Lauren to do what I want, not what she wants and—

A white CR-V pulls up to my apartment complex and stops in front of me. The driver's side window rolls down to reveal Lauren in sunglasses, her hair pulled back in a ponytail. She's wearing a maroon quarter zip pullover.

"Get in, camper," she says with cheek.

I love this side of her. I grin and Mags follows me as I walk to the back of the car. The hatch lifts and I toss in my backpack. I open the back seat door and toss in a dog bed. Mags follows, settling into the spot I made for her.

"Hey there, girl," Lauren says from the front seat, reaching back to scratch Mags behind the ears.

"Want me to drive?" I ask.

"You be the guide and I'll drive. Plus, that means I get to control the music," she says.

"I am a radio DJ. I should get music privileges by default," I say, climbing into the passenger side.

"Enjoy the break then," she says, reaching for her phone and plugging it in. A deep male voice sounds over the car speakers.

"Do you like that?" the voice says in a deep, sultry tone. "That's a good girl taking my big cock. Just like that. Scream my name. That's it, good girl."

We both freeze, then Lauren jumps into action, fumbling with the volume knob. But the narration continues. "You squeeze me so good, baby. Ride me. Ride your daddy."

Finally, Lauren manages to twist the volume knob to zero and yanks the cord out of her phone. She fumbles with the screen, then turns it off.

"Was that—?" I ask.

"Don't say it," she says. She's scarlet, heat practically radiating from her face.

"Lauren Landau. What tawdry audio do you listen to?" I demand, my cheeks straining as I try to keep my smile under wraps.

"It's not tawdry," she defends, still not looking at me. "It's just an audiobook, okay? Nothing wrong with that."

"There's certainly nothing wrong with it," I agree. Then I lean into her space, close to her ear and drop my voice down a register, infusing it with heat. "Is that what you like, Lauren? Want Daddy to call you a good girl?"

Her head whips to look at me, her eyes glassy and . . . *fuck*. I think she likes it. I grin like the Cheshire cat. She shoves me back to my seat.

"Quit messing with me. That's not nice."

"I agree. It's practically devilish. I wish I would have known that's what you were into sooner, birdie. I could have given you a good spanking when you turned down my dinner invitation that night we cleaned up the beads."

"Seriously, Max. You got your point across." But she's fiddling with her phone and still refusing to look at me. Oh, this is too good. "Besides, there's nothing wrong with listening to romance. We all want a little fantasy in our lives. To read men written by women who praise us and recognize all the good things in a woman. Someone who knows what she wants inside and outside the bedroom and gives her a happily ever after."

Oh. *Oh.* "You're right. Not a thing wrong with it. I like it."

She plugs her phone back in and a GPS map of our drive fills the screen.

"Should I turn the volume back up?" I taunt.

"I'll get the music going, just hang on," she says a little too quickly.

"Or, if you prefer, I could read one of those books for you. After all, my whole job is using my voice."

Her cheeks blush so hard, I swear they turn purple. "I'm well aware," she mumbles.

Oh *shit.* Does she like my voice? Does it turn her on? Did I just find the magic key to finally unlocking the affections of Lauren Landau?

Do I want to? I don't want to ruin this friendship that's blossomed between us. It's been nice. Comfortable. But damn, if she turned to me right now and pressed her lips to mine, I'd kiss her right back, no question. Probably push her into the back seat and do much more than just kiss. I look to the back seat to gauge the space there and see a romance novel. It's hot pink and black with the back of a high heel on it. I reach for it, flipping to somewhere in the middle. I scan the page, then start to read.

"His hand slid along my thigh, rising to meet my aching core," I say, voice as low as I can make it. I make it extra dramatic. "His cock pressed hard into the seam of his jeans—"

"Give me that," she says, snatching the book from my hands and securing it in the driver side door pocket.

"Oh birdie, you naughty, naughty little minx."

She reverses and starts driving. "Freebird" blares to life over the speakers, drowning me out.

I laugh, my whole body vibrating with it. "Slow down there, birdie. We've got a lot of hours before we get to our rental."

Finally she cuts her eyes to me and something between a laugh and a cough escapes her lips. "God, I can't believe that just happened."

And then she makes the sound again, covering her mouth with her hand. She's embarrassed, but now I know something unexpected about her. Something that will take center stage in all of my fantasies from now on.

I make a mental note to snag that book out of the car pocket again when she's not looking, and read up on just what my birdie likes to dream about.

Interlude

THE RUSTON DAILY LEADER

February 8

Black Bear Attacks: Tourist Destination Nearly Turns Deadly for Local Man

By Rhett Hebert

While dangerous wildlife is usually contained to alligators and water moccasins in Louisiana, bigger predators lie just north in Arkansas. One local man, Eric Smythe, discovered just how dangerous wildlife can be while visiting Hot Springs National Park last week.

"I was following the marked path, minding my own business, thinking about stopping for a snack and some water. I heard some rustling and thought it was another hiker," said Smythe. "I moved to the side of the path to let them pass, and that's when I saw that my fellow hiker was a black bear! Nearly made me jump right outta my skin and over the cliff."

"Black bears are common in Arkansas, though are usually only seen in late spring and summer. This one, though, made an early appearance," said Ranger Florence Fisher of Hot Springs National

Park.

"I stood real still, hoping it wouldn't notice me, but it kept coming closer, sniffing the air. I swear I saw my life flash before my eyes. I grabbed my beef jerky, and threw it past the bear in the other direction. And, lucky for me, that big fella walked right over to it," Smythe continued. "I scuttled behind a big boulder and hid there until he ate that jerky and moved along."

According to Ranger Fisher, the best thing you can do when you encounter a black bear is to remain calm. "Make yourself big and bunch up your shoulders. Then slowly back away. Do not attack or try to hurt the bear."

As the warmer weather approaches, tourists are more likely to encounter Arkansas wildlife. Be vigilant, educate yourself, and have a plan of action. Visit Hot Springs National Park's website for more information.

Chapter 23

LAUREN

The cabin is . . . not what I expected. When Max said he booked us a tiny house, I imagined, well, a tiny *house*. Not this box. But he booked it and I'm not going to complain. I wanted an adventure, a break from the headaches of everyday life, and he has certainly delivered. Besides, the booking said it does have plumbing, climate control, and a couple of mattresses.

We walk inside the one-room space with a makeshift kitchen, one couch, a small bathroom, and a ladder on either side of the room, each leading up to a loft bed.

Could have been worse, I suppose. At least this isn't an "only one bed" situation, though the romantic in my head sort of wishes it was. I need to shut her right up. Especially after that embarrassing incident with my audiobook in the car.

I still can't believe that happened. I am never going to live that down, and I suspect that Max won't let me either. I shiver remembering the sultry things he rumbled into my ear. .

"Cold?" Max asks, dropping his backpack on the couch as he walks in with Mags. "There's a heater in here. I can turn it up."

I'm the opposite of cold, but I won't tell him that. I shake my head.

"Okay then. Well, I packed some groceries to tide us over while we're here. I just need to get them out of the back of your car."

"Me too," I chime in.

"Perfect. So why don't you change your shoes and we'll do a short hike today. Then we'll get back here and light the campfire and cook some dinner. Tomorrow we can do our longer hike."

I nod. This is way out of my comfort zone. I glance at my phone and notice it barely has a signal. I think about work and start to regret coming on this adventure. On a deep breath, I assure myself my staff has everything handled. I have to be able to trust them. To live for myself a little more.

Internal pep talk accomplished, I sit down on the couch and reach for my brand new pair of Columbia hiking boots. I grab a rain jacket and a beanie, noting the fifty degree temperatures and chance of rain.

Max sits down next to me and changes into his own pair of well-worn hiking boots and rifles through his bag. By the time I look up, he's also donned a beanie. His long, brown hair that's normally tucked into a bun, is down and skims the tops of his shoulders. Paired with his beard scruff, the man looks like he could have stepped out of the pages of an L.L. Bean catalogue. And fuck if I don't love it. I swallow.

"Ready?" he asks, eyeing my shoes.

"Let me grab my water bottle."

Max booked a place near several trailheads and he chooses the path marked as "easy." It's a little over a mile loop through the woods. Mags, who dons a neon pink harness, which is frankly adorable, floats along beside us on her retractable leash as we begin our short trek through the woods.

The sky is gray and the trees are still in winter mode, but the first buds of spring have started to emerge at the tips of their branches. It's a study in contrasts and opposites. The dipping and rolling hills, even in Southern winter, are wondrous. I realize that I can't remember the last time that I stopped staring at a phone or computer screen long enough to take in the nature around me.

Wistfulness twinges in my chest. God, I really am missing out on life.

"It's beautiful, isn't it? It's my favorite thing. Escaping the demands of work and family." Max winces. "Out here, no one can get to me. No one can bother me."

"I hope this isn't a prelude to you saying that no one can hear me scream," I tease.

"Don't worry, birdie. If I'm making you scream, it won't be because I'm trying to hurt you." And he actually winks at me. I'd cringe if it wasn't so damn sexy. And that was definitely crossing the friend zone line. Or is this just playful banter?

I try to think about how I act with my friends. Or how I used to before I lost them to neglectful attrition. I really need to have that coffee date with Janessa.

"Look," Max says. I glance to where he's pointing. It takes me a minute and then I see it: a hawk flutters its wings where it rests on a branch. Mags seems to notice at the same time, pausing her walk and snapping her head up to look.

"It's beautiful," I whisper.

"I agree," Max murmurs. I grin and turn to look at him. But he's staring at me, not the hawk. The air seems to pull taut between us and my breath catches in my throat. He leans toward me, just the tiniest bit. I catch a whiff of his pine scent, noting the way his jaw feathers. My body seems to move on its own, closing the distance between us. My tongue darts out and licks my lower lip. His eyes follow the movement. He moves in closer.

Barking echoes through the air as Mags takes off at a run, jerking Max's arm with her leash. "What the hell, Mags?" Max grumbles as he locks the leash and tries to reel her back in.

The leaves crunch as a rabbit darts off on the trail next to us. The hawk cries and follows it. I wince, knowing that's not going to end well for the rabbit.

"Is this a bad time to sing 'The Circle of Life?'" Max deadpans.

I elbow him in the ribs and he chuckles. The tension from a moment ago has dissipated and we're back to throwing barbs again. I love watching Mags explore, her furry, gray snout dipping into hollows and rocks. It's still February and there are almost no bugs or creepy crawlies, which makes the walk much more enjoyable.

"So tell me the truth," I say, eager to start a friendly conversation. "How did your grandmother convince you to become Mardi Gras king?"

"You don't think I campaigned for the position?" Max says with mock offense.

"I think your grandmother was probably the one doing the campaigning."

He chuffs a laugh. "She really didn't have to say much. She's always had my back and doesn't ask much of me. Helps keep the peace the best she can with the rest of my family." He shrugs. "You?"

"Guilt and my career," I say. "Gladys's funeral home does a lot of advertising with the paper. I didn't feel like I could say no. And, I think maybe, deep down, I wanted to do something different. I love my job. I'm grateful for the work and position, but something's been missing for a long time. Maybe Lauren from fifteen years ago was shoving me out of my comfort zone."

"Well, thank you, Lauren from fifteen years ago, because this whole gig is a lot better with a friend."

"I'm sure you would have befriended any queen who took the role," I say, though I don't like the knots that form in my stomach when I say it.

"Maybe," he agrees. "But none of them would challenge me or make me laugh like you do."

"Or swoon from trying on a dress into your arms," I say with a laugh.

"Or skate across a pile of beads right into my chest."

"Or expertly guide you through a waltz," I defend.

"So there, you see, meant to be."

As we near the end of the hiking loop, my right knee starts to tweak a bit. Max notices my slight limp. "You okay there, birdie?"

"Oh, it's nothing. I've had trouble with it on and off over the years after a dance injury in high school. And turning forty certainly didn't help. Nor does always wearing heels. I'll need to stretch it and ice it tonight to prepare for our longer hike tomorrow." I hesitate, realizing I've just told him my age. Not sure what he'll think about our age gap. "Does that bother you?"

"What, your injured knee? Why would that bother me?" he asks.

"No, that I'm forty." I've never been embarrassed by my age, so I don't know why I suddenly am now.

"Why would that bother me?" he asks, genuinely confused.

"It's just that you're what? Thirty-three?"

"And? Once adults get past a certain age, it's really more about connection than age, right? Unless you're worried I'll make you look bad?" He raises an eyebrow and smirks.

"It's just that we spend a lot of time together, or at least we have recently. People might talk. Your family—"

"I don't care what they think," he says, cutting me off. "I'd much rather be around you than any of them."

"What if I were a worm?" I ask seriously, trying to hold in a laugh.

His head whips around and he studies me for a second. "Well then, if you were a worm I guess I'd have to get a little pot to carry you around in. I'd plant little seeds in it so you'd have some shade and put a lid with holes in the top so the birdies wouldn't eat my birdie."

I chuckle. *My birdie.* "Good answer," I admit.

"Oh, I'm not done. I'd prop you up on my nightstand in the evenings. And, because I want to make sure that you have all the things you love, I'd grab that little book out of your car, open it up to the smuttiest part I could find, and read those dirty, dirty things to you in my deepest, most come hither voice."

My mouth drops open and I stop walking. "You wouldn't."

He smirks. "Oh, I most certainly would."

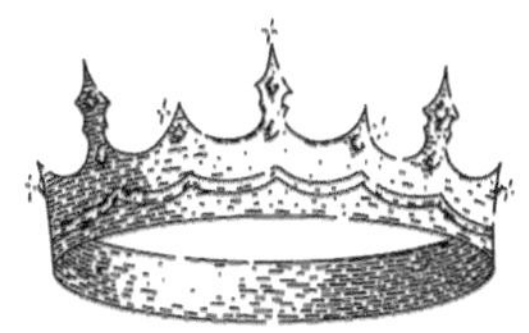

Chapter 24

MAX

Hiking alone with Mags is usually the only way I do it. But hiking with Lauren has been good for me. She's gotten me out of my head and my usual spiraling thoughts about my family. Mostly with our banter . . . and the way her ass looks in those leggings she's been wearing. Ten out of ten experience. Would do again.

And maybe I shouldn't be flirting with her, but I can't seem to turn it off. Especially when I so desperately want her to say "fuck it" and fall into bed with me. Or hell, I'd take a kiss. I'm not picky. Anything Lauren wants from me, she can have.

When we get back to our matchbox-sized cabin, I pull some firewood out of a covered alcove and stack it up in the fire pit. Lauren's inside, taking a few minutes to freshen up. I want to have it crackling before she comes back out here. I light a firestarter and put it into the log pyramid I built, then start feeding in small branches until it's going nice and strong.

Lauren emerges with her hair tied up in a bun and wearing an oversized sweatshirt over leggings. She looks domestic. Like this is something we do everyday. My heart tugs at the thought. I turn back around and stare at the fire to avoid staring at her.

She holds up a couple of sticks. "Hot dogs sound good? Not something I usually do, and in the spirit of having fun, I thought—"

"Perfect," I say, taking them from her. She smiles, encouraged. "Grab a seat."

I point to the fabric camping chairs I pulled from the tiny storage closet. She does, and Mags takes that as her sign to leap into Lauren's lap.

"Mags, get down," I chide.

"No, it's alright," Lauren says, scratching her between the ears.

Mags sighs with contentment and settles in. Never have I wanted to be a dog so much in my entire life. I like the sight of them snuggled up like this. My girls, right next to me, ready for me to take care of them.

I walk over to the ice chest Lauren packed and pull out a couple of flavored seltzers. I put them in koozies and hand one to Lauren, then pull my chair closer to hers and settle in. Dusk has settled over the forest, painting the sky in bruise-colored patterns. With each passing second, the fire seems to grow brighter and the temperatures cooler.

Lauren sighs and leans back in her chair. "This is so nice. I can't remember the last time I relaxed like this."

"It's good for the soul. Quiet, nature, campfire, a dog in the lap."

"You're onto something here, Max. I do believe this is the perfect recipe for peace."

That warms my whole body. The thought of pleasing her, of giving her something she needs but won't do for herself.

"You know, I could pick up some wine or something for you tomorrow, if you'd like some," I say.

"Nah, I'm good. Don't need anything else to help me relax out here."

"Nothing else?" I say, unable to stop myself.

She glances over me, light from the flames dancing across the planes of her face. "The company's not bad," she says.

"A meal wouldn't hurt either. Though, I should warn you, Mags will expect you to roast a hot dog for her too."

"I think I can handle that," she says, starting to rise.

"Nah, stay there. Enjoy the peace. I'll get everything ready for us."

Lauren relaxes back, murmuring, "Thank you."

I prep the hot dogs, skewering them. "How do you like yours cooked?"

"I like my weenies roasted and hot," she says.

"Lauren, was that a sex joke?" I say, dropping my voice register to mimic the audiobook narrator.

One of her eyelids opens. "Maybe."

"Well damn, girl. You really did just need some time away to loosen up a little."

She chuckles and sits up, reaching for one of the sticks. "Here, let me do it. It's part of the adventure."

I hand over the stick and she scoots forward. Mags doesn't move, happy to be crunched as Lauren leans over her.

"I can't believe you do this all the time," she says. "No wonder you're always so happy."

"Well now, I don't know about all that. I'm not always happy. I've got a lot of shit going on in my life with my family. And, I admit, I'm a little lonely. Sure, I've got friends I can go out to a concert with, but they aren't the kind of people I call and talk about deep life shit with. But yeah, the hikes with Mags help."

"So you rather like the company tonight too, then?" she asks.

"Yeah, I guess I do. Wouldn't mind having some company with me more often." I grin at her.

"Even if that company makes you look bad when you dance?"

"Oh birdie, I do that all on my own. You make me look good."

We fall into comfortable silence, enjoying the crackling fire and the smell of woodsmoke. I grab the buns and slide the hot dogs into them, extending one her way. She takes it, then nods to my offer of mustard. Mags does her best to try to snag Lauren's dinner.

"No you don't, Maggie Magnolia," Lauren says. "Plus this one isn't ready yet. Still needs ketchup."

I sigh. "And here I was thinking you were perfect. Good to know that you do have one fatal flaw. Who puts ketchup on their hot dog?"

"Everyone."

"Lies," I say, but I dig in the tote bag Lauren brought and unearth the ketchup bottle, popping the lid and squirting a line down the center of hers.

"Expertly done," she says as I hand it over, then she takes a bite and groans. That sound electrifies my body, and I shove my own hot dog in my mouth to keep from answering her groan with my hungry mouth on hers. This camping trip might just kill me.

"I guess I should clean up," I say, once I finish my hot dog.

"Not yet," Lauren says, sitting up. She gently scoots a reluctant Mags off her lap and walks over to her car. When she returns, she's holding Hershey's bars, marshmallows, and graham crackers.

"A little birdie told me that the birthday boy likes s'mores."

My body clenches. "How did you know?"

"Janessa. Rude of you not to tell me today is your birthday, honestly."

I look down at my lap, unsure of what to say.

"What's wrong?" Lauren asked. "Do you not like s'mores? I'm going to kill Janessa if this was all a prank—"

"No, it's not that. It's just. I don't really like my birthday. I don't do anything for it, ever. I don't tell anyone about it. Janessa knows that."

The dead leaves crunch under her feet as Lauren walks over to me. She kneels, then slides a hand around my cheek and tilts my head up to look at her. "Why don't you like your birthday? Is it the getting older thing? Because thirty-four is hardly something to be sad about. I wish I were still thirty-four." She smiles with her lips closed.

Hell. In for a penny, in for a pound. "No, nothing like that. It's just. My birthday always brings back the day that my dad kicked me out of the family for good. We were having dinner at my parents for my twentieth birthday. I had one too many drinks. So did Dad. He told me to get in line on the family business. I told him to fuck off. And then he told me I wasn't welcome back at their house. Mom tried to intervene. When I turned my back and started to walk away, Dad grabbed me by the shoulder and jerked me back. I shoved him. Then," I take a deep breath, "he swung at me. Clocked me right in the jaw."

Lauren gasps.

"I wanted to hit him back, but I knew it would upset my mom and my brother. I turned and walked out. Dad screamed at me the whole time. Telling me that if I walked out I was done. No more money. No more family time. But I didn't stop."

I pause, and run my hand over my head, fiddling with my bun. "And I haven't been back since. Not in more than ten years. Mom begs me to. Hell, even Dad has threatened me to toe the line, to do it for my family. But I refuse. And now, I can't look at a damn birthday cake without feeling sick, without being immediately transported back to that night."

Lauren's eyes study mine. Her hand slides across my jaw to the back of my neck. She massages the spot, telling me it's okay without words. A moment passes, her hand threading through my hair, massaging my scalp with her fingernails. It's divine. A physical comfort I didn't know I craved.

"Well," she finally says. "Good thing I didn't bring cake then. Besides, who else is gonna help me eat all of this chocolate? And," she leans down conspiratorially, "we should replace those bad memories with good ones. Because fuck your dad."

My eyebrows raise. "How could I possibly say no to that?"

"So tell me, how do you take your marshmallows? White and firm, or dark and flaming?"

"Gooey on the inside and crispy on the outside is heavenly."

Chapter 25

LAUREN

"I'm stuffed," I say, laying on the single couch in the shared living area and rubbing my over full stomach. "And sleepy."

"Same. But it's only 9 p.m.," Max says.

"Says the nighttime DJ. It's nearly my bedtime in my world."

"Good thing you're in my world then," he says, walking to hover over me. "Move your legs, scoot over. There's only one couch and I want to sit down."

"Floor," I mumble.

"Now where are your manners, birdie? Plus, I have a game for us to play." He holds up Scattergories.

"Brave of you to challenge an editor in a battle of words."

"Bold of you to assume I'm not good with words."

The challenge ignites me, and he knows it too. Dammit. "Fine, I'm in for a few rounds."

I sit up and scooch over as Max hands over a word pad, pencil, and category card. I'm ready to write down a word for each category that matches whatever letter he rolls. He tosses the dice and it lands on "Z."

"Starting with a challenge right out the gate, I see," I say.

"Ready to forfeit so soon?"

"Not on your life."

"Timer starts now!"

I scan the card, reading through the categories, struggling to come up with kitchen appliances that start with Z. Does that even exist? Oh wait, zester! I fly through the category card, skipping over ones that don't immediately come to mind and then going back to them. The timer speeds up, alerting us that it's about to buzz. When it finally does, Max shouts, "Pencils down!"

"Okay, one point for every unique word you got that I didn't get and vice versa," he instructs. "Let's do this. Animal?"

We both say, "zebra" and wince.

"Musical instrument?" he asks.

"Zither," I say immediately.

"That is not a real thing," he scoffs.

"Hell yes it is. It's this stringed flat thing. I know because we did a story on it when the Shreveport Symphony played a show in Ruston. Google it if you don't believe me."

"I would but there is zzzzero service out here," he says, emphasizing the "zzzz" sound.

I roll my eyes. "What did you write?"

"Zylophone."

"You can't be serious."

He lifts a shoulder. "It's a real instrument, unlike yours."

"First, mine is absolutely a real instrument. But xylophone starts with an X."

"Does not," he protests.

"Does too!" I grab the pencil from his hand and spell it out correctly on his sheet, our shoulders bumping as I write.

"Hmmm. That spelling does look correct," he admits.

"Nice try, buddy. But you're not pulling one over on me."

He leans over my shoulder and studies my list. "Oh come on now, zinnia is not a real flower."

"You really need a dictionary, you know that?"

"Oh, they have one," he says, leaning over my lap and reaching for a book on the table. "Clearly we're not the only ones to debate this game." His chest presses into my lap as he leans over me. I fidget from the little burst of desire the action unleashes. But just as quickly he's sitting up again, flipping the dictionary open. "Ah ha!" he says, running his finger down the page. "Zinnia is…. a flower. Dammit."

I smirk. "What did you put?"

"Zephyrlily."

"Not a flower," I say immediately.

"Au contraire," he says. "And the only reason I know that is because that's what my grandmother brought me to cheer me up after I had my appendix removed."

I grab the dictionary. "Dammit. You're right. Don't look so smug."

The game continues through five more rounds, each one getting more absurd than the last. We bump hips and shoulders, shove each other over answers, and smile into each other's faces. It's a comfortable shared intimacy, and damn if I don't want to climb right into his lap and snuggle in close.

But it's not long before a yawn escapes me.

"Alright, bedtime," Max says. "We've got a long day of hiking tomorrow and we both need our rest. I'll take Mags out if you want to get ready first."

He slips outside and I rummage through my duffle bag to get everything I need for bedtime. I duck into the tiny bathroom and exchange my leggings for a red, silky pj shorts set. I brush my teeth, then step back into the living area.

Max is holding his pj's and a toothbrush, waiting his turn. He scans me head to toe, eyes blazing. He must like the silky pj's.

"Bathroom's all yours," I say, then turn to the ladder that leads up to my bed and start climbing. I glance behind me to find Max eye level with my ass. He doesn't even pretend to look away. So when I start climbing again, I go a little slower, with a little more side to side movement. Letting him look. Liking the way his interest makes me feel.

When I reach my bed, I hear a cough, then the bathroom door closes. I grin to myself.

Moments later, the door hinges creak when it opens again. I glance down over the bed loft and see Max in a pair of flannel sleep pants . . . and nothing else. His back muscles ripple as he leans down to scoop up Mags. The sight unsettles me, but I can't look away. Suddenly I'm very, very warm.

He moves toward the ladder, reaching for it with his free hand, then pausing. He swings his head around and catches me staring and grins wickedly. "Night, birdie," he says, then climbs up with Mags tucked into one arm.

I let myself watch his back muscles as they bend and flex. My eyes skirt his forearm tattoo. And, for just a moment, I allow myself to imagine climbing into that bed with him.

Mentally slapping myself, I roll over, pop my earbuds in, and hit play. My audiobook resumes right where it left off. That is, right in the middle of a particularly hot intimate scene. Relieved Max can't hear what I'm listening to, I relax and pull up my favorite phone game to play while I listen. Eventually, I drift off to sleep.

BOOM!

I startle awake, my heart leaping in my chest. The window beside my bed lights up with a flash of lightning. Branches slap across my window, sounding like skeleton fingers trying to claw their way in through the glass. It's dark in a way that never quite happens in the city. There's a depth to it, one that makes me open my eyes as wide as possible and hold my hand up in an attempt to see it. I can't. At least not until the lighting flashes again, lighting up the entire cabin.

BOOM! I jump at the immediate thunder. The storm is right on top of us. Mags whimpers.

"Are you awake?" I whisper loudly.

"Yeah," Max says from his loft across the room. "You okay?"

"I think so?"

BOOM! Then the rain begins, hard and earnest. From the flashes of lightning I can see that it appears to be raining sideways, the sound of it hitting our tiny cabin like an ocean wave crashing on top of us. The branches pick up their speed, fighting at the cabin's exterior. It's like a scene out of my childhood nightmares. A loud crack sounds like a gunshot.

"What was that?" I ask, fear coating my voice. It sounds like trees are falling down on top of us. And suddenly, I wish very desperately to be back in my house where it's safe and secure with my cat snuggled up against me.

"It's okay," Max says. "Come over here with me."

I don't even stop to question it. At the next lightning flash, I note where the ladder rungs are and move to it. I shimmy down the ladder in the dark, then throw my hands in front of me to feel my way to the one that leads up to his bed. I climb up slowly, careful not to fall. When I reach the top, Mags greets me with licks to my face. "Hey girl," I whisper.

"I'd have come to you, but it was too hard to navigate with Mags," Max says.

"No, this is good," I say, scrambling to lay down next to him.

His arm slides around my back and he pulls me in close to him. I press my forehead into his chest and listen to his heartbeat. Its rhythm is quick, like mine, and that scares me even more. If Max is scared, then this storm must be something to fear.

Max's hand makes slow strokes up and down my spine. "It's okay. It will pass quickly."

"You don't know that. What if it rips the roof off this place?"

"It won't," he says, his arms still stroking my back.

"How do you know? I can hear your heart racing. You're scared too."

"Oh birdie, that's not why my heart is racing," he says.

"Then why?"

"I have a beautiful woman in my bed. Why do you think?"

"Oh."

"Yeah, oh," he says, a soft chuckle rumbling through his chest. His bare chest. Pressed against my face.

I slam my eyes shut when another flash of lighting lights up the room, the thunder immediately crashing with it. The rain seems to pound at the windows even harder.

"What if it's a tornado?" I squeak.

"It's not."

"How do you know?"

"Don't hear the train noise that comes with them."

"That's not reassuring."

"I do the weather report on the radio, you know. I've learned quite a bit about weather systems over the years. Yet another thing I beat you at," he says with a chuckle, his hand shifting even lower.

"Still didn't help you beat me at Scattergories though."

"No, I suppose not," he allows.

I snuggle in closer, sliding my arm beneath his and around to his back. Allowing this dark, small space to hide my movements and grant me a safety net as I trace my fingers along his back and shoulders. I allow them to slide along the divots and ridges of muscle. It's intoxicating.

Boom! I pull myself in closer to him, hooking my leg around his hip. He doesn't stop me. Instead, he tilts his hips so he lines up with me perfectly, his center to mine.

"Birdie," he groans.

His mouth ghosts along the top of my head, his hand moving until it rests just above my ass. I pull myself into him, feeling his rising erection against me. I should stop this, but not a single fiber of my being wants to. The tension between us has been building for too long.

I tilt my head up, brushing my lips along his bearded jaw.

"You probably shouldn't do that," he says.

"I probably shouldn't," I whisper. "Want me to go back to my bed?"

He pulls me in tighter. "No."

Boom! The thunder sounds farther away, like the storm is moving past us. But I don't let him go. I allow my body to take over, my hips slowly grinding into him. He thrusts back, both of us chasing friction through our pajamas.

Max groans then pushes me to my back and moves his hand to my stomach. He's on his side, body pressing into mine. His breaths come in shallow bursts and tickle along my jaw. "Tell me to stop."

"I can't do that."

"Birdie," he warns.

I turn my face into his throat and press a kiss right where I feel his pulse thrumming. His palm comes up to cup my jaw, the rough scratch of his stubble grazing my cheek as his mouth moves to find mine.

I gasp, the soft feel of his plump lips exploring mine is intoxicating. He brushes his mouth over my bottom lip, then my top one. He bites gently at my mouth and whispers, "I've wanted to do this for weeks. To know how you taste."

And fuck if that isn't straight out of one of my books. But this is better, because this is real life and his deep voice unlocks a piece of myself I chained up years ago. I mirror him, nibbling on his lips, pressing my mouth into his. And then his mouth opens and I follow him, my tongue tangling with his.

He explores my mouth, slowly, deliberately. My body moves on instinct, grinding into him, breaking the kiss to press more along his jaw, his neck. Biting his ear, exploring his stubble with my tongue. It's been so long since I've done anything sexual and I feel like I could eat him alive. He seems to like it, because his hand coasts down to the waistband of my pajamas and teases there, running his fingers along the band, over and over again.

"Can I touch you?" he whispers into my ear.

"Yes," I moan, as if I could say anything else.

His hand dips below my pajama bottoms, finds my panties, and slides beneath them. Lower until we both gasp.

"Lauren, you're so fucking wet for me," he says, voice low and sultry, right in my ear. Just his words, his voice, are enough to nearly make me come.

And he knows it. I know he does. He clocked it from the moment he first overheard my audiobook. Then again when he picked up my romance book and started reading the damn thing to me. Teased me about listening to spicy scenes. Used that voice that has been seducing me over the airwaves for longer than I care to admit. All of it, his touch, his heat, his voice, cast the perfect spell over me.

I feel my pleasure begin to build and he's barely even touched me. His hand finds my clit and circles it. He laughs, deep and seductive. "You like that, don't you, baby? Like how I touch you?"

"Yes," I groan. "More."

His fingers drift lower and one dips inside me easily. Another. "Yes, Max. Just like that. Please. Keep going."

And he does. He curls his fingers, pumping them in and out of me as his thumb finds my clit again. I've had plenty of boyfriends over the years, but none of them have known how to touch me like this, where it feels good, how it feels good.

He keeps moving his hand, building me higher and higher. "Yes, birdie. Ride my hand. That's it. You've got it. Just like that."

I dissociate, leaning into the pleasure, letting him talk me through it in that perfect voice. I feel like I've tumbled into a fantasy. I whimper, pleasure building. I pick up the rhythm, riding his hand, pushing him deeper into me.

"Right there," I gasp. "Yes, Max. Just like that."

"That's it, birdie. Fuck my hand. Be my good girl and come on my fingers."

And then I'm soaring over the edge. My whole body convulses, electricity shooting from my core to my toes, making them curl. Wave after wave race through my body. Lights flash behind my eyes. Thunder rumbles again, further away now, but I don't care. Not anymore. It's impossible to care when my entire body has transformed into a boneless heap of pleasure.

The waves of my orgasm finally stop and I'm boneless, my heart thundering in my chest. I can hear Max breathing roughly above me. Lightning flickers outside, briefly lighting the room. In that brief flash I see his long hair tousled, the wild look in his eyes.

He grasps my hand and moves it closer to his face. He lays his hand on top of mine, lining up our fingers. And then he pulls two of my fingers inside his mouth with his still on top of mine. The two that were inside me. I whimper and his laugh rumbles around our fingers.

He pulls them out. "Fucking delicious," he whispers.

I reach for him, moving my hand down his chest, his abs, to his pajama pants. His hand lands on mine, stopping me.

"Let me make you feel good, Max," I whisper.

"Another time," he replies, pressing a kiss to my temple.

"I don't want to wait."

"You'll have to. It's too late for that tonight," he says with an embarrassed laugh.

Wait, there's no way Max came without me even touching him, right? I mean I know we grinded on each other a bit and things have been heated between us, but that would mean him just touching me was enough to get him there. Is he really that attracted to me?

"You came?" I ask cautiously.

"Yeah. Haven't done that since I was a teenager. Thanks a lot." But he says it with humor.

And, damn, I can't believe he wanted me that much. I do a little happy dance in my brain, complete with a pirouette. Between the orgasm and Max's desire for me, I'm a content little kitten, ready to snuggle up and purr against his chest.

Thunder rumbles, but it's distant now. Soothing.

"Stay here with Mags," he says. "I'll be right back."

His phone light flashes on and he uses it to climb down the ladder. He disappears into the bathroom for a few minutes, then returns. He's in fresh pajama pants. Green plaid this time, and I blush knowing I'm the reason he had to change them.

He climbs back into bed and I sit up to move to the ladder.

"Where are you going?" he asks, holding onto my arm.

"My bed?"

"Stay. Please."

I hesitate. This is a lot. This is more than a one night stand. I know it. And I think he knows it. But I want this, want him. Resigned, I lie back down with a sigh.

"Here. A warm washcloth is pressed into my hand. "Thought you might want to use this."

It's so damn thoughtful that it brings tears to my eyes. Not a single man I've ever been with has thought to care for me in this way after sex. I reach down and clean up quickly.

"Just toss it over the rail to the floor. I'll grab it in the morning." I do as he says, then he curls up next to me. "Roll over. I want to be the big spoon."

With a smile, I do as he asks, rolling to face the dark open space of the cabin. His hand snakes around my stomach and pulls me in close. His chest presses into my back and it feels amazing. He feels amazing.

We lay in the dark for a few minutes, the occasional lightning flash briefly illuminating the room, showing me his large hand on my stomach. Doubt starts to creep into my mind. Was this a good idea? What does this mean for our friendship? The Mardi Gras ball? Will he still want to be around me after all the Mardi Gras stuff is over? Do I want him to be?

"Lauren," he says quietly. "I can hear you overthinking. It's okay. We're good. Better than good. Don't overthink it. Just go to sleep. I'll still be here in the morning, ready to give you hell and be a better hiker than you."

I relax. There he is. My Max.

I close my eyes, allowing my breathing to slow. I feel Mags shuffle around and lay down on my feet. Max's warmth seeps into my bones, and, in a blink, I'm fading to sleep.

Chapter 26

MAX

February 9

This will not be awkward. I won't let it be. Part of me feels like last night was a dream, but I know better. Because Lauren is still in my bed. And I am in a different pair of pants. I grin.

Lauren stirs in my arms, snuggling deeper into me. I want to hit the pause button and never leave this ideal tiny house in the middle of the woods. Ignore my job, the Mardi Gras ball, her job. Spend every day hiking and every night making love to this beautiful woman in my arms.

She stirs again, turns. Her mouth lands on my chest. And yep, I could definitely wake up to this everyday. God, what am I thinking? I've never wanted to end my bachelor life before. But Lauren makes me want to. She makes me want to take care of her. I bend to press a kiss to the crown of her head, savoring the moment.

"Is this real?" Lauren says against my chest.

"Yeah, birdie. It's real."

She pulls back, her eyes flickering open and finding mine. I grin at her and she blushes. Her blonde hair is a mess, sticking out in all directions.

"Oh God," she squeaks. "There is a hickey on your neck."

"You marked me, you naughty little minx. Claimed me. I like it."

She giggles and relaxes. "I can't believe we did that. Is this going to be weird?"

"I'm not going to be weird about it. Are you?"

She glances away, then back to me. "No?"

"Good, because I want to go hiking today and then do it again."

"Max!" she squeaks. But she's smiling and I know we'll make it through any awkwardness. I thrust into her, just enough for her to feel my morning wood.

"You're insatiable," she giggles.

"Only when you're around." I drop my voice. "After all, I do love the way you scream my name."

"Max!"

I laugh. "Come on, birdie. I'll make breakfast. Let's get you some coffee and let Mags out to go to the bathroom."

She gets up and moves to the ladder, making her way to the bathroom. I watch her boobs bounce on the way down, and don't even try to hide my stare. She glances up when she reaches the bottom.

"You're staring."

I shrug. "Guilty."

When she closes the bathroom door, I move to the ladder, scooping Mags up in one arm and slowly making my way down. I grab a t-shirt out of my bag and pull it on, then slide my feet into a pair of flip flops and open the door to the crisp morning air. Fog has settled over the ground, everything wet and blown over from last night's storm. Mags wanders away to do her business.

I walk over to Lauren's car, inspecting it for damage, but it survived mostly unscathed. A small branch lays on the hood, but it barely left a scratch. I grab it and toss it away. It's colder today and the trails will be muddy. I wonder if Lauren will still be up for a hike. I hope so, but I wouldn't mind staying in the cabin with her all day, either.

The door clicks open and Lauren steps out. She's put on her

leggings and oversized sweatshirt that still smells like campfire.

"Everything still standing out here?" she asks, shivering in the cold.

I walk over to her and slide my arm around her shoulders, rubbing her arm for warmth. She doesn't pull away and I'm relieved. Now that I've had a taste of her, I don't want to let her go. And all the boundaries I set for myself to keep from touching her were destroyed last night when she gave me the green light to touch her. If she wants me to stop, she's going to have to tell me to. But when she leans into me, practically purring, I know I'm golden. I grin, leaning down to kiss the top of her head.

"Did you say coffee?" she asks.

"That I did. Come back in and snuggle up with Mags on the couch. I'll fix coffee and breakfast." I want to reach for her hand, tug her back inside, but I'm trying to play it cool. Interested, but not obsessed. Sexy, not awkward.

But she takes matters into her own hands. Literally. Her fingers tangle with mine as she turns to walk inside. "Sounds perfect. I don't think anyone has taken care of me like this since I lived with my parents," she confides.

"I find that hard to believe," I scoff. And I truly do. How has no one scooped her up? Lauren's perfect. Smart, independent, gorgeous.

She shrugs. "It's true. But, to be fair, I'm not great at letting people take care of me either. I'm very much a first born, overachieving daughter."

"Well, I know it will be a burden to let me cook for you," I say lightly. "But I guess you'll just have to deal with it."

"I'll try my hardest," she says, bumping shoulders with me.

Inside, she drops onto the couch and Mags jumps up to settle beside her. Lauren snags a blanket and tucks herself in.

I get to work on the coffee. The kitchen is tiny with an induction stove top, but I make it work. Coffee first. As it starts to brew, I pull out a pan and set it on the small stove. I ask her about food allergies, but she says she has none. I keep it simple—scrambled eggs and toast. Protein and a few carbs for our hike today.

"How do you take your coffee?" I call over the sizzling pan.

"I don't like it very sweet. A little cream, the tiniest bit of sugar."

"Coming right up!" I fix the coffee and walk it over to her.

Lauren takes a sip. "Perfect," she sighs with satisfaction.

"That's what I like to hear."

I fix us both plates and grab forks and napkins. I settle in next to her on the couch and hand her a plate. She leans forward, setting her mug on the coffee table, then digs in. Mags lifts her head, interested in what we're eating. I break off a corner of toast and hand it to Mags, who quickly scarfs it down, crumbs getting stuck in her little Schnauzer beard.

"You're spoiling me, you know," Lauren says. "Nature, campfires, breakfast."

"Orgasms," I quip.

She blushes and dips her head. "Yes, those."

I grin. "I'd say I'm sorry, but I'm not. I liked making you feel good. You deserve all of this, you know."

She sighs. "Thank you."

"Please don't thank me. Let's just enjoy our full day today."

Her eyes smile over a forkful of eggs. "Deal."

It's cooler today, and our hike will be longer and muddier after last night's storm. I've prepared the best I can, filling my backpack with protein-rich snacks, lunch, and even some light duty first aid supplies, just in case.

Lauren has made several comments about enjoying being away from work, about living life more, and I want to deliver on something that will help with that today. I have a plan, but it will require a little effort.

"Are you up for a moderate hike today? Nothing too crazy, but not quite an easy, flat trek either. It will be worth it. It's one of my favorites. But say the word and we can do something else."

She looks up at me from where she's sitting on the couch and lacing her hiking boots. "Sure, why not?"

"We're going to have to drive to the trailhead though. Mind if I drive your car?"

She glances down at her shoes. "I know it's silly, but I have this control thing about my car. It's not that I don't trust you, it's just my anxiety and—"

"No problem," I say. "You can drive. But you will have to listen and do everything I say." I raise an eyebrow, loving the way her cheeks heat.

"I think I can handle that," she says quietly.

"Good. Let's go."

Chapter 27

LAUREN

I park my car and study the trailhead sign. "Falls Creek Falls. Is that really the trail name?"

"That it is. Original, I know," Max says as he fastens Mags into her harness. "This trail is about two miles. It's going to be muddy after last night's storm, so just watch where you step. If we hit a rocky patch, move slowly. They get slippery with this weather."

"Got it," I nod, looping my arms through my backpack straps.

"We're not in a rush. Let's just enjoy our day off in nature. Take breaks whenever we want. For once, this is not a competition," he emphasizes.

"You're just scared I'll beat you."

He smirks. "Normally, I'd be up for the challenge. But today I care more about safety."

"Fine, Daddy."

His gaze heats immediately. "Save that mouth of yours for later."

My core tightens, remembering the way he used his mouth last night. The dirty things he said that set my blood boiling. I swallow.

"Let's go," he says, letting Mags walk in front of him. I move beside him and we head onto the trail.

Our hike starts out painless. It's marked and easy to follow, if muddy. But fifteen minutes in my new hiking boots are caked in heavy mud and keep sticking to the ground. We have to pause and kick the mud off our boots every ten minutes or so, and my old dance injury has flared back up.

Max seems so determined and excited though, and I don't want to disappoint him, so I press on.

"Not much longer now," he says, reaching for my hand to help steady me as I walk over a patch of slippery rocks.

I look to his back where Mags rides in a perch on the top of his backpack. She's got the right idea. She gave up ten minutes in when her dainty little paws kept getting caked in mud.

A moment later, I hear it: the rushing sound of water.

I follow Max out to a clearing and stare, amazed. The falls aren't huge, but they're beautiful. Pouring off of a curved rock in a grove, down into a small lake. It looks like something out of an adventure novel.

I look at Max to tell him how amazing this is, but he's staring at me already, a grin plastered across his face.

"There's more water than usual because of the rain last night," he says.

This time of year, there's no one else here but us. Max gets Mags down from his backpack and lets her off leash to roam and drink from the water. We wander to a nearby rock and sit to take in the view. Max reaches into his bag and grabs a couple of protein bars, handing me one.

"This is beautiful," I say, taking in the gallons of water that crash over the rocks. The white noise is the exact opposite of what I experience nearly every other day of my life. I want more of this. But my knee tweaks, reminding me that my body isn't used to this kind of activity anymore. I flex and extend it, moving through some of the stretches my physical therapist taught me ages ago.

"I'd like to do this more with you. After all this Mardi Gras stuff.

Take you somewhere beautiful that you wouldn't normally get to see." He shrugs, slightly awkward in a way I'm not used to seeing.

"I'd like that. Just worried it won't always be easy to get away. My work is demanding and I don't want to hold you back, be the reason you don't go somewhere or miss an opportunity." Saying that out loud rips a little piece of my heart that was just beginning to heal.

He extends a hand and places it on top of mine where it rests on the boulder. "That's the thing though. If we want to make it work, we'll figure out a way. You've done that with all the Mardi Gras stuff, with this weekend. It may not always be perfect or happen when we want it to, but we can figure it out."

I stare into his rich brown eyes, seeing the sincerity there. And I think he's talking about more than just a getaway like this. I think, perhaps, he's talking about something more between us.

"Max," I sigh. "I'm scared I can't give you what you want. You deserve someone who will drop everything for you. Someone who's always up for an adventure. Hell, maybe someone who wants kids."

"Lauren. Stop worrying about what I want for just a minute. What do you want? Because, birdie, I want to have fun with you in whatever time you have available to share with me. And if you can give me that, then that's damn near perfect for me."

I stare at him, emotion clogging my throat. "No one's ever said anything like that to me before in my life. I've always been expected to be the accessory to whatever man I've dated. I . . . I don't know what to say."

He scoots in closer, sliding an arm around my shoulders. "Just say you'll give us a chance and see what happens."

"You're serious? You want to try something more with me?"

"Serious as a heart attack." And then he leans in and presses his lips to mine. The kiss is soft, sweet, a promise. Butterflies take flight in my stomach. I don't think I've felt those since my first kiss in middle school.

We stay like that for another thirty minutes: his arm around my shoulders, watching the waterfall together. I'm not quite ready to go back to the hustle and bustle of real life. But when I do, at least I know that my life has expanded to include a Max-sized shape in its rigid lines.

"Ready to get back?" he asks, breaking the comfortable silence.

"Not really," I sigh.

"Come on, birdie. Best to make our way back before the sun starts to set. It still gets dark early this time of year and it will take us some time to make our way back through all that mud."

He scoots off the boulder and reaches to help me down. When I land, pain jolts through my knee and makes me wince.

"Better ice that tonight," Max says.

The way back is at an incline, which makes the hike even more difficult. Mud makes us slide backwards and Max has to help prevent me from falling more than once. I keep reminding myself that once I'm back at our cabin and warm in bed, I'll be able to remember the good parts of today. But, right now, I'm cold and my knee is screaming in pain.

One step in front of the other, I coach myself. We're close, the trail marker telling us we only have a quarter mile to go. I can do this.

That's when Mags lets out a low growl from her perch on Max's backpack. He freezes, so I do too. We both scan the area, trying to figure out what she's locked onto. We haven't seen anyone else on the trail at all today, and don't see anyone ahead of or behind us. I glance to Mags and see that she's locked onto the treeline, her growl growing louder, the hair along her back ruffed up. Goosebumps spread along my arms.

"Max," I whisper urgently. "What's going on?"

"Lauren, listen to me and do exactly what I say. Don't panic and don't run."

Fear launches through my chest and my heart speeds to double time. "Max?" I squeak.

"It's going to be okay," he says soothingly. "But there is a rather large black bear right through the trees there."

I look to where he's pointing and see it. Distantly, I recognize how beautiful it is. Part of me wants to take a photo, to capture this moment. It's insane, I know it's insane. Good thing my instincts are much smarter than my brain—and they're telling me to get the hell out of here.

"Don't run," Max says quickly. "Raise your arms and make yourself appear as big as possible. We're going to talk to it so it knows we're people and not prey. Move slowly. Keep going."

I do as he says, raising my arms and moving up the trail. "Hey there, Mr. Bear, or are you a Miss Bear?" Max calls out. "Nothing to see here. We're just two humans having a little walk through your nice forest here. How about some jokes?"

And now I really feel like I'm hallucinating. Is Max really raising his arms over his head, wiggling them around, and asking the bear if it wants to hear a joke?

"What do you call a bear who is out in the rain? A drizzly bear!"

If we survive this, I'm never letting him live this down.

When he runs out of jokes, Max switches to singing. I would have never pegged him as a Swiftie, but I've got to give the man credit. "Shake it Off" seems to be the thing that finally makes the bear decide to move on.

We keep moving, adrenaline temporarily chasing away all the pain in my knee. We don't stop until we've cleared the trailhead, Max rambling off lame jokes the whole way. But it worked, because we're finally back at my car, safe and sound.

"What are the chances that bear is going to appear before we get out of here?" I ask.

"Slim to none. I doubt it wants to leave the woods."

We both do our best to kick the mud off our boots. I finally give up and yank mine off before tossing them into the back hatch. I'll drive sock-footed. Max does the same, helping Mags into her little back seat dog bed.

I start the car, relieved to finally rest and feel safe.

"Well, that certainly was an adventure," Max says.

"And I've never felt quite so alive," I agree. "My heart definitely works."

He chuckles. "I've been hiking a lot. Never seen a black bear this early in the year. It was probably still sluggish coming out of hibernation."

"Or maybe you just hypnotized it with the sweet sounds of Taylor Swift."

"Whatever works. If I have to sing the entire Eras Tour to keep us safe, I'll do it."

"Can you sing the whole Eras Tour?" I ask.

"No, but I'd make a valiant effort for you, birdie."

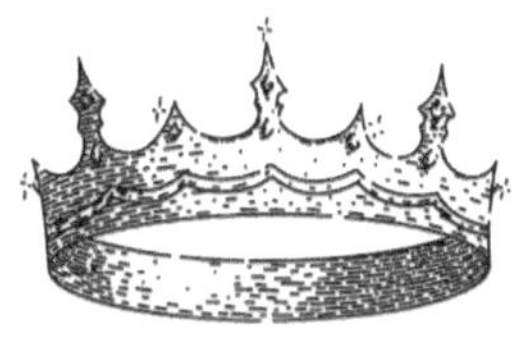

Chapter 28

MAX

I was a little worried that Lauren would be irritated after how chaotic and difficult our hike was today, but I think she's just relieved to be sitting on a couch again.

She's got ice on her knee and I moved a kitchen chair in front of her so I can sit and rub her feet. She winces as I work them over. Her feet may be used to the demands of high heels, but hiking on an incline up a hill in the mud while being followed by a bear is a new level of stress fitness.

"I brought red beans and rice for dinner tonight. Simple, but easy to make indoors. That work?"

"It's the ideal seasonal food to gear us up for our Mardi Gras sprint next week."

She's not wrong. The ball is next weekend and my grandmother has a list of tasks for the entire krewe to complete. From media interviews to picking up costumes, every day has something packed into it.

"But I'm glad you'll be with me for all of it," she says. "It's nice to know someone has my back."

"I'll always catch you when you fall, birdie. And I'll be extra prepared the next time we're around Mardi Gras beads."

She tosses a throw pillow at me. I dodge it and laugh when it smacks the wall behind me.

Dinner is quick and easy. We sit side by side on the couch eating and talking about our childhood antics. I tell her about how Janessa and I were constantly pranking my brother, Charles, and get to hear about her mom teaching her to bake the perfect pecan pie.

It seems like we just sat down to eat, but it's already closing in on 11 p.m. I urge her to shower first. She does, then climbs the ladder into my bed without comment. That does something funny to my heart. I want to sprint up there and join her immediately, but I've got mud all over me.

I let Mags out, wipe her down, and help her up to the loft. Then I go take a shower.

When I'm done, I open the bathroom door with a towel wrapped around my waist, and steam billows out behind me. I walk to my bag and pull on a pair of underwear and my green plaid pajama pants. I make for the ladder, eager to climb up and pounce on Lauren.

But when I get to the top of the loft, I'm greeted by soft snores. Mags is curled up next to Lauren and they are both sound asleep. I stare at her, noting the way her soft lips part just a little. How, in sleep, her face is relaxed and a faint blush tints her cheeks. Her pale hair is scattered around her, and I want nothing more than to bury my face in it and inhale.

I ease into bed, carefully scooting in behind her. I slide an arm around her waist and lay down. She fits my body like she's meant to be there. I don't think I'll be able to sleep with Lauren so close to me and touching me everywhere.

But I needn't have worried. Today's hike and the rush and crash of adrenaline win out, and soon I'm fast asleep.

Chapter 29

LAUREN

February 10

As soon as we exit the woods and get on the interstate, my phone lights up like a Mardi Gras float. Texts and emails that couldn't make their way to me while I was deep in the woods in Hot Springs National Park all flood in at once. I'm driving, so I can't look at them, but the barrage of pings makes me anxious.

What if something happened while I was gone? What if Rhett and the rest of the team couldn't handle it? What if my sister needed me?

"Hey," Max says, reaching over to place a hand on my knee. "You okay?"

"Honestly? No. I can't stop thinking about how many people I've probably disappointed while I was out of reach. How many things probably went belly up because I wasn't there. I don't like it."

He gives my thigh a gentle squeeze. "It can all wait a little longer, birdie. Why don't you pick the music? Let's enjoy these last few hours together?"

"You pick the music," I insist.

He nods, scrolls through his phone, then plugs it into my car. The first notes sound and it hits me.

"Is this . . . did you put on the Eras Tour playlist?"

He grins. "Whatever it takes to scare the bears away. Especially the anxiety bears."

And, without realizing it, I've relaxed. I lean back in my seat and drive.

That night, alone in my apartment, I scroll through all my missed messages while my gray cat, Lola, curls into my side. I'm relieved that there was nothing pressing, but feel vaguely ill thinking about how much work I need to catch up on while trying to juggle the Mardi Gras ball responsibilities this week.

I feel guilty putting so much onto Rhett and the rest of my staff. I should take care of them. Take care of all of it.

But then my phone buzzes and a photo pops up. It's a selfie of Mags and Max. I grin and immediately save the photo. Another text follows.

Max: It's lonely not sharing a loft bed with you.

My heart tugs. It feels good to be wanted.

"Vacation agrees with you!" Rhett says when he walks into my office Monday morning. "You look rested, happy. You should do it more often."

I sigh. "I have responsibilities here."

"And we handled everything just fine. Only ran into one small thing trying to decide which article should be the headline. I made the call and hoped it was the right one," he shrugs.

"Which is exactly what I would have done," I concede.

And I consider, not for the first time, if I should ask Rhett if he's interested in becoming managing editor. We haven't had one in years after a round of budget cuts that left our staff lean and overworked. But our advertising dollars are back up and the promotion of an internal employee might not be out of the question. And with a managing editor at my side, I can turn over some of the responsibilities to someone else—with oversight of course. I'd have more time for my sister, nieces, and nephew. More time for Max.

"I've got a few things to go over with you. Got a few minutes?" Rhett asks.

I nod, and he shares what I missed while out of the office. Together, we start planning for the week ahead. Reporters and photographers walk in and out of my office while we meet. And when they ask questions, I pause and look at Rhett, allowing him to respond. He makes the right call every single time.

I make a note to call the publisher later today and run it by her.

Interlude

PEACH 103.1

February 14

You're listening to Peach 103.1. I'm your DJ, Beau Baxter, and tonight on the show we are talking all things Valentine's Day. From the perfect candy, to romantic gestures, we want to hear your recommendations. Log onto our app and use the message button to share how you're celebrating today, and we will do our best to share your stories and advice on the airwaves.

Here are what a few of our listeners are up to today.

Sabine says that she and her husband have been together fifty years and he still takes her to their favorite diner for heart-shaped pancakes every Valentine's Day. Well if that isn't sweet as syrup, I don't know what is.

Rhett says that each Valentine's Day, he writes a short song and plays it on the guitar for his wife, Amelia. Well now, take it easy there, Rhett. The rest of us guys are going to have a hard time living up to that level of romance.

According to Beth, the best way to spend Valentine's Day with her husband is a nice, distraction-free walk around the park while remembering their favorite parts of their wedding day. Your husband sounds like a lucky guy, Beth.

And there's one last one here from Max. He says that even though he's working tonight, he's going to make sure his girl, Birdie, gets a slice of king cake for the two of them to share before they go to sleep tonight. I think that one might be my favorite romantic gesture of all.

That's the end of our show tonight, folks. I'm signing off. And, remember, tell your mom you love her.

Chapter 30

MAX

February 15

The week leading up to the Mardi Gras ball has been chaos. Between shifts at the radio station, I've been running unending errands for my grandmother. And Lauren has been frantically trying to catch up on work and picking up extra work while her copyeditor is out with the flu.

It's beginning to feel like that moment we had in my loft bed at the cabin was a dream, like it never happened at all. Sure, we've talked to each other, mostly through text exchanges. The banter is there and it doesn't feel awkward.

I did get to see her briefly and give her a kiss on Valentine's Day. I swung by Leslie's house after my evening shift to see Lauren and bring her a piece of king cake. She was at her sister's house watching her nieces and nephew so Leslie and her husband could have a kid-free night together for Valentine's Day. I admire her for doing that, even if I was disappointed that we couldn't have our own evening together.

But—I miss her. I miss the domestic intimacy we formed in the cabin without outside demands or stresses. I miss having her in my space, taking care of her. And sure, all the extra running around for my grandmother this week isn't usual for me. But the workload for her? That's par for the course.

And I need to decide if I can manage sharing her with it. Because I don't expect her to change for me. She's been pushed enough in her life to try to conform to what others want her to be. Hell, so have I. And I'm not going to do that to her.

Regardless, the Mardi Gras ball is tonight. And I know we will both be in high demand by everyone there. But we are king and queen, and we will be together for most of the night. I just hope I can steal a few moments of her attention.

God, I really am a simp for this woman.

I fire off a text right before I get in my car to go pick up my suit for the night.

Max: Ready to dance tonight in your birdie outfit?
Lauren: Definitely. I just hope you can keep up.

I grin. I'm so ready to see her again.

I feel like a groom on his wedding day in this small room with a group of men straightening our suit jackets.

Although these are decidedly not wedding suits. Every one of us is bedazzled in sequins and feathers. And we don't even have our gigantic, feathered back pieces on yet.

I'm ready to see Lauren. As much as I joked with her about dancing in that insane dress, I am worried about her. Between the passing out risk and her injured knee from hiking, I hope she's okay. She reassured me that her knee is feeling much better, and even took the precaution of wearing tennis shoes to work this week.

But still, I'll feel better when I see her.

I look in the mirror. I've got my hair down for once. I got it trimmed so that it falls just below my chin. I turn my head side to side, noting that the crown has been secured and isn't going anywhere. Its golden color matches my bowtie and custom Mardi Gras beads draped around my neck. A medallion hangs at the bottom, white with a giant pelican in the middle, beak agape and shiny gold.

My silvery coat with intricate beading is meant to reflect the colors of the pelican. Overall, it's kinda snazzy. I don't look half bad—just a little shiny.

My grandma pops her head in. "Five minutes everyone. Get ready for introductions. Like we rehearsed, you'll meet your partner at the back of the space and walk with them to the front and take your place when your name is called."

Butterflies dance in my stomach. Why do I feel like a middle schooler with my first crush all of a sudden?

As a group, the men walk out to the lobby and glance around, looking for our even more bedazzled partners. My grandmother disappears into another room, then reappears a few moments later looking anxious.

"They're coming," she says. "Just a few more minutes. Those dresses are pieces of art, and art takes time."

Before I can stop myself, I've threaded through the assembled men and make my way to my grandmother. I lean down and whisper, "Everything okay?"

She looks past me, then back and whispers. "Fine. Nothing to worry about. Just a little boob tape mishap, but all the girls are getting tucked into place now, if you know what I mean."

I raise my eyebrows. She shrugs. "Being a beautiful woman takes work."

Not Lauren, I think, remembering her in leggings and a messy bun, covered in mud in our shared cabin. I wish we were back there now. Comfortable, no room full of people ready to stare at us. Climbing into a bed together...

The door swings open and a flock of sequined women emerges that would knock the heels off a drag queen. Every one of them shimmers in hues of purple, green, and gold. And, right at the front of them all, stands Lauren. Her peacock blue dress is nipped and tucked to fit every curve of her body. The silver detailing is a perfect match to the hue of my coat.

She's stunning. Absolutely, take-my-breath-away gorgeous. Her hair is down and styled in flowing, golden waves that land just past her shoulders. There are peacock feathers woven into her locks, and a golden crown that mirrors my own rests atop her head. Her makeup is dramatic, all smokey eyes and dark maroon lips. She looks like she stepped right out of some dark fairy tale—probably one of those smutty ones she's always reading.

I smirk, already imagining how I could read it to her. How I could be her dark prince or, what is it that I read people call them? Oh yes, I could be her shadow daddy. I like that much better. And something tells me Lauren wouldn't mind it either.

I walk over to her and reach for her hand. It settles in mine, despite the oversized peacock feather ring on her pointer finger.

"You look like a queen," I say, my voice husky.

"And you look like a disco ball," she says solemnly. I cackle, grateful that she brought us back to, well, us.

"Line up," my grandma says, shooing us into our practiced places.

Lauren and I walk to the front and she loops her arm through mine.

I lean into her, inhaling her pepperminty scent. My favorite. "You feeling okay?"

She turns to look at me, hearing the serious note in my voice. "I'm okay, I promise. They loosened the dress a bit. Didn't pull the laces so tight. I can breathe." She smiles sweetly and I relax.

"Good evening, ladies and gentleman!" A female voice calls from behind the closed door. My grandmother, of course. "Welcome to the first ever Ruston Krewe of Persici ball. We want to thank you for helping make this such a resounding success and selling out this event. And a special thank you to our sponsors. A reminder that donations from tonight will help support two local nonprofits for children. We hope you're enjoying your specialty cocktails. Take an extra sip and make that little extra donation."

Laughter rumbles across the room. "But it's time to take a pause and introduce you to your court. The krewe court is voted on by our steering committee. And for this year's event, we asked members of our local media to step into the roles. All graciously agreed, and put in the work to not only make this event a success, but to support our local nonprofits as well. Without further ado, let's get this party started!"

A collective cheer rises and the jazz band starts up playing "The Second Line."

"First up, we have our king and queen. Please join us in welcoming Peach Radio DJ, Beau Baxter, and *The Ruston Daily Leader*'s editor-in-chief, Lauren Landau. Beau is representing Louisiana's state bird, the pelican, and Lauren is a beautiful, regal peacock fit for a queen!"

That's our cue. The double doors in front of us open wide and I'm momentarily blinded by all of the decorations. The jazz band is lit up with spotlights. Every round table and high-top has beads and candles on its surface. And the community has outdone themselves in costuming. Everywhere I look there are feathers and masks, sequins and beads. It's a fever dream of opulence.

We enter the room, Lauren's arm tucked into mine, and everyone cheers. And as the two of us stride down a makeshift aisle, arm in arm, with people standing and clapping for us, it's easy to imagine a different aisle, with different clothes, a white dress, a dark suit, forever on the horizon. I blink away the absurd fantasy.

In a moment we're at the end of the walkway and taking our places. As the rest of the krewe royalty is called out, we wave and smile, blinded by the spotlights directly in our faces.

Finally, once we all make it to the front, Amelia, who is the night's emcee, announces our royal dance. It's showtime.

Lauren and I take our places front and center, assuming our practiced waltz stance. And I swear my heart is going to dance right out of my chest. Where our hands clasp, Lauren gives me a reassuring squeeze. We've got this.

The music starts and I let the three-count run through my head. We look past each other, like we were taught, but I steal glances of her out of the corner of my eye. I can't believe this beautiful, regal woman is in my arms tonight in front of all these people. I revel in the small details I'm able to take in. Her golden feather earrings on her slightly pointed ears, the long line of her neck tilted for the dance. The way her lips purse, the dark color on them enhancing their round shape.

We move through the steps and turns and the whole thing is an out of body experience. I'm grateful that my feet somehow take on a mind of their own—and do so correctly. Colors, lights, and faces blur around us, the music hypnotizing. Every step is synched, like Lauren and I have been doing this our whole lives.

And then, just like that, it's over and everyone's clapping. Lauren leans in, pressing her lips to my ear. "We did it."

I close my eyes and smile. "And we both managed to stay on our feet. This calls for a celebration later."

"I won't say no to that."

Chapter 31

LAUREN

That dance didn't feel real. I was so worried about moving in this ridiculous dress, with visions of toppling over like a crumbling cupcake or sweating right through all those layers of fabric. It doesn't help that Max looks like some insane version of Prince Charming. Where does he get off having luxurious hair on top of all his other ridiculously handsome features?

And yet, somehow, we managed to practically float through that dance together. I feel oddly proud of us. Kind of like when Leslie and I performed for my parents as children and they'd give us a standing ovation.

And now? Now I just want to take my king back to my house, make him take off everything. Except the crown. The crown can stay. Sounds like the perfect celebration to me.

I'm just about to lean in and tell him so, when Gladys steps in and whisks me away. I'm only half-listening as she details how people are making donations to dance with krewe royalty tonight. She'll keep me updated and let me know when it's time to change partners. She shoves a glass of champagne into my hand, and tells me I have a five minute break before we get started.

I look around for Max, finally spotting him getting what must be the same rundown from Amelia. He glances up, sees me, smiles, and gives me a little wave. I wave back, then sip my champagne.

Gladys pops back into my line of vision. "Time's up!"

I listen as Amelia announces how this will work, and a moment later I'm dancing with a familiar face. I grin, delighted.

"Jacob Edwards! What are you doing here?" I reach in and hug him, I can't help it. Jacob was one of my best reporters for years. He went viral after a video of him going face first into a pile of boiled crawfish at a festival a couple of years ago hit the internet. He and his fiancée, Katie, one of my former photographers, moved to Dallas to grow their careers there. I haven't seen them in ages.

"Good to see you too, boss," Jacob says in his deep, easy timbre. He looks handsome tonight, hair shaved close, white suit in perfect contrast to his brown skin. I can see how he swept Rhett's sister right off her feet.

"Is Katie here too?"

"Say cheese!" a familiar voice says.

I turn to find Katie holding up a camera, snapping a photo of the two of us. She lowers it, then darts in to give me a hug. "So good to see you, Lauren. You look gorgeous."

"Good to see you too, Katie. Working tonight?"

"Yep! Amelia asked me to come cover the ball. We wouldn't have missed it either way, but it's nice to have a paying gig while I'm here," she says easily, tossing her auburn ponytail over her shoulder. "Speaking of, I'm on the clock. Have fun dancing!"

Jacob sweeps me back up in a comfortable dance and we catch up as we move. I love hearing about his success in Dallas, about the happy life that he and Katie have found there. Their wedding will be this fall, and I promise to be there.

The song ends and my next dance partner steps up. "Frank!" I smile. "Surprised to see Margie's let you out of her clutches tonight."

He winks. "Anything to raise money for our nonprofit."

I'm relieved that, so far, my dance partners have all been people I know. I was nervous about dancing with strangers, especially in heels and this dress. My knee is twinging a bit, but I took ibuprofen right before the ball started. It'll have to do.

Another dance partner moves in. He's older than me, probably in his early sixties. Dark salt and pepper hair. Handsome. He looks familiar, but I can't quite place my finger on where I know him from. I smile and we hold a formal posture as we begin to move.

"Beautiful night tonight," he says.

"Yes, it is. And we appreciate your support of our programs," I say, practiced. I'm glad I have Lauren-the-reporter to fall back on in situations like this.

"I bet you do. The money makes it nice, don't you think?"

I frown. "For the kids? I hope so. That's certainly our goal."

He sweeps me around, moving me more aggressively across the dance floor. "Sure, the kids. That's who you want it for."

My arms lock up. "I'm not sure what you're implying, sir—"

He rolls his eyes and smirks, then leans in a little too close. "Don't play dumb now, Lauren. We know what you're after with my son."

My expression must change, because his false smile turns devilish.

It takes me a moment to process what, exactly, is happening as we continue to dance. My memory of that night in the restaurant snaps into my mind and I finally place him. This is Max's dad. And he . . . wait, is he threatening me?

I try to pull away, but he won't let go of my hand. He squeezes tighter, just enough to send a warning.

"Let go of me," I hiss.

"It would be a real shame if anything happened to Ruston's newspaper. Such a staple in the community."

I gasp. "You can't do that—"

"Oh, trust me darlin'," he sneers. "I own half the businesses in this city. I know the two of you need to put on a show until the Mardi Gras thing is done. But after that, the two of you are over."

I finally rip my hand away. "Max would hate you for this."

"No darlin'. Max is blood. He's family. We have had our setbacks. But I'm his father."

And with that, he turns and walks away, leaving me reeling. My head spins, my breaths coming shallow and quick. Too quick. I turn, looking for an exit.

"Lauren," a familiar voice says, but it's far away. "Lauren! Are you okay?" My vision gets black around the edges. I feel someone sweep me off my feet into a bridal carry, and then I'm moving out of the room and into the men's dressing room. I'm settled onto a chair.

"Hey birdie, you okay? Is it the dress? Look at me."

I blink, seeing Max kneeling in front of me. "Hey, you okay? Do I need to unlace this thing?" he says with a forced smirk.

I burst into tears.

"That motherfucker. What did he say? I saw him dancing with you and I got to you as quickly as I could. I was dancing with someone and didn't see you at first. But, fuck. Lauren. What did he say?"

I allow myself this moment with Max, allow myself to lean forward and push into his shoulder, crying into his silver suit jacket. His arms wrap around me, holding me close, his fingers tracing light strokes up and down my shoulder blades.

"It's okay, baby. It's okay. Whatever he said, it's not worth getting this upset over. He's an asshole. I know it, everyone knows it. I'll deal with him in a minute, but I need to make sure you're okay first."

Amelia walks through the doors and looks to where I sit and Max kneels on the floor in front of me. "Lauren! Are you okay?"

"Stay with her? I have something I need to take care of," Max says to Amelia.

She nods. I try to reach for Max, to hold him to me, but he's up and out the door in one swift movement. I can practically see the fire blazing behind his eyes as he exits. I'm grateful. I'm terrified. I'm going to ruin everything if I stay with Max. Everything I've spent years building. My career. My livelihood. My newspaper. My staff.

I swallow, reeling, knowing that we're making a scene. Terrified that Max is about to make it worse. This isn't the time or place.

I stand, swiping at my tears. "Let me just clean myself up. I'm fine. We have a ball to get back to." I hear the quiver in my voice and hate it.

"Lauren, you don't have to," Amelia says, standing in front of me and pushing back strands of my hair from where they've stuck to my tear-streaked cheeks.

I force a smile. "I'm fine. Just let me freshen up."

I go to the connecting bathroom and flip on the lights. Turns out all that waterproof mascara they piled on me really is waterproof. My eyes are red and a little puffy, but everything else is miraculously in place. I comb my fingers through my hair, count to ten, straighten, then walk back out to the dance floor.

The sudden clash of lights and music is overwhelming. I spy Max trying to escape someone who's caught him in a conversation. He's weaving his way though the crowd, making his way to his dad who stands by a window with his mother. This can't happen. Not now.

I make my way to Max. I'll think about all these consequences later. Right now, I need to stop this fight before it ruins the ball. Several people try to catch my attention as I go, but I offer quick "hellos" and keep going. I'm almost there. I've almost caught him. But then, the crowd before him parts and he reaches his dad. Shit.

I keep going, trying to figure out the best way to help handle this. Fury blazes Max's face, his cheeks flushed and eyes laser focused. His jaw and fists clench. This is not good. Will it be worse if I interfere?

"How dare you!" Max shouts.

And then, a fairy godmother seems to descend on them both. Pale blue, feathered gown, styled gray hair. Gladys.

I halt, watching as she gently places a hand on each man's chest, never losing her smile. In one clean motion, she turns Max toward me, whispers in his ear, then gives him a light shove. Then she turns to deal with Maxwell Senior.

Max spots me and his gaze melts from livid to concerned. He glances over his shoulder once, seeing that Gladys has ushered his father away, then walks toward me. In a moment his arms surround me, pulling me tightly into him.

I inhale, feel the tears, push them down, exhale.

"Lauren," he whispers. "What are you doing? I told you I'd handle him."

"And I don't want you to make a scene at this ball that your grandmother has so carefully planned," I say. "Your dad isn't worth that, is he?"

Max tenses, hesitates, then sighs. "You're right. But this isn't over. I need to know what he said to you and make sure he knows that he can't ever talk to you again. Not ever."

I already know that it's not that easy, not that cut and dry.

"Not tonight," I say. I pull back and slide my hands down to his. "Let's go dance. Show the guests that everything is okay. They're starting to stare."

He glances over my shoulder. "Fine," he huffs.

I tug him back to the dance floor, but the jazz music does little to inspire us. We're both upset and acting celebratory is impossible. I'm grateful when the music shifts to a slow dance. This, we can do. This is what we both need.

I can worry about his dad after tonight. We have a week until the parade. A week together before Mr. Beaumont's threat is pushed into action. I need to figure out how to emotionally untangle myself from Max between now and then. But all I want to do is fall into his arms and kiss him senseless.

Tomorrow. I'll figure it out tomorrow. I'm giving myself tonight.

I lay my head on Max's chest as we dance, listening to the thrum of his heart beneath my ear. His dress shirt is a little sweat-damp under that ridiculous coat. But it makes his laundry detergent smell stronger. I inhale and close my eyes, reaching my arms up and around his neck, and holding him close.

Max leans down and presses a kiss to my forehead. It sinks into my heart and nestles there, a cozy cat on a fireplace hearth. My heart wants this, desperately, in a way it never has with anyone else.

But can I have Max and my job?

I've never let any man stop me from reaching my career goals in the past. And I certainly don't plan to let another one do it now. Not even Maxwell Beaumont, Senior.

Tomorrow. I tell myself. I'll talk to Max about it tomorrow.

Chapter 32

MAX

Adrenaline courses through my veins. I still want to tackle my dad to the ground. Scream at him to leave Lauren alone. To leave me alone. I still don't know what he said to her, but it was enough to bring tears to the eyes of the strongest woman I know.

And I didn't get the chance to blow off that anger. One yell from me and my grandmother was stepping between us, just like she always has.

Logically, I know that we would have caused a scene and ruined the event. And I don't want that, not even a little. But the raging animal part of my brain doesn't care. I want to make my dad go the fuck away and never come back.

But then I saw Lauren, eyes puffy, fear and pain on her face, and I crumpled. It turns out that the only emotion that's powerful enough to keep me from wanting to punch out my father, is wanting to care for Lauren.

And it's weird. Never have I felt this tug to anyone. But now that she's in my arms, tucked in close as we dance, I feel like I can breathe again. We sway, our bodies finding the rhythm. And this is no formal king and queen dance. This is the dance of two people who want to crawl into each other's arms and live there. I pull her into me a little bit tighter, skating my hands down the back of her dress, wishing it was her skin.

I kiss her forehead again, but I want more. I need more, something to take the edge off. I slide my hand up her back, to her neck, and land on her jaw. She leans into my hand and I tilt her face up. Our eyes lock and study each other's.

I see so much there: worry, anger, and something fiery.

We move at the same time, two magnets seeking each other. My mouth lands on hers, her lips pressing into mine. Our mouths move, slow and steady. Seeking, exploring. I taste champagne as my lips dance along hers. The desire is there, simmering deep in my stomach. But this kiss is one of comfort, of two people seeking each other out and finding a rightness amidst the chaos.

I nip at her bottom lip and she chuckles, pulling back to look at me. Her eyes are shining, joy chasing away the worry. I press back in, brush my lips against hers.

An announcement sounds over the PA system. It's time to don our oversized back pieces and walk in a second line through the room. This is when we'll ask our fundraising beneficiaries to collect donations.

I escort Lauren to the lobby. We separate to get help with our costumes. In short order, my white feather fan backpiece is strapped on and my ridiculous pelican mask is on my face. My arms are weighed down with beads to throw to the guests.

I spy Lauren and my jaw drops. Her peacock feather plumage is stunning. She looks like a goddess pulled straight out of a painting. Blue and gold feathers arc all around her, and the peacock mask that was her undoing weeks ago has been trimmed down to a more modest, and oddly beguiling, fit. She also has beads draped across one arm.

It's showtime.

As our names and titles are announced, we form a line, walking through the crowd and tossing beads to guests as jazz music echoes through the room. Some of the young beneficiaries of our nonprofit programs join us, tossing cups out to patrons.

As we move through the crowd, I see a lot of familiar faces, but my parents are gone.

When our walkthrough is done, we gather at the front of the room for a round of photos with the entire krewe. This moment is the crown jewel of the evening. All that's left to do is send off guests, change, and rest up until next weekend.

I stretch and roll my shoulders, relieved to finally have all the heavy costuming off. I tilt my neck side to side, cracking the joints. Pulling on a t-shirt, I say good night to Rhett and a couple other krewe members leaving the dressing room. I walk out to the lobby, and see Lauren in her leggings, oversized sweatshirt, and purple tennis shoes. She's digging in a duffel bag, looking for something.

"Hey there," I say, stepping up to her and tracing my fingers along her back. I'm still desperate to have my hands on her, hungry for more kisses.

Her makeup is still on, eyes still smoky, hair still curled and down, stiff with hairspray.

"Hey, you," she says, standing.

"Can I help you find something?" I ask, nodding at her bag.

"Oh, just looking for my keys." She yawns. "Got them."

I reach for her hand and tug her into me for a hug. "Hey, I know things were weird tonight with my dad. But I want you to know that I'm here for you. I'm on your side in whatever this is."

She hugs me back. "I know. Tomorrow, okay? I just want to ride out the good parts of the rest of this night. He doesn't get to ruin that for me."

"Okay."

"Hey Max?" she asks, leaning back to look at me. Her face is serious and my stomach flips. Is she about to tell me to get lost?

Anxiety starts to churn in my stomach. She ducks her head and, when she looks back up, her cheeks are pink. She clears her throat. "I know it's late. And maybe I'm being too bold. You can say no."

"Spit it out, birdie," I say, trying to make light of it, but desperate to hear what she has to say.

"Do you want to come over to my place?" she says it in one, rushed breath.

I blink, stunned. Then I grin. "You sure?"

"I mean, only if you want to. You don't have to. I just thought, well, I have tomorrow off work for once and we've barely seen each other this week and we both might need some comfort after tonight."

"Oh birdie. I want to come over, but if I do, I should warn you: I'll comfort you, but I don't know how much resting we'll be doing." My voice has dropped low, her suggestion driving me wild. I want to hoist her over my shoulder, toss her in the car, and drive her straight home.

"I'm okay with that," she says. "But what about Mags?"

"She's staying with Janessa tonight. I knew I'd be home late and Jan insisted."

"Okay then," she says. "Let's go." She smacks my ass, then walks out into the night.

I'm left stunned and grinning. Then my brain catches up to what's happening. I run to her, reaching out to grab her ass as I speed past her and to my truck. I open the passenger side door and throw my bag in. She catches up, giggling. She does always love a challenge.

"I need your address, birdie."

"Nah. You just need to follow me and keep up," she taunts.

She leans in for a kiss. I follow her, but she pulls back just before our lips make contact. Then she runs around to her driver's side, opens the door, and turns on her car.

I jump in mine, just as she backs out and goes to exit the parking lot.

Game on.

Chapter 33

LAUREN

I don't know what tomorrow looks like, but I know what tonight could be. And I love that Max is willing to play. Love that he's chasing me, competing with me.

I gun it out of the parking lot and his headlights flash behind me. He wasted no time. I crank up the radio and note the time. It's nearly 1 a.m. I wince. It's late. But when was the last time I stayed up this late for fun and not for work? Screw it.

It's only a few miles to my house, and the whole drive home I dream about the ways Max will touch me, replaying that kiss from earlier tonight as we danced on repeat. By the time we reach my house, my whole body is on fire and aching for his touch.

I park in my driveway and get out, just as Max pulls up and parks on the street in front of my house. He's out of his truck in a flash. I yelp and try to run, but he's on me in seconds.

Max reaches me and wraps his arms around my waist. "Gotcha!" he growls, and that's it. That's all I need. I spin in his arms and kiss him, mouth open and needy. I drink him in, tongues tangling in a way I haven't made out since college. It's wild and free and desperate.

Delicious.

Lust consumes me, licking up my core, spreading into my breasts, reminding me of our cabin trip and the way his fingers dipped into me.

"Bedroom?" he pants.

"I'll show you." I tear myself away and fumble with my keys. It's dark outside with only the street light to help me see by. I drop them twice before I finally land on the correct key and open my front door. I reach for the light switch, flipping it on.

I look around my house, suddenly realizing I was not ready for company. Shoes are in a big pile by the front door, this morning's coffee cup still sits on the end table next to my couch, a romance book spread open over the couch arm, spine up.

I gasp as I'm lifted off my feet, legs dangling over one of Max's arms, the other supporting my shoulders.

"I said, *bedroom*."

And damn that man for hearing my audiobooks and knowing exactly what to say to turn me on.

"That way," I squeak and point. He marches in the direction I showed him while I plant kisses on his beard, down his neck. I love the way his pulse thrums beneath my lips. I nip at it.

"Fuck," he groans, then tosses me on the bed.

I giggle, loving being tossed around like this.

I roll to my back and push up on my elbows. This would be much sexier in anything but a sweatshirt and leggings, but Max doesn't seem to care. He reaches for his t-shirt collar and yanks it over his head, exposing lean muscles and the full scale of his phoenix tattoo up his arm. I lean back to turn on the lamp. He turns and flips the overhead lights off. The shadows lick up his body, highlighting every dip and curve of his chest, biceps, abs.

And when he chuckles, low and deep, I realize I'm staring at the bulge in his jeans.

"Your turn, birdie. Shirt off."

I don't hesitate. I scramble for the hem of my sweatshirt, ripping it off and taking the cami beneath it too. I glance up and see Max staring at my cleavage in my purple push-up bra. My boobs do look good tonight.

I run a hand over my stomach, ready to hide the stretch marks and loose skin that come with time and age. But a hand grips my wrist and pulls my hand away.

"I don't think so, birdie."

Max lets go, unbuttons his jeans, and yanks them off. I swallow, taking in the sight of him. Black boxer briefs cling to toned thighs. He pulls a pony tail holder off his wrist and ties his hair up in a bun. And then he fucking winks at me.

"Don't want my hair to get in the way."

I swallow and imagine all the ways his hair might get in the way. My gaze trails downward again. Max climbs onto the bed and reaches for the band of my leggings. He yanks, pulling them off me. I watch his face so I know when he realizes it.

"Birdie. You're not wearing any underwear."

"Very astute of you."

But he doesn't look away from where I hold my legs closed. And suddenly, I'm nervous. I'm no virgin, but it's been a very long time since I've done anything like this. What if I mess up? What if I can't climax? What if I do something he hates?

"Hey," he says, gaze softening. "You want me to stop, just say the word. We stop. No questions asked."

"It's not that. It's just. It's been a long time since I've been with someone. And I want to make you feel good. I'm worried I won't be able to have an orgasm and—"

"Babe, let's just go with it. There are no expectations. We just do what feels good, okay? And tell me if you want me to do something."

"What if you don't like what I'm doing? My ex hated it when—"

"There is nothing you could do to me that I would dislike."

"Oh."

"Yeah." He glances down to where he's rock hard in his boxer briefs.

"What if I spanked you?" I ask, feeling daring.

"Babe. I'd love it if you spanked me." He lifts an eyebrow in challenge.

"Oh," I say, processing. "Oh."

He moves to crawl on top of me and I lean back on the bed, giving him the space to do so. He kisses along my neck, down across my collarbones. Lower, until he reaches the cups of my bra. He pulls one to the side, exposing my nipple. He leans down and sucks it into his mouth. I gasp and he chuckles, the laugh rumbling against my sensitive flesh. He takes his time, licking and sucking, sending zings straight to my core. Little lightning strikes of pleasure.

He pulls back.

"Don't stop," I plead.

He chuckles and yanks the other bra cup down, giving my other breast the same delicious treatment. He's holding his weight above me some and I squirm beneath him, seeking friction.

Max takes that as his cue. He releases my nipple and then starts kissing and licking his way down my stomach. When he reaches my pubic bone I'm panting. I want this. I'm scared he doesn't. My last ex hated going down on me.

"You don't have to," I say, breathless.

In response, he loops his arms under my thighs, pulls my legs apart, and stares. He keeps staring until I'm embarrassed.

"Max," I whimper.

He seems to snap out of it.

"I've been fantasizing about this ever since I got that small taste of you in the cabin. I don't want to rush it. And you are so wet for me, baby."

God, the way his voice drops makes my whole body shiver. He smirks, "That's right, my birdie likes a man who uses his words. Well, that's going to be hard to do here in just a second, but I'll do my best."

And then he descends on me. He parts me with his tongue, taking one long lick and groaning. "You like that don't you, baby?

Want more?"

I'm helpless. This is beyond anything I could have imagined would happen to me in real life.

"Use your words," he says.

"More," I whisper.

"Good girl."

He licks me again, making slow circles around my clit with his tongue, sending waves of pleasure washing through my body. He pushes his face into me, his beard scratching my thighs and all around my center, providing the perfect friction and pain to the soft, warm movement of his tongue. Never has anyone paid this kind of attention to my pleasure. I start to worry that he's spending too much time on me, and I'm not giving him anything in return.

"You can stop if you want," I whisper.

He slaps the side of my ass. "Max!" I squeak.

He chuckles and keeps going, sliding a finger inside me and curling it. Another. Oh fuck. I can't stop the wave building inside me. One minute I'm dancing along the edge of pleasure, the next I'm falling over it in blinding bliss. Wave after wave washing over me, my body pulsing with it.

Distantly I hear Max saying, "That's right. Just like that. Give it to me, Lauren. Give me all of it." He keeps his voice low, amplifying every second of my orgasm.

When it's over, he leans back, grinning wildly. He looks a little unhinged, his beard covered in me. I love it.

I sit up and reach for him. He comes willingly, crawling back on top of me.

I reach for his boxer briefs and yank. They get caught on his erection and he laughs, then helps me get them off.

"We can stop here if you want to," he whispers.

"Not a chance," I insist.

And then I look down. Holy shit. Those boxer briefs didn't lie. Max is . . . big. I swallow.

"Like what you see?" he asks.

Yes, yes I do. I nod.

"I am on the pill. And haven't been with anyone in more than three years. I was clear at my last checkup." I wince, realizing how that sounded.

"I just got tested at my physical. I'm all clear. But Lauren, I can wear a condom. I just want you to feel safe." He strokes himself, watching me.

I swallow, tears forming in my eyes. His thoughtfulness is so fucking refreshing.

"I don't have any. And it's fine. I promise."

"You're sure?"

I nod. And then he climbs over me.

Chapter 34

MAX

Lauren's scent is all over me, driving me wild. I kiss her, loving that she doesn't shy away from me even after I've had my mouth all over her body. I ease back, pulling her up to sit with me. I work the back clasp of her bra, getting it undone and tossing it away. Finally, I have all of her, skin to skin.

I move my knees between her legs, grab the outside of her thighs and flip us so that she's straddling me as I lean against the headboard. I want her to be in control tonight, want her to show me her limits, what she likes.

She settles into the position. We look down between us. I'm so hard it's painful. She reaches, and when her hand wraps around me, I nearly come right then and there.

She giggles.

"Temptress," I gasp.

"Tell me what you like. What was it you said? Use your words," Lauren says, voice all sultry.

"I want this," I say, moving to grab her ass. She yelps. I lift her and line her up on top of me. "And I want you to control it . . . while

I talk you through it."

"Max," she sighs.

And I love that I know this thing about her that no one else does. That my words, my voice, turn her on so much.

"Now. Ride me."

She slides onto me slowly, taking me inch by inch. It's agony and heaven all rolled into one. "That's it," I say, my voice rasping. I reach back and cup her ass, helping to guide her down. "You take me so well. Almost there."

Another inch. Another. And then I bottom out. I hold her still. "Don't move," I gasp. "Give me just a minute." I clench my jaw, my chest heaving. I open my eyes and see Lauren watching me, amused. She pushes her breasts forward and in my face. Fuck.

I massage them. She groans and starts moving on me again. "Slower. Yeah, that's it. Just like that." Lauren undulates on me, her tight heat ratcheting me up, higher and higher. "You fuck me so good, Lauren. So wet, so tight. Move like that. Good girl."

My mouth keeps running. Telling her what I like, what to do, my lips moving between her breasts, neck, and lips. It's addictive, and I'm lost to it.

I slide my hands around to her ass again, adjusting the angle. "Faster baby. Yes. Just like that. Faster. That's it. I can feel you. Come for me, baby."

Lauren's chest is flushed, her head thrown back. A rush of pulsing and panting and crying out and then I'm there, her name on my lips. My orgasm explodes through me, both of us calling out each other's names, over and over.

When Lauren shudders and falls forward onto my chest, I hold her while she tucks her head under my chin.

"You good?"

"Hmmm. Perfect," she sighs.

I chuckle, rubbing my nose into her hair, noting the smell of the unfamiliar hairspray. I hear her breathing start to slow, and realize that she's dozing off with me still inside of her. As gently as I can,

I roll her off of me and onto her bed. She grumbles a little, then resumes sleeping.

I stare at her, adoring the way her lips pout out, how her hair slides into her eyes, how all the stress melts from her face. I stare at her kiss-swollen lips, wincing at the beard burn on her jaw that's sure to sting in the morning. But also loving that I left my mark on her. Just like she did with those beads on me over a month ago.

I reach down and brush her hair back. She hums when my fingers graze her flushed cheek.

I climb out of bed and head into the bathroom, cleaning up. I return with a warm wash cloth and gently nudge Lauren, offering it to her. Her eyes squint open, she takes it, cleans up, then tosses it to her wood floor.

Well then. Okay.

She lifts a lazy arm. "Snuggle."

"Yes ma'am," I say, crawling under the covers and letting her be the big spoon. Her arm snakes around my chest and her hips tuck against my ass. Her body touches my whole back, skin to skin, and a moment later, we're both asleep.

Chapter 35

LAUREN

February 16

Meow.

Ugh. Lola. Dammit. Every morning at 6:30 a.m. like clockwork.

Meoowwww. My brain starts down its practiced trajectory: Cat, coffee, clothes, work. Groaning, I roll to get up and feed her.

Or at least I try to, but I'm trapped by something large and warm. Something that is decidedly not part of my routine.

My eyes flutter open. Max.

My brain trips over itself replaying last night. The dancing, the kissing, the sex. My body heats just thinking about the way his mouth was all over me.

His arm is draped across my stomach, his head tucked into the crook between my neck and shoulder. His breathing is slow and steady with the hint of a snore sneaking through every few breaths.

I run a finger over his arm that rests across my waist, tracing the lines of his tattoo, marveling at the line work, how it was designed to perfectly fit the dips and curves of his forearm muscles and bone structure. Max flinches away from me. "Tickles," he murmurs.

I chuckle and do it again. He pulls away again. I try one more time. But when I skim my finger along his skin this time, he moves his arm up and wraps it around my waist, pulling me on top of him. He makes quick work of pinning my arms to my sides.

"I said that tickles. Now you're in trouble," he says, eyes still closed.

"Maybe I should get in trouble more often," I tease and wiggle against him. We're both still naked and that little shimmy of skin on skin finally makes his eyes fly open. "What, does that tickle too?"

"Watch it, birdie, any more of that wiggling and we're not leaving this bed today."

"Hmph. Doesn't sound like much of a punishment to me." I kiss his cheek.

He turns his head and his lips find mine, brushing across them in a soft, sweet caress.

MEOW!

I wince. Right. Lola.

The little food demon materializes beside us on the bed, her gray fur a sharp contrast to my white bedsheets. My Russian Blue is mouthy, and she starts letting me have it for not getting up to feed her on time. She meows and rubs against us, turning to headbutt Max directly in the chin.

"Hey now," he protests and releases my arms.

Max holds a hand out to let her sniff it. When he seems to meet her approval, he strokes the top of her head. Lola's purr comes immediately.

"Well, that is a surprise. Lola doesn't like anyone but me."

"Does getting Lola's purr of approval mean we can have a slumber party again?"

"I suppose so. But only if I get up and feed her. Otherwise she's going to associate you with the reason she's getting a late breakfast."

I push up and reach for the t-shirt that Max tossed away last night. It hangs off the side of the bed. I pull it over my head, then walk over to my dresser, pulling out a pair of cotton panties and sliding them on.

"Hurry back," he says.

I look at Max. It's a bit jarring to see a man in my space. It's a place I've protected for a long time. One I've shared with Lola and, occasionally, Leslie. After years of bad boyfriends and botched dating, I didn't want any man to come back to my sanctuary and disrupt the peace I've so carefully built here.

And yet, I didn't think twice about inviting Max over after the ball last night.

Even though—his dad. Right.

I turn and leave the room before Max sees my face fall. We need to talk about his dad, what he said to me. How to handle it. Our relationship? Is that what this is? Or is this just a fling?

My thoughts continue to spiral as I walk into the kitchen and get Lola's food out, dropping it into her bowl. I check her continuous flow water bowl and make sure it's full. Part of me wants to run and jump back in bed with Max, pretend like that situation last night with his dad never happened. My stomach flips and twists at the thought, and I know I can't avoid the topic. I've fought too hard for too long to get to where I am, both in my career and with my personal peace, to let someone like Mr. Beaumont try to upset it.

My body resumes its usual routine. I move to the coffeemaker, adding the filter and grinds—enough for two—fill the water, and turn it on. As the machine warms up and makes its comforting gurgly brewing sounds, I pull out two mugs, both a matching shade of candy apple red.

I take my time in the kitchen, wiping down my pale gray counter tops, even moving to the white cabinet doors to give them a quick dusting. My body moves in time with my anxious thoughts. Cleaning, throwing away scraps, removing dust. I'm so lost in the tornado of my mind that when an arm wraps around my waist, I startle.

"Hey," Max says gently. "Everything okay? I didn't upset you, did I? Do something you didn't like?"

Shit. I turn in his arms, facing him. He moves one hand to my chin, tilting me up to look at him.

"Talk to me, birdie."

I sigh and plant my forehead into his chest. "It's not you."

"Please don't say, 'it's not you, it's me,'" he tries to joke.

"It's not you, it's your dad," I mumble.

I feel his muscles go taut beneath my hands and forehead. I look up and notice the tick in his jaw.

"I should have kicked his ass last night."

"No," I say immediately. "No, that would have ruined the evening. I'm not upset about you not defending my honor or anything like that. It's just. We need to talk about what he said to me. What we're going to do about it."

"Lauren, you don't have to do anything," Max says, lightly stroking his hands down my arms. "He's my dad. My problem to fix."

"Oh but I do," I insist. "Because he threatened my livelihood, the career I've fought to build for myself. And I'm not going to take that lying down."

Max startles back like I slapped him. "He did what?"

I sigh, moving away to pour us each a cup of coffee. I hand one to him, then move to the fridge to pull out my favorite cinnamon coffee creamer. I pour a splash in my mug, then motion with it to Max in question. He nods and takes it from me, adding a bit to his mug as well. I put it back in the fridge, grab a spoon, give my coffee a quick stir, and offer it to him.

"Come on. Let's go sit and I'll tell you what happened," I say, nodding to the blue suede couch in my living room.

Max follows me over. I sit in one corner of the couch and he settles into the other. We turn to face each other, both of us propping our feet up on the cushions, our legs tangling comfortably. Max is wearing his t-shirt and boxer briefs. I find the look oddly endearing. We're both in our undies and t-shirts, like this is something we do every day.

But his dad. Right.

I grab the blanket that sits on the back of the couch and toss it over my legs. Lola takes that as her cue and comes running, leaping up to settle on my lap. It grounds me.

I look up at Max. He's watching me, waiting for me to begin. I take a sip of my coffee. "So. Your dad threatened me last night. Told me if I didn't leave you alone, didn't stay away from your family money, that he'd sink the newspaper and my career. He wants me to get lost after the Mardi Gras parade is over. I think the only reason he didn't use threats to separate us last night was because he didn't want to ruin Gladys's work on all the Mardi Gras stuff."

"Fuck," Max says, running his hand through his dark hair. "Lauren, I'm so sorry. I knew he was a piece of shit, but I expected him to come for me, not you. I should have intervened, kept an eye on him, kept him away from you—"

"His behavior isn't your fault, Max."

He looks away. "I'm the reason he's harassing you though."

I shrug. "I think he's the reason he's harassing me, actually. You've done nothing but take care of me, ask me what I want, show up when no one else does. I don't want to end whatever is growing between us, Max. But I don't know how to stop your dad. And I won't let the newspaper fail because of his personal vendetta. So the question is, what can we do?"

"I'm going to talk to him," Max says, resigned. "That's what he wants. I've held that boundary with him, kept him out of my life for so long, that he'll do anything to force me back into the fold. Even threaten people I care about." He looks at me when he says that, emotion shining in his eyes.

"Max. You've worked hard to protect yourself, your peace, from him. I don't want you to break it for my sake. There has to be another way."

"There's not. My grandmother has run interference between us for years. Did it again last night. She shouldn't have to do that. I have to figure out a way to stop this, once and for all."

"How? You've already cut him out of your life and that didn't stop him. What else can you do?"

Max takes a sip from his mug, then sets it down on the coffee table next to us. He moves his feet to the floor and scoots over close to me, pulling my legs into his lap.

"I don't know. But I'll figure something out. I don't want to lose you, just as I'm finally getting to have you."

He runs his thumb over my knee and I slide my hand down to cover his. Lola meows in protest at us jostling her in my lap.

"We have a week before the parade, before he makes his move, right? I'll figure out something before then. Just don't give up on us, birdie. Not yet," he pleads quietly.

I squeeze his hand. "I won't. And I'm going to work on figuring out something too. We're in this together."

He pulls my hand up to his lips and presses a kiss to my knuckles.

Chapter 36

MAX

"There's something else I want to ask you about," I say, rubbing her calves. I want to steer her thoughts away from my terrible father. He is a problem that I'll take care of. He's taken my family from me, he doesn't get to take Lauren.

"Oh?" she asks.

"You had fun hiking and going to the cabin?"

She smiles and dips her head. "You could say that, yes."

"I thought so." I move my hand down to her foot, bending her knee until it's in my lap. I massage her foot, taking my time with every inch. She groans.

"And I was thinking," I continue. "About what else you might like to do. Some things that maybe you've always wanted to try, but never had the time or energy or person to do them with. And I was curious. What might those be?"

I know I'm walking a delicate line here. Know that she might shut down and tell me to mind my own business any second. But I've gotten the sense that she yearns for more time to explore her interests, despite adoring her work. I wait for her to answer, staring at her foot as I continue to work it over.

"Do you mean like a bucket list?" she asks.

I turn my head side to side. "Something like that. More practical. Small things that bring you joy. Or big things. Like, I've always wanted to try haggis," I offer.

"You've got to be kidding me," she barks out a laugh. "Sheep guts and oatmeal? No thanks."

"Hey, sounds like an adventure to me. Why not? Your turn. What about you?"

She hums, taking a moment to think it through. "I don't know. I guess I always thought it would be nice to learn another language. Something beautiful like Spanish or French."

"So academic," I tease.

"Better than haggis!"

"What about experiences?"

"Like what? Sky diving or something?" she asks.

"If that's what you want to try, sure."

"No, I don't think jumping out of a plane is for me," she laughs. "But I did enjoy our dance lessons. I wouldn't mind more of them. Maybe a different style. Something contemporary. I don't know."

"You'd be phenomenal at it," I say, studying the way her muscles flex in her leg. Imagining how they'd bend and twist while dancing.

"Anything else?" I ask.

"Honestly? I want to write my own book. And I'd love the time and space to do it in," she says like a deeply held confession. "Maybe rent a cabin, bring my cat. Stock up on all my favorite foods. The perfect girl dinners like charcuterie, fizzy drinks, wine. And I'd allow myself to sit in the quiet, let my imagination take over, and just write whatever I want. Write for the joy of writing, not because I'm on a deadline, but because the words need to fall out of my mind and fingers."

I study her face, the joy lighting up her eyes. There it is. There's the thing I knew was tucked down in there somewhere. The thing that makes her feel alive.

"And what would you write?" I ask. "Something naughty like all those books you listen to?" I smirk.

She blushes and looks away, then returns her stare to me, eyes heating. "Maybe."

Oh I like that answer. I like it a lot.

"I bet you'd write a delicious novel. And I'd read it to you. Record your audiobook. Or, maybe…" I say, bending down to kiss her knee, "I'd help you figure out exactly what to write in those spicy scenes of yours."

I reach behind her back and pull her into my lap. She gasps, nearly spilling the last drops of her coffee. Lola darts out of her lap, tail shaking in protest. Lauren turns and sets her mug on the coffee table then wraps her arms around my neck.

"Oh would you now? What do you have in mind?" she asks, dipping her mouth close to mine.

I take the invitation, bending to capture her lips.

Distantly, I hear a buzzing sound in the background. A phone. We ignore it and it stops. It starts again. Lauren pulls back and looks around.

"Sorry," she says. "It's just that it might be work."

Sighing, I release her and she gets up and heads to the kitchen, picking up her phone off the counter. I watch as she looks over the screen.

Her shoulders relax and a smile lights up her face. "Not work, but I think Janessa is anxious to turn Mags back over to you. And she somehow guessed that, when you didn't answer your phone, that you were with me." She looks at me with mischief. "Now, I wonder why she would think that?"

I try to hide my smile and fail. "I may have told her that I had intentions where you're concerned."

"Is that why she wants to be my friend?" her smile falls.

I laugh and Lauren balks. "Sorry," I say. "No, it's not you. Shit, bad reaction. It's just that the thought of me telling Janessa who to be friends with is hilarious. I have never been able to convince my cousin to do anything she doesn't want to do. If she has selected you and decided she wants you as her friend, that's all on you, birdie."

Her frown fades. "And if it doesn't work out between you and me?"

"I don't like that. But she would still be your friend. Hell, she's my cousin, my dad's sister's daughter. You see what's happening in my family. And she still chooses me. My grandmother too. Those two seem to have gotten all the goodness in our family." I glance at the floor, heart aching over a topic I usually avoid.

I hear footsteps and then an arm slides around my shoulders as the couch dips next to me.

"Not just those two. You are good through and through, Max Beaumont." She kisses me on the cheek. "I just don't have the best track record with friendships, or any kind of relationship for that matter. I work a lot. People don't like that. I've made my peace with it."

I turn and look at her. "Huh. Seems to me that a lot of people want to be in your life. Leslie, her kids, my grandmother. Hell, your whole staff is willing to do anything for you. They love you. And Janessa sees what I see."

She looks at me, studying my expression. "And what's that?"

"Someone genuine. Someone who doesn't apologize for being who she is. Someone who cares deeply, so deeply that she's willing to sacrifice herself to keep her work alive, make sure her staff has jobs. Don't sell yourself short, Lauren. Say the word and a hundred people would come running to help you."

"I don't think anyone has ever said anything like that to me before," she says, searching my eyes.

"Well, it's about time someone did." I press a kiss to her lips.

She leans her head on my shoulder and I pull her into my side, both of us holding each other through these wounds that have chased us most of our adult lives.

Her phone buzzes again. I wince, knowing I need to meet up with Janessa and pick up Mags. "I'll go get my phone out of your room. Sorry she's bugging you because of me."

"She's not bothering me," Lauren says, reaching for her phone.

"Maybe not. But she's bothering me. I'm trying to have a moment here." I lean in and kiss Lauren below her ear. Move down her neck. Linger at her collarbone.

"Max," she gasps. "I really should check that. Because—"

A knock sounds at her front door and I halt. "Ignore it," I decide, then pull the collar of her t-shirt to the side, moving to her shoulder, drinking her in with my mouth. She groans.

The knock comes again, followed by a bark. "Open up, I know you're in there, Maxie."

"I may have given Janessa my address so she could drop Mags off on her way to Pilates," Lauren says in a rush of air.

I growl, but pull away. Lauren hops up and skitters to the front door. It's then that I realize that I never put a shirt back on after last night. Janessa is never going to let us live this down.

The door swings open and a combination of woofs and "Lauren! So good to see you!" fills the space. I spy Lola peering around the corner and realize that I don't know if her cat has ever been around dogs before. Probably not the time to find out.

I stand and Mags spies me, jerking away from Janessa's grasp, her purple leash trailing behind her as she darts to me. I bend down and am instantly covered in licks and happy whines. "Whoa, calm down girl. Daddy's here." I look up just in time to see Lauren raise an eyebrow.

"Well damn, Maxie, I knew you were comfortable around me, but half naked in your girlfriend's house is next level," Janessa says.

"Please, Jan. We grew up together. You've seen me shirtless—and pantless—more times than either of us cares to remember."

"But you've always hidden your dalliances. This must be serious, hmmm?" Janessa waggles her eyebrows.

I notice Lauren fidgeting, looking uncomfortable. Time to pivot.

"Not my fault you showed up over here this morning. You get what you get."

"All the same, can't say I mind it. You deserve some happy. I imagine you both do and I won't get in the way of it. I'm headed to Pilates. Enjoy the rest of your day. And Lauren, don't be a stranger. Coffee this week? I'll text you."

I stand and give my cousin a side hug. She wraps Lauren up in a tight hug, then departs.

When the door closes, Lauren turns to me. "Sorry, I tried to warn you—"

I steal a kiss. "Don't apologize. I'm glad she likes you."

A low growling snags my attention. I turn to see Mags facing off with Lola, who is arching and hissing.

"Shit," I mumble. "I'll grab Mags."

But before I can scoop her up, Lola lunges at her, batting her nose. Mags turns tail and hops up on the couch, huddling behind me, trembling. Well that settles that then.

"Lola has always been a bit of a baddie," Lauren sighs. "Is Mags okay?"

"Yeah," I say, scooping up my pup. Mags's eyes never leave Lola. "I think she just needed to learn who the top dog is around here." I rub the top of her head, making her ears swish from side to side. "Don't worry, Mags. She'll get used to us."

"Is that right?" Lauren asks, strutting toward me.

"As long as the two of you will have us," I smirk.

"Deal."

Chapter 37

LAUREN

February 18

With less than a week until the parade, the newsroom is consumed by the preparations. From the final touches on float assembly, to the upcoming float loading party, and detailing the parade route, Mardi Gras has officially consumed my small staff. And me.

Between my insane daytime workload and Max working evenings, it's been nearly impossible to spend more time together this week. But we call and text constantly.

We need to figure out this thing with his dad. He insists he's going to take care of it, but it feels like a doomsday clock is ticking down on our situationship, and I'm mad that Maxwell Beaumont, Sr. has placed this added stress on Max and me this week, of all weeks.

I look at my ever-expanding inbox and groan. Maybe I'll finally take the vacation my staff has been pushing me to take once Mardi Gras season is over. Though I already feel a little guilty about all my time away from the office recently. Even if my participation as krewe queen is bringing us more advertising and interest.

My phone buzzes.

Janessa: Coffee?

I wince and glance at the clock, it's 1 p.m. and I haven't taken a break or eaten anything today. Then I look at my inbox. Three more emails come in.

I shouldn't leave. My stomach rumbles.

I'm going to burn the midnight oil tonight anyway with all this additional work load and special edition of the paper leading up to the parade. Might as well go get the caffeine to get me there.

Lauren: Meet you at Lattes and Lagniappe in 30 minutes?
Janessa: See you there.

When I walk into the familiar coffee shop, I glance around, noting the beautiful photos on display. The little shop always has a Louisiana artist up on the walls, and I'm delighted to see that right now the framed photographs are by our former newspaper photographer, Katie.

"Lauren!" a familiar voice says. I glance to one of the tables where Janessa sits in her deep purple yoga gear, already a couple of bites into a chocolate croissant with some sort of latte resting on the table. "Sorry to start without you. I was starving."

"It's fine," I smile, wishing that I was in yoga gear and eating a chocolate croissant. Yep, it's definitely time for some self-care of my own. "I'm going to place my order and come join you."

A few minutes later, I'm walking to the table with a honey cinnamon latte and a breakfast sandwich. I settle in, feeling a little awkward. It's almost like I'm dating a potential friend. Where do we start? Common interests? Am I overthinking this? Or maybe I should go into reporter mode and investigate the scene?

"I'm so glad you had some time to hang out," Janessa says, interrupting my thought spiral. "I had fun bowling a few weeks ago, but it was hard to chat when my cousin was dead set on trying to win you over," she laughs.

"He did a pretty good job of it," I smile.

"I'll say. You're definitely the best woman he's ever dated."

Are Max and I dating? I decide now isn't the time to hash that out.

"You barely know me," I say instead.

"I know you have a stable job, a cute cat who is well taken care of, and you're willing to let Maxie teach you how to bowl. Plus you both work in media and you're both gorgeous. What else am I missing?"

I laugh. Her candor is refreshing. I remember she mentioned that she and Max were born in the same week, so she's just a bit younger than me then.

"That's sweet of you," I say, taking a sip of my latte. "And you really want to be friends? I admit it's been a while since I made a friend who wasn't a coworker. I'm probably not very good at this."

She shrugs. "You have the right vibes. I like you. And I'm of the opinion that we can't have too many smart, strong women rooting for us, you know?"

"I do," I agree, settling back into my seat. "So tell me about you. What do you do? What do you like? Got any pets?"

She takes a bite of her croissant and I'm tempted to go back and order one. "Yep, I have a cat I rescued from a dumpster as a kitten named Francis. And then a black cat that found me named Binks. I do social media for my grandmother's funeral home business—I know, weird. But it's strangely fun. Um, I like to read."

"What do you read?" I cut in. This is a topic I can work with.

She smirks. "Give me all the romance books. I love them all, from sweet and swoony to monster erotica."

I laugh, delighted. "Oh, you and I are going to get along just fine then."

The conversation turns to our favorite audiobook narrators and I find myself relaxing into the conversation, enjoying Janessa's frank way of saying everything that comes to her mind. I was so worried about what we were going to talk about that I'm shocked to realize an hour has already passed and I need to hurry back to work.

"Let's do this again," I say. "Or we can go out for drinks sometime."

"You should join my book club," she says. "Everyone would love you. Plus, we only read romance, so I already know you'll enjoy what we pick." She grins.

"I worry about the commitment with my busy job," I hedge.

"So read the first book. I'll send you the meet up time. If you come, you come, if not, maybe next time?"

Can it really be this easy? Have I psyched myself out of making friends for so long for no reason?

My phone buzzes.

"Sent you the information. Our next book is *Sweet on You* by Dani Galliaro. Cowboy romance. Hot! Am I right?"

I giggle, my shoulders loosening. I'm excited about the idea of having someone to talk romance books with. Someone who gets it.

"I'd love that. Thanks, Janessa."

"Looking forward to it!"

Chapter 38

MAX

I turn the problem of my dad over and over in my head.

I need to get ready for work, but I can't focus. Finally, I pull up the Notes app on my phone and start listing things out:

1. He wants me to be part of the family again.

2. He wants me to take a leading role in the family business.

3. He wants me to marry a wealthy woman who will create better business connections for him.

4. He wants me to forgive him for hitting me.

He won't say that last one, but I know it's buried beneath his narcissistic facade.

I read through the list again. The only item that's even remotely negotiable is being part of the family again. But even thinking about it makes my stomach churn. I want to spend time with Mom, my brother, Charlie and his wife, again. But I don't know how to do that without seeing Dad.

Maybe the better option is to push back and shut him down. But what power do I have here? I'm a radio DJ with a modest income. I have some savings, but there is nothing I can do financially to sway my wealthy father.

I hate him for laying down this deadline, especially because I know he'll act on it. He'll destroy Lauren's career if we don't come to heel.

We could hide our relationship?

I immediately hate myself for even thinking it. Absolutely not.

I reach for my phone and pull up Janessa's contact. My creative thinking only goes so far, but Janessa? Well, no one crosses her for a reason. I hit the call button. It rings twice before she picks up.

"Were your Spidey Senses tingling?" she asks.

"Why do you say that?"

"Just finished having coffee with Lauren. I like her. I don't know how you managed to snag her, but good job."

"Very funny. I'm not that terrible."

"No, you're wonderful. I'm just glad to see you finally going for a woman you deserve."

That makes my heart ache. "Lauren's great. I'm glad you two are on friendly terms."

"Oh, I invited her to my romance book club. Look out. She's going to be my best friend in no time."

I smile, imagining those two hanging out together and laughing over spicy books.

"Everything okay, Maxie?" she asks.

I usually text, rarely calling unless it's something serious. Like things with my dad right now. "Not really," I admit. "Dad is up to his shit again."

"What did he do this time?"

"He threatened Lauren to stay away from me. Implied that she's a golddigger after our family's money and that he has a better plan for my future."

"That motherfucker," she hisses.

"Exactly. He told her that he'll stay away until after the Mardi Gras parade so nothing's ruined for Grandma. But he threatened to ruin the newspaper if she doesn't stay away from me after the parade is over."

"Why is he always such an asshole?" she yells. I don't say anything, because what can I say? "Okay, so what are we going to do about it?"

"I'm not asking you to do anything about it," I say immediately. "I just need . . . I don't know. Some insight? Advice? Thoughts? Prayers?"

"Support," she says solemnly.

"You don't need to wade into this with me. You and Grandma are the only family I regularly get to see. I don't want anything to destroy that."

"Oh Max. So selfless. So noble. So dumb."

"Hey!"

"I hate your dad, too. And I love you. And Lauren is my friend now. Uncle Maxwell does not get to kick her out of our lives."

I'm relieved to hear her say that. To know that some family really does stick around no matter what.

"Maxie . . ." Janessa draws out. "How do you feel about breaking and entering?"

"I suppose it depends on the target."

"Okay, so hear me out. I'll get Grandma to lure your dad out of the house. And then you and I are going into his office for some investigating. I'll bring the gloves. Leave your moral compass at home. If he's going to fight dirty, then dammit, we're going to stoop down to his level."

"And what are we looking for during this little adventure, exactly?"

"If anyone keeps a record of his dirty deeds, it's your dad. So when he comes for Lauren, we come for him."

"This sounds very cloak and dagger, Jan."

"Cloaks, yes! But leave the dagger at home. We don't want to be caught with weapons."

I chuckle, reminded of the shenanigans Janessa and I got up to as kids. "And when will this little heist take place?"

"When's your next night off?"

"Wednesday. But I was hoping to hang out with Lauren."

"Well, there will be no more nights with Lauren if we don't solve this daddy issue. Reschedule your date night and pull out your black sweatshirt. I'll talk to Grandma and confirm."

"Okay. And hey. Thank you, Jan," my tone turns solemn.

"You're welcome, Maxie. I love you, you know?"

"Yeah, I know. Love you too. Good night, you menace."

She cackles and hangs up. I pick up my phone and pull up my texts.

Max: Change of plans Wednesday. Something came up. Reschedule for Thursday?

Lauren: *sad face emoji* Can't. I'm spending time with Leslie and the kids that night. Unless you want to join?

Max: I'll tag along if your sister doesn't mind?

Lauren: Are you kidding me? An extra adult on hand? Leslie will kiss you when you show up, and then hand you a baby.

Max: I've never had sister wives before, but if you're up for it . . .

Lauren: Ha ha! Very funny, mister. I get all your kisses. But you can hold a baby.

I smile at my phone, imagining hanging out with Lauren's tight knit family. How much I want that. How much I want that with Lauren in particular.

Max: I can handle that.

Max: I have to work tonight. Call later?

Lauren: Looking forward to it.

Interlude

PEACH 103.1

Beau: On the show with us tonight, we have Amelia Hebert. In her role as vice president at the Chamber of Commerce, Amelia is the center of many festivities in the Ruston area, including our newest: Ruston's first Mardi Gras parade. Amelia, welcome to the show.

Amelia: Glad to be here tonight.

Beau: There's been a lot of build up to this first Mardi Gras parade. Fundraisers and a ball among them. The parade is this weekend. What can people expect as we head into the event.

Amelia: Before the parade we have a very important party, one we're asking anyone in the community to join who wants to. All the parade floats are being stored in the krewe's den, a warehouse near the site of the Fall Festival. And we need your help to get the floats ready to go for the parade.

Beau: Do you mean paint and decorations, or—?

Amelia: (laughs), No, all of that is already done. We're having a float loading party! And that's exactly what it sounds like. We have thousands and thousands of throws. Beads, cups, doubloons, a few other special things. Right now they're all in boxes, and we need to get them loaded onto those parade floats so our riders are ready to toss them to parade attendees.

Beau: And I'm guessing that means more than just loading boxes onto floats.

Amelia: Right you are. There are special hooks on the floats for the beads. We will sort them by color, and place them so riders can reach them easily.

Beau: So a special behind the scenes look, then?

Amelia: Yes. And there will be plenty of Johnny's Pizza to go around for anyone who joins us. And, helpers will get to see the special beads designed for this year's inaugural parade only.

Beau: A little once in a lifetime moment.

Amelia: Certainly the only time you'll get to be part of the prep work for our first-ever parade.

Beau: Well, sounds like fun to me. Can you give us the details?

Amelia: Sure, we're loading at the krewe den on Friday evening, beginning at 5 p.m. We'll keep going until we're done and the pizza's all gone.

Beau: We hope to see you there.

Chapter 39

MAX

February 19

"Janessa. I don't know if this is a good idea."

The two of us are staring at my childhood home, dressed entirely in black like a couple of tweens ready to steal Mom and Dad's vodka after watching a heist movie. Ridiculous.

"What if we get caught?" I'm trying to be reasonable.

She shrugs. "I mean, it's your parents' house. Not like it belongs to a stranger. If we get caught, then we were just stopping by to tell them hi."

"Plausible. Especially since I haven't been to visit them in ten years," I deadpan.

"It's fine. Besides everyone knows your dad does shady business dealings. If we get caught and handed over to the authorities, we'll just throw him under the bus and make a run for it," she says easily. "Think the garage code is the same?"

Turns out that it is, which makes this little heist a helluva lot more boring. But I'm glad for it. Keeps things simple.

My parents' house is gigantic. A two story sprawling ranch with endless hallways and bedrooms. Entirely too much house for two people. Though I know Mom has aspirations of having places for her grandbabies to come stay one day. I wince, my heart aching at the thought. I've never had a desire for children, not that I'm opposed to them if I met the right person and she wanted them. Mom hopes for so much, yet stays out of Dad's way while he attempts to manipulate our whole family.

The anger that ignites in my chest spurs me on. Before we head inside, I walk over to the circuit board in the garage and kill the power. No need for all those inside cameras to send alerts to Dad's phone that someone's inside the house. Besides, he should be at Grandma's by now, and the signal at her house is terrible. We're betting on that being our backup cover.

We unearth our flashlights from my backpack and head in, making for Dad's office.

With the power out and flashlights on, this really does feel a bit like a heist. And I can feel Janessa practically vibrating with excited energy beside me. Just like when we were kids.

When we get to Dad's office, I head straight to his desk, tugging at the drawers there. I shouldn't be surprised when they don't open. Even Dad is smart enough to lock anything that might be damning away.

"That feels like such an obvious place to hide something," Janessa protests.

I shrug. "Check the obvious places first, right? He probably still keeps the keys in his night stand. I'll go look. You keep searching here."

I walk out of Dad's office and into their bedroom, swishing the flashlight around the space. Its beam catches on their bedspread, an abandoned pair of pants on the floor, and a portrait on the wall of our family when I was about sixteen. My cheeks are round, hair a messy mop on my head. But I'm smiling, unaware of all the dark things ahead of me.

I tear my gaze away and head for the night stand. I shuffle around a few things: a flashlight, a pocket knife, a box of tissues. And there, a small ring of keys. I grab it and head back to Dad's office.

When I get there, I find Janessa looking through the bookshelf, moving books around.

"Find anything?"

She shakes her head. "You?"

"Got the keys. Let's take a look."

I unlock the desk drawer and pull it open to find a line of file folders. I scan through the labels, unsure what I'm looking for. They are mostly client files. Dad's longtime work as an investment banker has allowed him to secure a lot of corporate partners. He's a consultant now, advising clients on when and how to invest in stock options, asking for businesses to step in and help startups.

It all sounds very official and professional, and it all seems to be above board. But Dad has a reputation for being threatening to clients and investors to make all the pieces work together. And that has never been part of my personality. I never wanted to follow in Dad's footsteps, not like my brother, Charles.

And although his business is legal, I have always wondered how he's been able to hold onto such large customers. Rumors have always circulated around him, but no one has been brave enough to say anything publicly. I have suspected for a while that some of his dealings aren't quite ethical.

While I'll do anything to keep Lauren out of his clutches, I still don't like digging into all this. It feels gross, like a coat of slime on my skin. Even though, if what he's done is as bad as I think, he deserves a lot worse than the two of us digging through his desk.

I thumb through the files, glancing at numbers, not really sure what I'm looking for. Janessa sits next to me and does the same.

"This is a waste of time," I sigh. "There is no way I can discern any of this. I won't know if he's cooking books by looking at balance sheets like this."

"I don't think we're looking for spreadsheets," Janessa hedges, continuing to look through files. She's heard the rumors too.

"Well then? What exactly are we looking for?"

She pushes the files apart and looks down. "I think we're looking for this." She reaches down through the files, down to the bottom of the drawer and pulls out a folder.

She flips it open, using her flashlight to scan the page. "Fucking bingo."

I scooch in close to her and glance at what she's reading. Handwritten notes on lined paper. Squinting, I start to read.

"Well shit," I mumble. "We can't take this with us though. He'll know."

"I'll hold the flashlight," Janessa says. "You take the photos."

I snap them quickly, tapping to make sure everything is in focus, feeling a little more ill with each capture. We finish up and close the drawer. I lock it, then jog back to my parents' bedroom to return the keys, my head spinning with everything I just read. I meet Janessa in the hallway and we head out to the garage. We don't talk, both of us mulling over our discovery. My estimation of my dad just dropped lower, and I already thought it was in the gutter.

I head to the circuit breaker, turning all the power back on. We walk to my truck and Janessa climbs into the passenger side, just as headlights flash across where I stand. I freeze, a deer caught in headlights. I want to jump into my truck and peel out, but the part of my brain that still works reminds me that would be really fucking suspicious.

Which means my only other option as my parents park and get out of their car, is to act like I intended to be here. Fuck.

"Well, this is a surprise," my dad drawls as he steps out of his Lexus.

"Max," Mom says, getting out of the car and running to give me a hug. I hold her, breathing in her familiar, once comforting flowery scent. I pray she can't hear my thundering heart. "What are you doing here?"

I have to make a flash decision. "I came to talk. To both of you. And," I glance to the truck where Janessa is hastily pulling a hot pink sweatshirt over her black outfit. "Janessa came with me."

Mom frowns as Dad walks to stand beside her. "Well, you are always welcome here, son," she says, throwing a worried glance at my dad.

"I must admit, I'm curious to hear what you have to say, why don't you come on inside. Janessa is always welcome too, of course," he adds, eyes flitting to my truck. I can see him shift into his business man facade—the wolf pulling down his mask. "I do wish you would have called first. We could have had dinner," he adds. "And made sure we were home. Your grandmother needed our help this evening advising her on a sour client relationship."

I nod and we follow my parents inside.

Dad pours a glass of bourbon and offers me one. I shake my head. He rolls his eyes and adds a little more for himself. He gestures to the couch in his home library and we both take a seat.

Mom already ushered Janessa into the kitchen, insisting on wine and charcuterie.

For the best. This conversation is one I've been avoiding for over a decade and we don't need witnesses. And if Dad decides to try to hit me again? Well, there's a reason I've frequented the gym over the last decade. And Dad's strength has deteriorated. He won't get the jump on me this time.

"What finally brought you to our doorstep, Max? Common sense finally kick in? Too bad you wasted your college degree. We'll have a lot of work to do to get you ready to run this business. It's a damn shame you've wasted so much time."

I clench my fists. There's still a chance to handle this the right way without dragging in tonight's discovery. I owe it to myself to at least try.

"Father. That's not why I'm here. I want to talk to you about Lauren. About what you said to her."

He lets out an amused chuckle and shrugs. "That woman is no

good for you. She's past her prime and poor. You deserve better than that. This family does."

"Shut the fuck up!" I yell, before I realize what I'm saying. "Lauren is a good woman. She doesn't give a shit about your money. But she cares about me. Far more than you ever have."

He chuckles, taking a lazy step toward me. "Is the sex really that good? I looked into her, you know, did some digging. She's got quite the checkered past. Dumped man after man after she got access to his money. Did she tell you that?"

My heart thuds. She wouldn't do that to me.

"Oh yes, son," he emphasizes. "I know many of her past flings personally. Clients of mine. They had plenty to share when I asked around."

The word clients shakes me out of my fear. It reminds me of the damning evidence now on my phone. The lists I still need to read through so I can make a stand. Because this? This isn't working.

"You're a liar," I throw at him.

"Am I? Ask her, then. Ask her about Frederick McAlister and Kyle Govern. See what she says. And when she comes clean, I'll be here ready to educate you on how your life should have always been. We'll match you up with a woman who can give you children. One who won't need our money. She'll be a good little wife to you, a good mother. And you can finally take your place where you belong—helping me run my business."

My thoughts are tripping over themselves. He wants me to ask Lauren about men she's dated? Does that mean it's true? What Dad said? But no. If that were true Lauren would already be with someone. Or am I her next target? Fuck, I hate myself for even thinking it.

I want to punch my dad. I swallow down the impulse and turn, stepping out of the library.

"Janessa!" I yell. "Let's go!"

My cousin arrives a moment later, her purse on her arm. "I thought you'd never be ready," she whispers.

And the two of us walk out the front door of my parents' house, not daring to look back.

We get in my truck and I start driving. We sit in tense silence for several minutes.

"Max," Janessa hedges. "What happened?"

My eyes are locked on the road, my thoughts in tumult. "I don't know what to think," I finally say. And then I tell her everything.

She leans back in her seat. "Well, I understand that your dad's got you all fired up, but I hope you're not over there steaming about Lauren. There's a simple solution here. Just ask her about those guys."

My stomach flips. I feel sick.

"What if it's true," I murmur, betrayal licking at me.

"Then better you find out now than further down the road," she says. "But Max. You saw what I saw in your dad's office. I don't think Lauren is the problem here. You owe her the benefit of the doubt."

My shoulders sag. "Fuck. I'm an idiot."

"Yeah, you are. But I love you anyway. Call her. Talk to her. And then decide for yourself."

"And what do we do about Dad? About what we found?"

Her grin turns mischievous. "Oh, I have lots of thoughts about that. Call Lauren. Talk to her. And then, let's work on stage two of our plan."

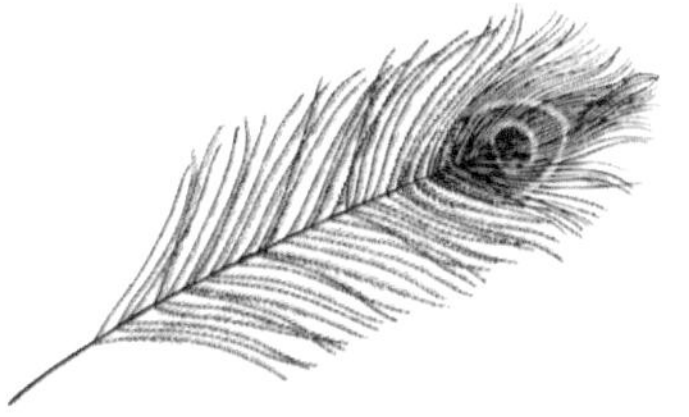

Chapter 40

LAUREN

February 20

Today kicked my ass. Work was one mess after another with employees calling out sick and having to stop the press when we realized the wrong version of a story was placed on the page. I'm in a terrible mood after Max canceled our hang out last night. Especially after he sent me a quick "talk tomorrow," text when I tried to call him last night.

What does that mean? Was this all just a fling for him? But no. There's something more between us. I know it. He probably had something come up with work and I'm just overthinking everything. Besides, we'll hang out with my sister later tonight.

If only I can get away from work.

"Hey, boss," Rhett says walking into my office. "Can you look over this front page story one more time? It's the right version this time, but it's on that church embezzlement scandal, so it could use another look-see."

I sigh and turn to my email, finding the story waiting on me. "Of course," I say, opening the file.

"Thanks, boss." He turns and walks out of my office.

I scan the story, my heart dropping. I know the basics already, but reading about the bad choices people make always lowers my morale. I really need snuggle time with my nieces and nephew.

And Max snuggles.

I glance at the clock. I can do this. One more quick run through the copy and then I can head out.

Except the quick run through turns into a fact-checking nightmare. With stories like this, we have to make sure everything is sourced, every potential accusation is backed up with police reports and eyewitness testimonies. Especially when it comes to churches in the Deep South.

I glance at the clock and sigh. Then I pick up my phone and text Leslie, heart sinking as I send the message.

Lauren: Late story with fact-checking errors. I'm stuck at work. I'll text you when I'm done?

The three dots appear and disappear multiple times and my guilt starts to eat at me.

Leslie: Of course. Miss you.

I want to hurl my phone across my office.

Instead, I pull up my text thread with Max and tell him the same thing. He replies with just one word: "Ok."

Unease prickles up my spine, but I shove it away to the back of my brain and return to my computer screen.

By the time I finally leave work it's 9 p.m. There's no salvaging this night with Leslie. But Max? Maybe.

I text Leslie and let her know, making promises to schedule something next week.

Then I text Max and ask him to come over. He replies quickly with another "Ok."

And as I close my phone and start my car, I can't help but feel like all the joy my universe has brought me over the past few weeks might not be mine to keep.

I see Max's headlights through my house's front window and jump up to meet him at the door. It's nearly 10 p.m. and anxious energy pulses beneath my skin. I changed into leggings and a tank top, fed Lola, cleaned up my kitchen—did everything I could to keep myself occupied. I can't help feeling like something is off.

By the time Max knocks on my door, I'm waiting. I open it and jump into his arms for a hug. He pulls me in close and the returned affection grounds me.

"I missed you," I whisper.

"Me too," he says.

I walk back into my house and he follows behind me, Mags at his heels. He wouldn't have brought her if he didn't plan to stay long, right?

I sit on the couch and he sits next to me, but doesn't look at me. That internal alarm bell starts ringing louder.

"Max, I'm sorry about canceling the thing at Leslie's house tonight—"

"No worries. I know how your work goes sometimes," he says, looking down at his shoes.

"Okay. Max. You're acting weird. Is something wrong?"

He finally turns to look at me then. "We need to talk."

Those four words are a gut punch. I feel like I'm going to be sick.

"Are you dumping me?" I need to know. Rip the Band-aid off.

"What? No!" he says, reaching for me. "Sorry. That was the wrong way to start this. I'm just. I don't know, shaken up. I talked to my dad."

Oh. *Ohhhhhh*. My stomach slows its flips, just a little. I reach for him, sliding a hand along his shoulder and squeezing. "Is this what we need to talk about?"

He nods. "Yeah. It wasn't good, Lauren."

And there goes my stomach again. "Is he going to try and sink the paper still?" My voice comes out shaky.

"I won't let him," Max says. His jaw clenches. "I have a plan, but I need to talk to you first. Lauren, when I spoke to my dad, he told me he had done some investigating on you. Mentioned two people, Frederick McAlister and Kyle Govern. Told me to ask you about them. Said that you took advantage of them. Went for their money. Told me I was just next on your list."

He can't look at me when he says those last words.

"And you believed him?" I say incredulously.

"No. I don't know. He got into my head, Lauren. I know he's the bad one here. Trust me. But I guess I just need to hear you say it. Say that he's insane for throwing these guys in my face." Max's cheeks are flushed, his eyes bright with fear.

"Max," I say, hurt churning in my gut. "Yes, I dated Freddy and Kyle." He winces, but I press on. "And yes, both are men from wealthy families. But, if you'll take a moment to remember what I told you on our hiking trip, both men wanted me to be their pretty little kept wife. They demeaned me and my career. And when I turned them down, they were humiliated. No one tells them no. God knows what they said about me. I walked away and didn't take any of their fucking money. And frankly I'm pissed that you would believe I did."

"Lauren, I didn't think you did. I just. My dad gets into my head. He always has. He knows what to say to make me question everything I think I know."

My heart twists with sympathy, but it's not enough to overcome the anger building from my hurt. "So what? You just take everything you've come to know about me over the past several weeks and throw them out the window? My character means nothing to you?"

It's my deepest insecurity. Feeling like I'm not enough. Being made to feel small. An accessory to men.

I stand and face away from Max, fighting back tears I don't want him to see.

"Lauren, I'm sorry. I didn't mean it like that," he says, pleading. "I've just been burned by women before. Women who were only after me for my family's money. And my dad knows that. He fed off of it. But that's not an excuse. I should have handled this better."

He slides a hand over my shoulder and I tug away, spinning to face him.

"He's trying to push us apart. He told me that to my face. And yet, you still believed him?" A tear escapes and trails down my cheek. I swat it away.

"No. I don't believe him. I'm just, God. I fucked this up," he sighs, running a hand through his unbound hair. "He told me to ask you. And I knew if he was pushing me to get your side of the story, he had some ulterior motive. Janessa told me you would never do anything like that. We're both on your side in this."

"You told Janessa about this? Before me?" I practically choke on the words.

"She was with me. It's a long story. Lauren. I want to be with you. I don't want my dad to destroy your life like he has mine. I'm trying to fix this so we can be together."

"But first you have to make sure I'm not after your money, right?"

He flinches, the verbal slap finding its mark. I feel simultaneously guilty and validated.

"I deserved that," he says.

"I think maybe you should go," I say. I don't want Max to see how much he hurt me. I need time to think this through. Figure out what's real.

"Birdie," he pleads. "Let's talk about this. I need to tell you about—"

"Just stop. I need some time to think."

His shoulders drop, but he nods. "Okay, I get it. But once you've had some time. Please hear me out?"

I shrug. He scoops up Mags and walks out, glancing over his shoulder one more time before closing the door.

As soon as he's gone I scream for as long as I can. It's always going to be like this, isn't it? Another man trying to ruin my career, not believing that, even at forty goddamn years old, I don't need them for anything but support and affection.

I kick a throw pillow and Lola skitters out of the room. I fumble for my phone and crank up my rage playlist. And then I start cleaning. Which probably isn't all that smart since I'm already exhausted, have to work tomorrow, and then go to the float loading party. But I need an outlet.

And as I scrub my grout lines with an old toothbrush, I sit with my anger. My past pain. How previous boyfriends treated me. And by the time I get to the baseboards, I'm onto Max's relationship to his dad. Two hours later, I'm physically and mentally exhausted, and I'm still not sure that I've made any emotional progress.

I get into the hot shower and let it burn as I wash this awful day down the drain.

Tomorrow is the float loading party. I'll see Max and it will be fine. For the best really. Saturday is the parade and then it's over. I'll walk away from him and won't have to worry about my job or the newspaper's future. And Max won't have to worry about me coming for his family's money.

By the time I crawl into bed, I've worn myself out enough that Lola approaches me, hopping into bed and curling into a ball. I reach out and stroke her head, loving the little lines of fur between her ears. I'm afraid I won't be able to fall asleep, but the adrenaline crash is real and makes the decision for me.

I spend the whole night enmeshed in nightmares where I'm running from the Monopoly Man and putting myself into jail.

Chapter 41

MAX

February 21

I have an early shift at work today, trading with another DJ to have tonight off for the float loading party.

Which is going to be a struggle because I slept for a grand total of about three hours while I tossed and turned all night. In hindsight, maybe going over to Lauren's last night wasn't the best plan. In my mind, she'd laugh off my dad's accusations, and then we'd kiss and I'd stay over.

But we were both exhausted. I was reeling and not thinking clearly. I panicked and needed to know about those men. And fuck. Of course they hurt her. And I was a damn idiot for throwing them in her face.

Max: I fucked it up.

Janessa: Whyyyyyy. How??? What did you say? Do I need to come slap some sense into you?

Max: I was hoping for some support actually.

Janessa: Perfect, I'll call Lauren right now.

Max: For me, you menace.

Janessa: Sigh. Tell me.

Max: Those two men Dad mentioned were Lauren's ex boyfriends who treated her terribly and dragged her name through the mud when she told them she didn't want to be their housewife. And I kind of came off like maybe I believed Dad.

Janessa: ...

Max: I know.

Janessa: What are you going to do about it?

Max: I'll see her tonight at the float loading party. Grovel?

Janessa: Start now, dipshit.

Max: She won't answer my texts or take my calls. And I'm about to head into work.

Janessa: You've got an hour. What does she like? Get it and drop it off at her office. Write a note. It's not rocket science.

Max: Damn, that is a good idea.

Janessa: Go. Hurry.

Janessa: And keep me posted.

Max: And what about the thing with Dad?

Janessa: I'll call you after your shift is over. I've got some ideas.

Max: Thank you, Jan.

Janessa: I'm doing it for her, not for you. *tongue sticking out emoji*

I change quickly, pulling on a Smashing Pumpkins t-shirt and taking Mags out to do her business. Then I get in my truck and make a plan.

Thirty minutes later I arrive at the newspaper office. I hit the buzzer and someone asks me my name and purpose. When I tell them who I am and that I'm here to see Lauren, there's a pause.

"Um, I'm not sure she wants to see you," the voice says.

"I brought things to grovel with," I insist. "Please."

A moment passes. "Fine, but don't you dare tell her I let you in."

"Ten-four," I respond.

The buzzer sounds and I step inside. This place is totally different in the daytime. People crawl all over the small office like ants. I turn toward where Lauren's office is, shuffling everything in my arms.

A young woman seems to apparate in front of me. "Hi, name please?"

"Max."

She jots it down with a sharpie on a name tag that says "Visitor" and hands it to me, but I don't have any available hands.

"Okay if I put it on your shirt?"

I nod and she obliges.

"Follow me."

As I pass through the maze of cubicles, everyone pauses to stare, their eyes following me all the way to Lauren's office. I didn't realize how much attention would be on me when I made my plan, and I suddenly wonder if this was a terrible idea. Will she hate me even more for drawing attention to us?

But before I have the option to bail, I'm standing in her office doorway. Lauren is at her desk, a young man with red hair sitting next to her—Rhett. They are busy discussing a baseball tournament. I clear my throat and both heads snap up.

"Lauren, you have a visitor," my guide says, then darts away.

"I'll just come back later," Rhett says, with a quick smile at me. And then he's up and out the door.

"What are you doing here?" Lauren demands frostily.

I had hoped for a warmer welcome, but I came here to grovel, and grovel I shall. "I brought these for you."

First, I hand over the bouquet of colorful gerbera daisies and then the box in my hands. She glowers at me suspiciously as she sets down the flowers. Then she takes the box from me and opens it. I study her expression. At first, nothing. And then, a quirk of the lips which she tries to stifle.

"Max Beaumont. Do you really think you can show up here with flowers and a king cake and I'll welcome you back with open arms?"

"No, that's just the appetizer." I reach into a bag I have hanging on my arm and pull out a romance novel. The one I saw in the back seat of her car that day. I flip through the pages until I find the one I'm looking for, and then clear my throat.

"Max. You are not—"

I hold up a finger, then start reading. I make sure to use the sexiest, most romance book narrator voice I can muster. I allow it to rasp and growl. "She stalks into the room, her cleavage spilling out of the tight red dress that hugs her in all the right places. I want to run to her, pull her hips into mine, and bury my face in those perky, delicious tits."

"Max . . ." Lauren hisses, glancing behind me. "This is not work appropriate."

I close her office door. But all it does is mute my voice to everyone outside this room, because her office walls and door are made up almost entirely of windows. Good enough for me. I continue.

"But I knew I pissed her off earlier when I didn't claim her as mine in front of my friends. And I have no right to demand she forgive me. Even if I know that she definitely wants me to bend her over my kitchen counter and fuck her into oblivion."

I glance up to see Lauren's eyes wide and her cheeks flushed. Her breathing has picked up too. She must remember this scene. Perfect. But she doesn't stop me, so I keep going. I'm going to be so late for work. Worth it.

"Chloe strides closer to me, hips swaying. I follow their saunter from side to side. I want to pull her beneath me, lick every inch of her curves until she's begging me to rip her clothes off and fuck her. But when she reaches me, she lightly touches one of my shoulders, then shoves me down, hard. I fall to my knees before her."

I pause and look at Lauren. "This is the part where you can act it out, if you want to." I smirk, beckoning her with a come hither motion.

She looks past me out the windows of her office, and then walks over to where I stand. She hesitates, searching my face for something.

And then, her hand rises and lands on my shoulder. She pushes and I fall to my knees.

I pick the book back up. "I look up into her face and beg for her forgiveness. I put all of my soul, my energy, my desire into my voice and make the best goddamn apology of my life. 'Chloe, my queen, my goddess, my everything. I'm sorry. You deserve so much better than how I've treated you. You deserve to be worshipped every single second of every single day. And I failed you today. I was a coward, an idiot. I don't deserve your forgiveness. But if you give me a chance, I'll spend everyday worshipping you, and proving to every person we encounter that you are mine.'" I growl the last word for emphasis and then look up to where said goddess stands above me.

Her gaze is so heated that I'm not sure if she's going to punch me or kiss me. I wait.

And then, when she slides her heeled shoe over my knee, I grin. She's replaying the scene from the book. And so, like the good boy I am, I reach for her foot, pull it up to my lips, and kiss it.

When I peer up at her from beneath my lashes, I see her grinning wickedly.

"Well, you do learn from the best," she whispers. She pulls her foot from me and offers a hand up. I accept. She steps in close to me and whispers, "I'm still irritated with you, you know. But maybe we can work through those emotions at my house tonight."

"I accept, my queen, my goddess, my everything."

She gives me a light slap on the shoulder and chuckles. "I can't believe you just did that."

"Believe it, birdie. I'll do anything for you."

I glance past her shoulder and see the crowd gathered there.

"Looks like I gave something for your coworkers to gossip about for at least the next week too."

"They already call me boss. This just adds to my lore," she grins.

And then she leans in and gives me a chaste kiss on the cheek. I pull back and smile, then turn her around. The entire office is watching and begins to clap.

She ducks her head and then, to everyone's surprise, takes a small bow.

"See you tonight, birdie."

Interlude

THE RUSTON DAILY LEADER

February 21

Floating Into Town

By Rhett Hebert

Have you ever wondered where Mardi Gras floats come from? The colorful, elaborate celebrations on wheels are often crafted in production studios across the country, but predominantly in New Orleans.

The majority of the Ruston's parade floats were made by Floating Through Life Studios. With decades of experience under their belts, owners Clifton and Jacqui Rex assemble hundreds of professional floats each year.

"We are honored to be chosen as the makers of Ruston's debut Mardi Gras floats," said Clifton. "We leaned into the traditional color palette of purple, green, and gold, while utilizing feathers as inspiration for the king, queen, and captain floats. I think the people will be real excited to see what we've made."

Parade floats are usually about thirty feet long and seventeen feet tall. They're built on a truck chassis and towed by either a tractor or truck. The Rexes say that up to fifty riders can fit in a standard float.

As with most Mardi Gras floats, the bases are built from plywood. While Floating Through Life Studios also designed the majority of the Ruston parade's twenty floats, a few were completed in town by the Boys and Girls Club members. Be on the lookout for the Birds of Paradise float to see how members of our own community helped contribute to our first parade.

And, of course, there will be other entertainment too.

"The local high schools are sending their marching bands to participate in the parade," said Gladys Beaumont, chair of the Krewe of Persici's steering committee. "And we even got the world-famous Grambling Marching Band to be part of it too!"

You'll have your chance to get a sneak peek at the Float Loading Party beginning at 6 p.m. on Friday, February 21. The parade rolls at 5 p.m. on Saturday, February 22.

Chapter 42

LAUREN

I'm still blushing as I wrap up work for the day. I couldn't concentrate at all after Max's little stunt. And by the way my coworkers kept smirking at me, I doubt they were working at a hundred percent today either.

I wave to Rhett as I pass by his cube, and see that he's packing up too. Right, he's a krewe captain. We have a busy night ahead of us. I pause so we can walk out together. He grabs his lunch box and nods at me.

"Excited about tonight?" he asks.

I shrug. "I don't know what to expect, but I bet it will be fun. I'm just tired."

"Same," he sighs. "But it felt good to finish up that baseball story today. It helps knowing what's going on the front page earlier in the day so we can relax tonight."

He's right. I've been letting him help more, take the lead on bigger stories, make some editing decisions. Feeling him out on all of it. And he's sailing through all of it and seems happy.

"Has the additional work been too much?" I ask.

"It's been thrilling, to be honest. I love the reporter work, but it's nice to do something new. Something that's more of a challenge. Thank you for trusting me to help you."

His words hit me hard. Trusting him to help me. Is that what my struggle is? I try to control and manage everything on my own, too scared to ask for help? Not trusting the most dedicated team I've ever encountered? I gnaw on my bottom lip.

We reach my car. "Rhett? Would you be interested in doing more editor type duties in the long term?"

He grins. "I'd like that very much, boss."

I nod. "Well then. See you tonight?"

He smiles back. "See you tonight."

When I get home, I'm shocked to find Leslie waiting on me in the driveway. I hop out of my car and run to give my little sister a hug.

"Where are the minions?" I ask, referring to her crew of children.

"I took the night off. They are home with Adam. And I am going with you to the float loading party. Figured my big sister could use some moral support after what you told me happened last time you encountered a box of beads." She smirks and I elbow her in the ribs.

"Hey now. That was just bad luck," I insist.

"I think it was good luck. You've been happier, you know. Since you got involved with this Mardi Gras thing. Since you met Max."

I sigh, knowing she's right. "Well, we've still got a couple more big nights of this Mardi Gras thing. Let me go change and we can drive over."

I head into my room and grab my purple Krewe of Persici t-shirt that I got at the Boys and Girls Club fundraiser. God, that feels like years ago now. I still think about how Max and I walked arm in arm together around the field. About those first nudges of attraction.

I'm still irritated with him, but a little time and space have allowed me to step into his shoes a bit more. Things have never been good between him and his dad. And there's a reason he cut all ties with him. He put aside his own boundaries to talk to his dad because of me. No, he shouldn't have doubted me, but maybe I need to sit with Max and listen. More than likely, he needs my support as much as I need his.

Satisfied with my internal pep talk, I change clothes, snag my crown and sash, and head back outside to meet my sister.

"You look fabulous," she declares as we climb into my car and drive to the float loading party.

The warehouse-turned-float-loading-site stands in the field next to the fall festival site, doors propped wide. The light from inside glows, a beacon in an otherwise desolate landscape. Inside is a kaleidoscope of purple, green, and gold. Every float is lined up along the sides of the cavernous room, creating a walkway of bedazzled birds and larger-than-life characters mounted onto floats.

Jazz plays over the speakers, and beignets and popcorn create a salty-sweet aroma that has my stomach rumbling. And then there are the people. So many people of every age mingle in the space, oohing and ahhing over the elaborate floats.

"Well damn, maybe I should have brought the kids," Leslie says.

"Nope. Mama needs a drink tonight," I say, nodding to the bar.

"Don't forget your crown now, queenie. And I'm not talking about the one you mix with Coke," Leslie winks.

I slide the thing on my head and we make our way through the room. But if I thought getting to the bar was going to be easy, I'm sadly mistaken. Someone stops me every few feet to say hello, take a photo with me, and tell me how excited they are about the parade. Eventually, I give up and send Leslie to the bar on my behalf with a twenty dollar bill in hand.

It's weird to have so many people wanting my attention—and so many of them are little girls. I never thought about being a role model while being Mardi Gras queen, but over and over again I find myself telling would-be princesses and queens about my work as a reporter and editor.

When someone taps my shoulder, I'm so relieved for my drink that I spin and start saying thank you before I realize that the tapper isn't Leslie.

"My queen," Max says, extending his arm.

I hesitate. Am I ready for this? I think back to my little pep talk to myself before I left. I sigh out a breathy "yes" and slide my arm through his. Max seems relieved, not proud, not victorious. And that, right there, is why he's different from the other men I've dated. He wants me for me. Not to be some prop for his ideal life.

I squeeze his arm, just a little, to let him know I'm in this with him. His skin on mine feels right, comforting. I glance up to admire the way his crown catches the purple, green, and gold lights.

Together we make our way through the crowd, stopping to admire each float since there won't be time to do so tomorrow at the parade. Gladys asked us to be at the royalty floats at seven tonight, ready to load them with all the throws. I glance at my watch. 6:50 p.m.

"Shall we?" I ask Max.

"After you, my lady."

"There you are!" a voice calls. Leslie's face appears in the crowd, flushed and holding my drink high. "Sorry, couldn't find you earlier, so I drank both drinks of our first round. Here," she says, handing me a pink drink that she just barely manages to avoid sloshing onto me. "A hurricane. I know it's a little touristy, but I thought there was no better night for it. Plus, they're delicious."

I take a sip. She's right, it's delicious. But whew, is it strong. I can't believe she's already on her third. Good thing I'm driving tonight.

"Oh my gosh!" Leslie says a little too loudly as she stares past me. "Lar Lar! It's your float!"

I spin and see the monstrosity in all her glittery glory. A giant peacock is mounted on the front of the float, painted gold with accents of purple and green in its feathers. Glitter covers every inch, and ornate feathers are perched on her head. Or maybe I should say he, but who really cares at this point?

I reach out and brush my hand along its surface, marveling at the level of detail put into it. And I get to be her first queen. I smile, knowing I'll always carry this experience with me.

"Oh good, you're here," Gladys says. "We're about to make the announcement that loading will start. These are your special beads to give out to people of your choosing tonight." She hands me a tote bag. "Max, here's yours. Each bag has about twenty special pieces in it. Both of you go ahead and climb into each of your floats. You'll be up top in your crowns where everyone can see you, taking the beads and placing them on hangers. Go on now, and good luck!" she says, hurrying off to the next person.

"I'll see you later," Max says, pressing a kiss to my cheek. And then he darts over to the float next to mine. The one with a giant pelican with spread wings on the front. He climbs up into it and then waves down to us.

"Well, hell yeah he likes you!" Leslie's too-loud voice cuts in again, and I wonder if I can sneak that hurricane out of her hand and deposit it onto a table somewhere.

"Hush you," I say, then grab her free hand and pull her up into the queen's float with me.

The whole thing is made mostly of plywood, but it's easy enough to navigate. There are labeled boxes sitting inside already. I note one that reads "Margie's Jellies and Jams Cups" and another says "Debbie's Delightful Brownies Cups." Sponsors, got it. The marketing strategy is brilliant, honestly. Everyone at the parade tomorrow will catch and go home with a tall stack of plastic cups with business names on them that will live on their shelves for the next decade.

A microphone squeals to life, causing everyone to mumble and look for its source. Gladys's voice echoes off the metal walls. "Thank y'all for coming out tonight and supporting our first Mardi Gras parade. I'm so proud of how much work this community has put into launching our krewe and all the fundraisers and events leading up to this weekend."

Everyone claps and Gladys takes a minute to let them celebrate. "Yes, yes, thank you. It's hard to believe that we're here on the eve of the parade already. And if this year is any indication, we will be doing this again for many years to come." More applause.

"But now it's time to get started on what we're all here for tonight: loading up our floats so they are ready to go for tomorrow's parade. Each member of parade royalty and captains are already stationed at their floats. Spread out and start passing up the beads. The people up top will fill the hooks and store the cups and doubloons, as well as any other special throws they have in store. And don't forget, there are special beads that will be handed out tonight. Keep your eyes peeled. Now, off you go! Go find a float and let's get them loaded up!"

Thunderous applause followed by jazz music echoes through the speakers. It's a bit overstimulating, so I take a swig of my hurricane and wipe the back of my mouth with my forearm. I glance over at Max and he's got a wicked grin on his face.

He cups his hands over his mouth and shouts over the noise, "First to fill their wall of bead hooks wins."

He points to the plywood wall behind him filled with metal hooks. I glance at my own bead wall, noting that it's about the same size. I'm reminded of our first bead toting competition and grin. We've come full circle on our Mardi Gras meet-cute, it seems.

I'm knocked out of my memories when Leslie shouts, "Lauren, there are people down there trying to hand beads to me."

Right. I take one more look at Max. He counts down from three with his fingers. When he drops the last one, my adrenaline surges. I tear open the first bag and notice that the beads are fastened with paper rings that contain twenty-five strands each. I loop them all on a hook, then keep going. I have no idea how much time passes as I grab and hang beads, over and over. I do know that each float has been assigned the same number of throws, so when we're out of beads one of us wins.

My team of helpers is mostly teen girls, giggling as they pass beads up to me. Leslie may as well be one of the teen girls for how much she's laughing too. I'm glad to see my sister having so much fun. Grateful we can do this together.

I'm closing in on the last four hooks and glance over to see that Max is looking right back at me. He winks, then keeps loading. We're neck and neck. And part of me wishes I could tackle him and steal the beads from his hands. Good thing we're on separate floats this time.

I spot Janessa helping Max load his float and flash a mock outrage face at her. She just winks and keeps going.

"Last box!" one of the girls calls from down below, the same time Janessa says the same on Max's float. My heart thrums like a bass drum with the thrill of the race. I refuse to look at Max as I grab the last two clusters of beads.

I hear Max shout in triumph right before I load them onto my hooks. My heart sinks when I glance over to see him gloating. I place the last two sets of beads on their hooks, then my fist finds my hip and I glare at him.

"You'll pay for that!" I shout, suppressing a laugh.

"Not so fast," Janessa says. "Looks like you missed one, Max." She grabs a cluster of beads off the floor of the float and hands it over.

Max's face falls and I shout, "Victory!" like I just won gold at an Olympic relay race.

I dance unabashedly all over the float and Leslie joins in, singsonging, "We did it! We won! Winner winner, chicken dinner!" and all kinds of other crazy nonsense.

When I look at Max again, he's laughing and pointing a finger at me like he's going to get me later. And I do believe that I'll be okay with that.

We spend the next hour organizing all the other throws. We stack open boxes of cups and doubloons, and I smile when I discover my very own little box of Moon Pies to toss as well. Tomorrow is going to be fun.

When we're done, I hand each of the teen girls one of the special queen's beads, the medallions on the ends of them glinting with that ridiculous peacock. I learn that several of my helpers tonight volunteered to ride on my float tomorrow, and I'm already excited to get to spend time with them and show them that you really can have both: a wonderful career and a life. I'm learning this far too late in my own life.

I glance over at Max and watch his biceps flex as he bends and lifts boxes and moves them out of the float. My cheeks heat at the memory of his arms flexing when he kissed my foot in front of my whole damn staff.

"Max and Lauren sitting in a tree, K-I-S-S-I-N-G!" Leslie sings. And yep, she's definitely drunk. I pull her into me and hug her tight. She squeezes me back. "I love you, Lar Lar."

"I love you too, Leslie. Now, let's get some food in you."

"I want another drink," she mumbles, eyes closed where she lays her head on my chest.

"Probably not a good idea tonight, sis," I say and kiss the top of her head.

"Leslie! Lauren!" a familiar voice calls from ground level.

I look over my sister's shoulder to see Janessa waving up at us.

"Oh good. I could use a friend right now," I say, and realize I mean it. I now have a friend who I can ask for help.

"Sure thing," Janessa calls.

"Can you climb up here?" I ask, not wanting to embarrass my sister.

"Yep," and she practically hops up the float ladder. Oh, to be young and agile again. "What can I help you with?"

I nod to where Leslie is now practically snoring on my chest. "Help me get her down?" I whisper. "I'll call her a ride share. I'd take her myself, but I think Gladys would murder me for leaving early."

"I'll take her home," Janessa shrugs.

"You don't have to do that," I insist. "You're here for the party."

"I'm here to support you and Max. And this," she says waving her hand at my sister, "supports you. And probably Max." She winks.

"Plus, you'd do the same for me."

My heart warms as the truth of that statement hits me. "Thank you," I whisper. "So how are we going to do this?"

"Max!" Janessa calls to her cousin, who is climbing down the ladder on the side of the king's float. "Can you come over here?"

He jogs over immediately and looks up at us on the float. "Everything okay?"

"Yep," Janessa says. She leans down and whispers something to him. Then she returns to me. "I'm gonna get people away from your float for a minute. Tell them we have some special throws. Max is going to help you get Leslie down. I'll meet you both outside by my car."

I nod. "And your car is where?"

"Max and I rode together. He'll know where it is," Janessa says.

I should probably be more concerned with how Max will get home, but that's the least of my worries at the moment.

Janessa makes quick work of drawing the crowd near the entrance of my float away. Then Max stands at the bottom of the ladder.

"Leslie, I need you to wake up," I say to her, shaking her a bit. She mumbles something and rolls her head across my chest. It really is good that I'm not wearing sequins and glitter tonight. "Come on, girl. Wake up." I attempt to hoist her off my chest and she finally blinks a few times, stares at me, and grins.

"To the ladder we go. Max is going to help you down."

I shuffle her over, making sure she doesn't topple to the floor in the process. Max does an excellent job of standing behind her on the ladder as they move down together, making it look like everything is perfectly normal. But when they both get to the floor, Leslie stumbles. He scoops her up and her head falls to his shoulder. We head to one of the "Staff Only" doors and dip behind the scenes.

"This way," Max calls. I follow him through an exit door and out into the dark parking lot.

We find Janessa's car, and Max settles Leslie in the back seat. I give Janessa Leslie's address and text her husband to let him know to help Leslie when she gets home.

I give Janessa a hug and thank her profusely. "No worries," she insists.

Max and I wave Janessa off until her headlights fade onto the highway.

I turn to Max. "Thank you for that. Leslie doesn't get out much and can't handle her rum anymore," I say with a little laugh.

"It happens to the best of us," he says. "Glad to help."

"I guess we better get back to our royal duties?"

He checks his watch. "Only another hour or so. Then it looks like I might need a ride home."

"Considering your ride just took care of my sister, I think that means I'm your default driver."

"Just my default driver?" he asks, reaching to tuck a stray strand of hair behind my ear. "Or maybe," his lips hover by my ear, making me shiver "you can be my spend the night company too?"

Heat floods my body despite the cold evening. "Well, King Max, I guess we better finish up our royal duties and see what happens."

He grins and extends his arm to me. I take it, and together we walk back into the party.

Chapter 43

MAX

The float loading party draws to a close with an air of celebratory anticipation. The lights dim, and all the float lights turn on, like some sort of Carnivale candlelight ceremony. Gladys reminds everyone riding tomorrow to be ready to get into costume and on the parade route by 3 p.m.

I spot my ride across the room talking to Rhett and Amelia. Lauren looks relaxed, happy. And damn, I'm proud that she might just be mine to keep if all the stars finally align. My stomach twinges knowing that means I'll need to commit to handling my dad once and for all. But I shake it off as I strut over to Lauren, straightening my crown as I go.

When I reach her, I slide my arm around her shoulders and she leans into me. A good sign. I say good night to Rhett and Amelia, then Lauren and I make our way to the staff room to get her purse.

"Have fun tonight?" I ask.

"I really did, actually," she says with a grin. "But I could be up for more fun. Still up for a slumber party?"

"Oh definitely. I thought we might paint fingernails and braid each other's hair." Desire burns through my exhaustion, waking me back up, followed closely by relief that she's forgiving me for being an idiot last night.

She laughs. "You do have the perfect hair for braiding."

"Like a viking," I agree.

She rolls her eyes playfully. "Come on then, Mr. Viking, let's get you home. We have a long day tomorrow."

As we walk out of the staff room, I spy a box of beads with "Krewe King" written on it. I reach in and snag a bag.

"Do I want to know what those are for?" Lauren asks.

I just shrug, place my arm back around her shoulders, and guide her to the parking lot.

I'm glad I cleaned my apartment. Not that I expected company, but I've been worried about Lauren's response to me losing my cool last night and, well, cleaning seemed to be a good way to deal with it.

Mags greets us at my apartment door, delighted to see Lauren with me. I bend down to pet her, then get Lauren a glass of water while I take Mags outside to do her business. Mags and I aren't out long, it's cold and Mags isn't keen on staying out longer than she has to.

When we get back into my apartment, Lauren is sitting on the floor next to my record player table and digging through my vinyl collection. "Great taste in music," she says, pulling out a Norah Jones album. I smile remembering the last time we listened to Norah Jones as we waltzed in an empty Community Center Hall.

I walk over to her and take the album, pulling it from its sleeve and placing it on the record player. I adjust the needle and "Turn Me On" croons through the speakers. I offer her a hand and pull her to stand. I tug her in close and start to sway.

"No need to waltz tonight," I say softly.

She lays her head on my shoulder and we move through my

small living area, feeling the music and our hands on one another.

"I'm sorry for last night," I say, eager to make a formal apology. "I let my dad get into my head and twist my thoughts around until I didn't know which way was up. It's not an excuse, but it didn't help that I was also tired and emotional."

"I forgive you," she says, her head on my chest.

"It can't be that easy," I insist.

"It can though," she insists, lifting her head to look at me. "Am I still hurt? A little," she shrugs. "But I spent a long time last night thinking about all of it. About how your dad has treated you, things you've experienced before. Hell, how I've been treated. It was the perfect storm. Your dad knew both of our insecurities and plucked at that string expertly. And it almost worked."

It did almost work. And fuck him for that. I almost let him rob me of this. Of someone who not only likes me exactly like I am, but is quick to forgive me when I mess up and apologize.

"I'm furious that I almost let him come between us. Let him manipulate me. We both deserve better than that."

"And," she says, hesitating a second. "I also realized that all those other assholes I dated? When I upset them, they made sure I knew I was the problem, the sole person to blame. I was given the cold shoulder, or, even worse, gaslit until I believed what they told me about myself. But dammit, Max. You came and groveled in front of an entire office of people. And you asked for forgiveness. How could I possibly not forgive you?"

I swallow, emotion clogging my throat. "I meant the apology."

"I know."

I dip my forehead to hers. We stay like that, offering each other silent comfort for a few moments. But as the sultry music plays in the low-lit room and our bodies move in closer to each other, guilt and relief give way to something else.

I slide my hand along her back, my fingers finding her spine through her t-shirt. When I get to the hem, I dare to slide my fingers beneath the fabric and trace circles on the small of her back. Lauren hums, so I continue my exploration. She nuzzles into my neck and plants a kiss on my pulse point. My hands trail down to her ass and give it a squeeze. She chuckles and moves her hands down to do the same to me.

"Always trying to beat me at my own game," I say, and kiss her forehead.

She tilts her head up. "Not just trying. I usually win."

"Oh, is that right?" I say, staring into her playful blue eyes, admiring the way they glint in the lamplight. I'm so damn happy to have her looking at me like that again.

"I beat you tonight, didn't I? When we were loading the beads?" she prods.

"That doesn't count. Janessa helped you win."

"There were no stated rules. I won. You lost. Case closed."

"And you celebrated my humiliation, you spoilsport."

She shrugs, her eyes crinkling.

"That wasn't nice, you know."

"Didn't know I was supposed to play nice," she says, leaning in to nip at my lower lip. I shudder, loving the teasing, the sexiness of having her here in my arms.

"Well two can play at that game," I say. Then I bend down and haul her up over one of my shoulders so her face is hanging over my back, and smack her ass.

She kicks and laughs. "Put me down, you brute!"

"Now, now, birdie. I thought those women in your books like to be manhandled a bit."

"Max Beaumont. Have you been reading more of my books?"

"Mayyyyybe." I carry Lauren to my bedroom while she lightly pounds on my back.

In my room, I gently toss her on the bed. "Oh, such big muscles!" she says with too much enthusiasm.

"The better to hoist you with, my lady."

I crawl onto the bed with her and find her mouth with mine. I don't want to push her if she has lingering feelings of anger, but she responds to my kiss eagerly, her mouth opening as soon as it touches mine, inviting me in. I push her wrists above her head with one hand, and hold most of my body weight off of her with the other.

We kiss, exploring every inch of each other's mouths that we've missed over the past week. I savor the taste of her drink from this evening still lingering on her tongue. And she groans as I slide my mouth down to her jaw, her neck. I let go of her wrists and reach for the hem of her shirt, pulling it over her body and exposing the gold-colored bra underneath.

"This is festive," I say, running a finger under one of the straps.

"I am the Mardi Gras Queen," she teases.

Then she grabs the hem of my shirt, pulls it over my head, and tosses it to the side. I lean down and kiss her again, loving the way our bodies connect skin to skin. Ready for more.

Lauren reaches for my jeans and I catch her hand, stopping her.

"Everything okay?" she asks, breathless.

"Yes, but you're skipping to the good part. I told you I was going to punish you for dancing all over my pride tonight."

I get up and head back into the living room. I return with the bag of Mardi Gras beads I snagged on my way out the door of the party.

"I do believe that in some parts of the state, women are willing to show off quite a lot to get some of these," I say, ripping the bag open with my teeth. I pull out a purple strand and twirl it around my finger. "Let's see what you got, birdie."

She gawks. "You can't be serious."

"Oh, I'm dead serious," I say wickedly.

"You know I can get as many beads as I want tomorrow."

"Ah, but not these special king beads."

"You gonna make all the ladies show you their boobs for those special beads tomorrow?" Lauren asks, raising an eyebrow.

"There's only one pair of tits I want to see, birdie. And they're currently hiding behind a silky golden bra. So, are you going to please your king and get some beads?" I lift an eyebrow.

She stares at me, debating. And I wonder if this is too weird, too silly for her. Finally she lets out a long-suffering sigh and stands.

And then, she turns it on. She slides a finger under one of those golden bra straps, slowly drawing it down her shoulder. She pauses to look up at me through her lashes. Then bats them, giving me a show. She reaches for the other strap and does the same.

She does a slow twirl and turns her back to me, then reaches for the clasp of her bra and undoes it with a twist of her fingers. When she spins back around, she's still in her jeans and has her arms folded across her breasts.

I swallow, forgetting our game for a moment.

"Let's see those beads, then," she says, voice low and taunting.

I let them untwirl from my hand and hold them up for her examination.

Then she throws her arms up in the air and shouts, "Throw me something, Mister!" the traditional Mardi Gras phrase paradegoers shout to people on floats.

I take her in, making a show of it, studying her nipples and the way her boobs bounce.

"God, how can women do this in public? I'm embarrassed just doing this for you," she laughs, folding her arms back over her breasts.

"Nope," I say, stepping forward. "Nope, show me if you want these beads."

Her arms drop and she looks at me shyly.

"Good girl, now lay back on the bed."

"Hey! Where are my beads?" she says petulantly.

"Oh you'll get them, don't you worry," I say, voice filled with desire.

She sits on the bed and crawls backward over the mattress. I resume the position we were in earlier, pushing her wrists above her head. But this time, I use the beads as makeshift handcuffs. They aren't tight, just a suggestion of what restraints would actually be, but I still check in with Lauren. "Okay?"

"Yes, Mister," she says.

"Good. Keep them there then, let me do the rest." I shuffle down her body and unbutton her jeans, grabbing her panties as I work them off. In a moment she's bare beneath me, except for the purple beads around her wrists. I study the dips and curves of her breasts, waist, and hips, drinking my fill.

"Are you just gonna stare all night, or are you going to do something about it?" she taunts.

"Mouthy tonight, aren't we, birdie?"

"I do wish you'd be more mouthy," she says, then blushes at her own words.

"Your wish is my command, my queen." Then I scoot down and put my mouth to work. The first taste of her is divine. I take my time exploring her, paying attention to when she moans and squirms, learning exactly how she likes my mouth on her.

"Max," she gasps. "I'm going to come—"

I stop immediately and she groans in frustration. "Why did you stop?"

"Punishment. Remember?" She lifts her wrists and I move to push them back down. "Nope, they stay there."

I reach to unzip my pants, pushing them down with my underwear. She stares at my cock.

"Sure you want me to keep my hands up here?"

"Yes," I say. Then I grab a pillow and signal for her to lift her hips. She does and I slide it under her lower back. Then I reach for one of her legs and lift it up in the air until it lays against my chest, exposing her to me. "This feel okay?"

She nods, watching where I tease her entrance. I slide through her, but not inside, teasing, playing.

"You're killing me, Max."

"In the best way," I insist.

She mutters a curse, but keeps her bead-bound hands above her head on the mattress. I draw out the beautiful torture, rubbing myself on her, stirring us both up. She's panting by the time I begin to slide inside her. I move slowly, loving the way Lauren pleads for more. When I bottom out, I pause for a second, enjoying the way she feels around me, the way she squeezes me.

"Just wait until I punish you," she growls at me.

I chuckle deeply, then thrust.

"Yes," she whispers.

I do it again, moving her leg down from where it was propped up on my chest so that I can lean between her hips and over her body. I keep my movements slow, kissing her lips, her neck, her breasts. I savor the control she's giving me tonight, the way she trusts me with her pleasure even when she desperately wants more. I pick up my pace, my pleasure building.

"Max, I'm about to come," she says desperately.

And this time, I don't hold back. "Give it to me," I growl. And as I feel her begin to flutter around me, I come with her, both of us crying out when our pleasure crashes into us.

After a moment, I reach up and pull the beads off her hands, making sure her circulation is good. She finally pulls her wrists down and drapes them around my neck, then kisses me. It's long and passionate. A comforting caress. I roll onto my back, pulling her with me. She settles onto my chest, tucking her head under my chin.

I wrap my arms around her, loving the way she fits against me, drinking up the way her body heat soaks into me.

"You okay, birdie?"

"Perfect."

Interlude

PEACH 103.1

Beau: We are coming to you live from the start of Ruston's first ever Mardi Gras Parade. The Krewe of Persici is getting ready to roll in just a few hours. We'll be on scene throughout the day sharing live updates. With us now we have Margie Murphy. Our local YouTube star is captaining and riding on one of today's floats. Thanks for joining us Margie.

Margie: Delighted.

Beau: Can you give listeners a feel of what's going on inside the float warehouse right now as everyone prepares for the start of the parade?

Margie: Utter fuc—um, I mean *fun* pandemonium, Beau. Everyone is gearing up to hitch their float to a truck or tractor and make sure everything's in the right order.

Beau: And it's going to get even wilder later as marching bands and first responders join the line up.

Margie: That's right. And rumor has it that Santa is on vacation from the North Pole and going to make an appearance on my float tonight.

Beau: Is that right? Well, you heard it here first. Come out tonight to catch some beads and be on your best behavior so you don't end up on Santa's naughty list. Speaking of, tonight the beginning of the parade zone is alcohol free and kid-friendly. We know a lot of you are already out there on the parade route partying, and that's just fine, but follow the rules and keep it safe.

Margie: And those beads can cause a mean sting when they're tossed at high velocity. We're gonna do our best to toss 'em up gentle like, but be careful.

Beau: And have fun! And remember—

Beau and Margie: Tell your mom you love her!

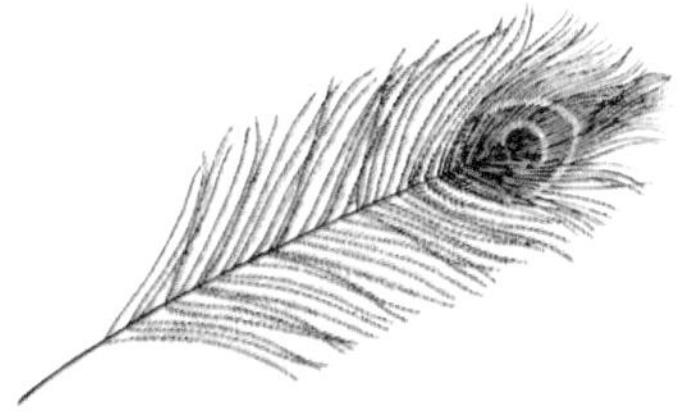

Chapter 44

LAUREN

February 22, Parade Day

I imagine that today feels a lot like a wedding day. Dress fittings, makeup, logistics, snacks. All of it flies by in a blink. I'm glad Max and I had an hour or so this morning to have coffee and breathe at his apartment before I ran home to take care of Lola, because now there's no time for anything but getting parade-ready.

I kept the radio on as I prepared, listening to Max interview participants in today's parade. He just turned it over to another DJ so he can get ready. I hope I get to see him before this thing rolls. My stomach feels like a swamp of gators is chomping around inside of it. I'm running on adrenaline and determination.

At 2 p.m., floats start hitching up to waiting trucks to move onto the highway and then downtown, where they'll queue up for the parade. As the parade's queen, my float won't roll until nearly the very end, so I'm stuck waiting and watching. I refuse to put on my peacock dress with its gigantic back piece until it's time to ride.

I sit down on the floor of the queen's float and scroll through my email on my phone, making sure there are no late breaking stories or people calling off work. Fortunately, the parade is the headliner today, and I'm on site if anything happens. A real cute picture I'd be in my giant sparkles and feathers interviewing people. I shake the thought away.

A ladder thumps against the side of the float and the whole thing jostles as someone climbs up. I'm prepared to see Gladys, but relieved when Max's face emerges.

"Finally off duty?" I ask, scooting over so he can sit beside me. Down on the float's floor like this, the sides give us a bit of privacy and I relish in this quiet before the storm.

"Yep. Good thing I got my work hours in this morning too. I'm going to need at least two days to recover from all of this," he says, gesturing to the warehouse around us.

"Same," I agree.

He slides his arm around my shoulders and I rest my head on his.

"When this is all over, you should come get in my bed and not leave for at least two days," he says, kissing the top of my head.

"Sounds delightful. But I'm not sure either of us would get much rest if I do that."

"Guess that means we better hydrate and grab some energy drinks then," he says, causing me to chuckle.

And then I remember. Our deadline with his dad is over after today. My stomach sinks.

"Max. Your dad though? Is he really going to try to ruin the newspaper? Are we going to need to take a step back from each other while we figure out how to handle him?"

I feel him tense. "You don't need to worry about that, Lauren. Janessa and I are going to handle it."

"Handle it how?" I ask leaning up to look at his expression.

"We're going to beat him at his own game." He sighs when I plant him with a look. "Don't look at me like that. I just wish I didn't have to do this, you know? I wish that I could have normal parents who love me and want what makes me happy instead of what makes them happy."

I move my free hand to one of his and hold it. "It's not fair. None of that is. And I know that this thing between us is still pretty new, but you have a family with Leslie and me. Her husband and kids too. With Janessa and Gladys. Just know that whatever happens, we've got your back, okay?"

He nods.

"So, you going to tell me what you're doing about your dad, or should I pull out some cash for bail money just in case?" I nudge him.

He sighs. "Janessa and I found something in his files and—"

"Alright Queen Lauren, your float's up. Climb down from there and come get in the truck cab for the ride over to downtown," Amelia calls up to us with a megaphone.

I look at Max. "Later," he promises, then kisses me quickly on the lips.

We climb down and he walks me to the passenger side of the big, white, all-wheel drive truck that will be pulling my float tonight. I open the door and climb in, nodding to the older man behind the wheel with kind eyes and tie-dyed shirt on. I turn back to Max.

"See you tonight?"

"Of course, birdie. I'll be right behind you. Literally." He nods to his pelican float. "I'll catch up with you after the parade. We'll talk." He gives me one more quick kiss and walks over to where Amelia waits for him at the king's float. She looks past him to give me a wink, then gives Max his instructions.

If I thought wearing that giant back piece at the ball was bad, I had no idea what I was in for on parade night. I'm supposed to wear it for the entire parade—all while standing and waving and throwing things. Already I'm dreaming of the bottle of ibuprofen waiting for me when this is all over. And there is no way I'm wearing heels tonight. Not even my well-conditioned feet can handle the extra weight of my costume in heels. It's hard enough on my tweaked knee.

Still though, when I put the whole thing on, I pause to admire myself in the mirror like a true peacock. I do rather look like a queen, especially when I fix my crown on my head. I leave the dressing room at the convention center and head to my float.

When I step outside the sun is just beginning its descent, casting that golden glow that makes everything feel a bit like a fairy tale. I allow myself to just enjoy this moment, one I'll likely never experience again. I stare down the line of floats, people crawling all over them like ants. Their lights are on, some flashing, reflecting off the golden, sparkled surfaces of the decorations. The cacophony of musical instruments drifts on the light breeze as band members do their warmups. Twirling batons and shimmering costumes glint and shimmer all up and down the street.

The town is holding its breath, waiting for the celebration to start.

I spy my float and walk over to it. I eye the ladder, then wiggle my shoulders, unsure of how I'm going to climb the damn thing with this costume on my back. One of the teen girls who helped me load my float last night appears above me on the float and extends a hand.

"I've got you," a deep voice rumbles behind me. I turn and see Max, handsome as ever in his sparkles and feathers. So he hasn't climbed into his ride for the parade yet. Lucky me.

"A quick photo!" Katie shouts, appearing in front of us.

It's hard to get close with our giant back pieces on, but Max and I turn toward one another and grin for the camera. The shutter fires and then Katie leans in to wish us both good luck.

"Up you go," Max says. "And this time, I'm not racing you. Easy does it."

I reach for my teen friend's hand who is waiting in the float above me, and place one Hoka-shoed foot on the ladder. I feel Max, a hand on my back to steady me. Slowly, steadily, I make my way up, and when I arrive safely at the top, I feel as victorious as when the two of us survived our black bear scare.

I turn to Max and wave. "Laissez les bons temps rouler!" I call the traditional Mardi Gras saying.

He responds in English, "Let the good times roll!"

The police sirens scream to life, letting everyone know that the parade is about to roll through town. My float crew is adorable in their peacock feathers and masks as they move to take their spots along the sides of the float. They're chattering and pointing to people they know, their youth and joy is infectious.

I move to my perch higher up and watch as each of the floats creeps forward. The music blares to life with each speaker system as they go.

Finally, it's my turn. "Killer Queen" blasts from our speakers. I laugh and start waving, reaching for beads to toss to the huge crowd of onlookers.

Riding in the float turns out to be one of the most exciting things I've ever done in my life. A few miles of crawling through downtown Ruston on a gaudy piece of wood may not sound like much, but crowd watching is its own delightful sport.

People of all ages, from all backgrounds, are out tonight. I love watching kids on the shoulders of adults dancing to music. Get a thrill when members of the crowd catch my eye, point at me, and scream, "Throw me something, mister!" I blush, remembering saying those words to Max last night.

And when I spot Leslie, Adam, and the kids, I reach for a whole bundle of beads and cups and toss them their way. They cheer as the girls chase down their throws and add them to their huge manes of growing bead collections around their necks.

Being at the back of the parade means that everyone is already shimmering with their catches by the time I see them. Stacks of cups lean in towers, kazoos sound as children blast them at each other. It's a Carnivale kaleidoscope.

I keep expecting something to happen. Something to suddenly go wrong and ruin this perfect night. But it doesn't.

The weather is always hit or miss in February, but tonight it behaves. It's chilly and comfortable with all my layers of costuming on.

The girls in the float with me make sure my throws stay stocked. And, as we near the end of the parade, I realize I need to unload them all. By this part of the parade, most of the people at the end have been outside tailgating for hours. Many of them are intoxicated, though they seem to revel in it by dancing and singing. It's entertaining.

And just as we're about to cross the threshold where the parade ends for the public, I see them: my newspaper staff. At least fifteen of them, all gathered together and wearing peacock masks. I jump and point to them and they all yell at once, "Throw us something, boss!"

I grab the last of my throws and toss them all to them, giggling as I watch the people I work with scramble along the ground for doubloons.

Yes, tonight is absolutely, positively, perfect.

Chapter 45

MAX

I love that from my float I'm able to catch glimpses of Lauren all night. Her arm extending as she tosses beads, her profile as she turns and smiles at someone on the parade route. She's happy. Living.

Of course most of the time I'm busy hamming it up and dancing to the music blasting through my float's speakers while I toss beads to the delighted crowd. I gotta give it to my grandmother, she really did a phenomenal job with this whole thing. Hell, we all did. I'm proud of us.

I get caught up in all of it—the music, the dancing, the cheering crowd. It's easy to pretend I'm actually a king and everyone loves me. Makes it even more fun.

So when we near the end of the parade and I spot him, it takes a minute for my emotional high to catch up with the realization of what I'm seeing: my parents waiting near the end of the parade. Mom is actually dancing, wearing beads, and appears to be having a good time. Dad catches my eye and nods, an attempt at civility or saving face?

I don't like it either way. Still, as we pass them, I toss Mom one of the special king's float beads, the one with the gaudy pelican on it. But just before it reaches her, my dad extends his hand and snags it out of the air, taking it for himself.

I frown, and then we're past them, our floats rolling into the unloading spot. My mind is still spinning, distracted by the sight of him, when Amelia walks past us with a megaphone, instructing everyone to dismount and take off any heavy parts of our costumes that we can without causing a public nudity incident.

With the help of my fellow float riders, I get my feathered back piece off and rest it on the floor of the float, then follow them down the ladder. I move to the passenger side of my driver's truck and wave to Lauren as she does the same. Joy lights her face, her smile spread wide.

No need to tell her my dad is here tonight and take away her happiness. I'll deal with him tomorrow. And then Lauren and I can finally be happy in peace.

When we arrive back at the warehouse, there's a sense of frenzied celebration. Champagne corks pop and glasses are handed around. I take one and then quietly discard it when no one is looking. Staying sober hasn't been easy over the years, but I'm not going to fail now.

I catch sight of Lauren through the crowd, wisps of her blonde hair straying from the coronet braided around the top of her head. She shimmers with body glitter and escaped sequins, a real life queen. And when she turns her gaze on me, I feel like I could both melt to the floor and scoop her up, toss her in my truck, and drive straight home.

She skips over to me and throws her arms around my neck, kissing me on the lips in front of everyone. She tastes like champagne—and she's the only kind that I would gladly get drunk on. So I pull her back to me and kiss her again, longer and deeper.

"About damn time!" someone calls. I glance over to see Grandma, champagne glass raised in toast to us.

My grin widens as Janessa materializes beside her and applauds us. Soon everyone is joining in and Lauren ducks her head, embarrassed.

"Nothing to be ashamed of, birdie. They're happy for us." And then I give her one more kiss for good measure.

By the time we make it back to our cars, both of us are ready to collapse. The adrenaline high of the parade followed by seeing my dad in the crowd is causing me to crash and burn, leaving me with a pounding headache.

The exhaustion hangover will be tough. Tonight it's water, ibuprofen, and Lauren in my arms.

Tomorrow, I'll deal with my dad. I'm not letting him steal our joy tonight.

By the time I pull into Lauren's driveway and turn my truck off, I feel like I could flop right onto her front yard and sleep there for the night. At least until I see her get out of her car. The sight of her with smudged mascara reaching into the air to stretch is a jolt straight to my heart . . . and other places.

I stroll over and bear hug her, rubbing my beard against her cheek. She laughs and sinks into me. We stand there beneath the stars and take a minute to just exist.

"Want to go inside?" she whispers, her voice muffled where she leans into my t-shirt.

"Yes, I'm sure Lola is ready to see you.'"

"And Mags?"

"Is with Janessa. No Pilates tomorrow morning, don't worry."

"Thank goodness, I could sleep for three days," she says, unlocking the front door and letting us both inside.

The cat in question trots over to us and yowls, scolding us for coming in so late. Lola drops a toy at my feet.

"She wants you to play fetch," Lauren yawns.

"Seriously?"

"Yep, toss it."

I do, then marvel as Lola skips over to the little fuzzy mouse toy, bites it, and brings it back.

"She's well-trained," I say, picking it up again.

"More like she's got me well-trained," Lauren says. "Get anything you want out of the kitchen. I'm going to take a quick shower and wash all this makeup off. You're welcome to get in after me."

She kisses me and then heads to her room. I hear the shower come to life and the bathroom door closes. I move to the couch and sit, tossing the little mouse toy again, making friends with Lola. As I rest, the adrenaline from tonight finally fades, replaced by a dull, throbbing headache. Exhausted, my thoughts take on a life of their own, spiraling into uncomfortable places.

I know Dad showed up at the parade tonight for many reasons, all of them self-serving. That's his way, as evidenced by what Janessa and I found in his desk drawer. He was there to appease my grandmother, get her on his side. He was probably there to intimidate Lauren, but failed in catching her attention. That, at least, was a win. His primary goal though was to remind me of who he is, and what he's capable of. What he'll do to the newspaper if I don't fall in line. He was flaunting my mother in front of me, showing me what I'll miss forever if I don't cave to his demands.

Mom. Thinking about her is a whole trigger that I've failed to ever come to terms with despite therapy. I love my mother. My whole life she was gentle with me, shielded me from my dad when he would drink too much. Doted over Charles and me. She's the reason my radio sign off is what it is. Most nights I hope she listens in and hears it, knows that I still love her.

But when it came to us or our father, she chose him every single time. And I'm not sure if it's intimidation, manipulation, or some combination of both, but all the hope in the world won't make her take my side in this standoff.

I hear the water from Lauren's shower, her voice humming a

familiar song. My shoulders relax just the slightest bit.

I allow my thoughts to go down the path of what it would look like if I gave in to my father's demands. Stiff family dinners. Business dealings that would never sit well with me. More money than God. The potential for scandal at every turn. A wife who would, no doubt, be young and beautiful, and be thrown into some marriage of convenience neither of us truly wants. No more Lauren. Nausea roils through my stomach.

I forcefully shift my thoughts down another path. One where I come home late from a shift at the station and walk into a home that smells of peppermint. I'd be greeted at the door by two gray scruffs, one that barks and another that meows her demands. I'd wander back to the bedroom and find Lauren in bed, waiting up for me, a romance book in her hands, or in her ears. She'd put it down and look up at me with a welcoming grin. I'd walk over to her and lean down for a kiss. She'd throw her arms around me and pull me into bed. We'd snuggle and talk about our days while our fur children join us there.

One word surfaces: *home.*

I realize I'm smiling, my chest warm at the thought.

I know what I have to do. Janessa has a plan. We haven't talked it through yet, but I already know I'll follow along with whatever it is. We only get this one life and I want to choose my home, my Lauren.

I stand and walk into her bedroom just as she emerges from her bathroom wrapped in a fluffy white towel. She smells amazing. I'm drawn to her, a moth to her flame.

"Hey, beautiful," I say, then lean down to kiss her still-wet lips.

"You're up," she says, nodding to the bathroom.

"Didn't wait for me to climb in with you?" I tease.

"There is no way either of us has the energy for that after today," she laughs.

"Try me," I say, bending to kiss the side of her neck.

"And you're all sweaty," she wrinkles her nose.

"Fine," I say with an exaggerated sigh.

I slip past her and into the bathroom, then start the shower. I take my time, letting the hot water wash away the stress and excitement of today. Let it wash down the guilt of the fact that I'll likely have to blackmail the blackmailer to be done with my father forever—and the other relationships that will likely disappear with him. I use Lauren's peppermint shampoo, loving that I get to rub her scent into my hair and beard.

By the time I'm done, my shoulders are finally relaxed and the adrenaline headache has faded away. I grab a towel and dry off, then wrap it around my waist. I notice an unopened toothbrush next to the sink and smile. Did she plan for me to stay over?

I open it and make quick work of brushing my teeth. I briefly consider putting on my underwear from today and then decide that naked is definitely better. When I open the bathroom door, a cloud of steam rolls out before me into Lauren's lamp-lit room. I'm fully prepared to be a giant goofball and make a show of removing my towel.

But when my eyes adjust to the low-lit room, I see Lauren propped up in bed, book open and dropped in her lap. She's asleep sitting up. It's adorable.

I walk over, grab her bookmark, and place it in her book—one with a muscled man chest on the front—and set it aside on her night stand. Then I gently lower her down onto her pillow and turn out the light. I wonder how many nights she's fallen asleep just like this, mid-book, lamp on. And think about how many of them I will hopefully get to be a part of in the future.

I walk around to the other side of the bed, taking my towel off and hanging it on the door hook. Then I crawl under the covers. I brush my thumb along Lauren's forearm, savoring the feel of her smooth skin beneath my fingers. I let my hand stay there as I close my eyes.

Interlude

KREWE OF PERSICI SOCIAL MEDIA POST

Birds of a Feather really do flock together. Pictured: Krewe King Beau Baxter and Queen Lauren Landau steal the show at the parade's afterparty with a storybook kiss.

Likes: 3,351
Comments: 432
Shares: 563

Chapter 46

LAUREN

February 23

I wake to the sound of my phone buzzing relentlessly where it rests on my nightstand. I glance at the clock, 9:30 a.m. On a Sunday. What in the world?

I roll out of Max's embrace and grab the phone, seeing the newspaper's office number. "Hello?"

"Lauren, thank God. It's Rhett. We have a situation. Can you come into the office? It's urgent."

I glance at Max sleeping in my bed, Lola curled up next to him. My heart tugs.

"Yes, of course. Give me just a few minutes."

The anxiety of not knowing what's going on, of not being there when whatever this is started going down, shoves me into a tailspin.

I put on the bra that I tossed on the floor last night. Then I go into my closet and grab the first thing I see, tugging on a pair of slacks and a blouse. I slide my feet into a pair of nude pumps, wincing at my sore feet, then duck into the bathroom to wrestle my wild hair into a bun and brush some mascara on. Not my usual poise, but it will have to do.

When I go to exit the bathroom, Max is standing in the doorway waiting on me. And he's naked. I whimper.

"Everything okay?" he asks, reaching up to place a hand on my shoulder.

I lean into him for a quick hug, then brush a kiss over his lips. "Work emergency. Gotta go. Feel free to stay as long as you like. I'll let you know when I'm done with whatever this is."

"Talk about shooting down a man's ego. Greeting you while naked didn't make you blink, even a little?" he smirks.

"Oh, it didn't make me blink. It made me stare," I smile, then it drops. "I'm sorry to run out like this, Max."

"It's alright," he says, gently. "I'll still be here when you get back. Or, if not here, you know how to find me. Go boss up."

His words are a balm to my anxious soul. A gift I've been missing for so much of my life. I make myself pause and be in this moment for just a few more seconds.

I reach up and cup his jaw, brushing a thumb over his cheek. "I'm sorry I have to dash like this. I'm trying to get better at work-life balance. But when it comes to urgent matters, I'm the boss. I have to be there. But I'll call when I'm done. We still have three more days until Fat Tuesday. Maybe I can snag us a king cake when I'm done."

He reaches up and holds my hand against his cheek. "Go do what you need to do. I'll see you later today." He bends to kiss my forehead.

I turn and walk out the bedroom door, grabbing my keys and purse. Just as I'm about to leave, I hear Max yell, "And don't forget that king cake!"

I smile as I hustle to my car.

When I get to work, Rhett is waiting on me. He follows me into my office and closes the door.

"You're freaking me out," I say. "What's going on?"

"There's been an accusation. A reliable source has reported that Maxwell Beaumont, Sr. keeps a list of his clients' indiscretions as blackmail. The source is good, and a junior reporter got the tip. Pushed it through without one of us here to okay it. Fortunately one of our copyeditors texted me before it ran and I came in immediately. The paper hasn't printed yet, thank God," Rhett says, running a hand through his hair and mussing it. He looks as tired as I do.

"We need to fact check it," he continues. "Find out if the source is willing to go on record, if it's been reported to the police. Go through the proper protocols so we don't get hit with a libel lawsuit. But also—"

"That's Max's dad," I say, horror churning like a tangle of snakes in my stomach.

"Yeah, that," he says, reaching up to rub the stress lines on his forehead.

"Well, we won't suppress it," I reassure. "Journalistic integrity reigns supreme. But fuck."

"Do you think Max would be willing to confirm it?" Rhett asks and winces. "Sorry, that wasn't tactful. Puts you in a bad position. If you want, I can lead this, keep you out of it."

I place my elbows on my desk and drop my head into my hands, my head spinning. Every fiber of my being that has worked this hard to get this far wants to take the lead on this story. But I don't want my feelings for Max to get in the way of good journalism. And Rhett has proven himself over and over again.

"And one more thing," he adds. I can hear the reluctance in his voice. He holds up his phone. A photo of Max and me kissing after the parade is on the screen. I squint, and then my eyes go wide when I see the number of likes, comments, and shares.

"There's no way I can oversee this story," I say immediately. "Everyone knows Max and I are an item now."

"Yeah. I mean, I didn't want to tell you what to do, boss. But that's not a good look."

"Okay," I say, spreading my palms over my desk. "Here's what we're going to do. First, do you know who the source is? Confidentially, of course."

Rhett swallows and nods. "Janessa Guiles. She has photographic evidence to back up her claim. And she approached us with the info willingly."

Was this what Max was telling me? Is this how he plans to handle things with his dad? Why didn't he say something last night? I'm not sure if I'm hurt, furious, or devastated for him.

"Okay. I need to call Max." My stomach lurches at the thought. "But I don't want to be accused of corrupted journalistic ethics. So here is what we're going to do. I'm going to call him and you're going to lead the conversation. Ask him to go on record. If he's willing, you'll take it from there. We need another witness." I consider. "Grab Gabrielle. She's been reporting the longest. We can trust her."

Rhett nods, then disappears. I try to slow my breaths, even as my heart threatens to escape my chest. When they both appear in my office and close the door, we brief Gabrielle. She looks at me with pity, but I can't stand it. I look down to my phone and call Max.

"Hey birdie! That was fast!" he says on answer. "Everything okay?"

My heart beats so loudly it nearly drowns out his words.

"Not really. Hey Max, I have Rhett and a reporter, Gabrielle, in the office with me and I need to put you on speaker phone. I'm sorry to have to do this, but it's cover for both of us, okay?"

"Baby, what's wrong? You're scaring me," he says, and my heart breaks, just a little more.

"Okay, you're on speaker phone," I say, trying to remain calm. "Max, Rhett needs to talk to you." I nod to Rhett and he takes over.

"There was a tip submitted to the newspaper last night. It involves your dad and the alleged blackmailing of clients. We have a reliable source who reported it."

He pauses, but silence is the only thing that greets us.

"I am taking myself off of this story," I say. "I don't want anyone to question my journalistic integrity and accuse me of being biased because you and I are together. Rhett is going to run lead on this.

But Max, if the source is willing to go on record, I can't suppress the article and keep my job." My voice quivers on those last words. My heart is a bass drum in my chest.

"I understand," he says, voice raspy.

"And," Rhett says, "we want to know if you know anything about this. And, if so, if you're willing to go on record."

"No comment," he says immediately.

And I know it's the right thing for him to say. But fuck if it I don't feel a little betrayed. He knew about this and he didn't tell me.

"I need to make a couple of calls. Confirm some things. Talk to my lawyer. I'll be back in touch in an hour," Max says.

And then he hangs up. My heart fractures with Max's pain at the end of the call.

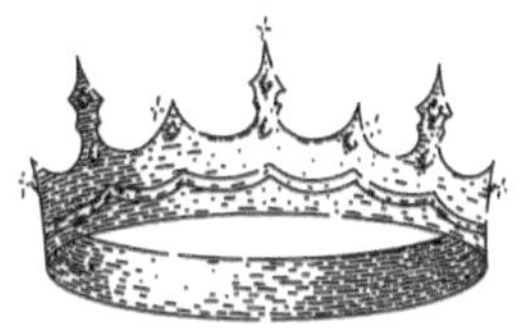

Chapter 47

MAX

I throw up again. Wipe my mouth, flush the toilet, and then quickly brush my teeth. Mags circles me, whining in worry. Janessa dropped her off here less than an hour ago, and I wish she was still here when I got that call from Lauren and Rhett.

Grumbling to myself, I call Janessa.

"Well, hello there, King Maxie," she says on answer. "Just saw a photo of you smooching Lauren. It's all over the internet today."

I'll have to process that last little tidbit later. Right now I have more important things to deal with.

"Janessa. I need you to be honest with me right now. I just got a call from the newspaper. Did you tell them about Dad's list?"

The phone goes quiet. "Oh."

"Fuck, Janessa! What were you thinking?"

"I was thinking that asshole has controlled and manipulated your life for years. That he's doing it to everyone he can squeeze a benefit out of. Everyone he can use. And it's not only horribly evil, but it's illegal. It's time karma came to bite him in the ass."

"Janessa," I say, trying to steady myself. "I thought we were going to confront him about that list. Not print it in the damn newspaper and turn it into a public scandal!"

"You tried talking to him. Remember how that ended?"

"And you didn't tell me you were going to the goddamn media with this because?"

"I knew you'd try to stop me," she says confidently.

"Did it ever occur to you what a terrible position this puts Lauren in as the editor-in-chief of the whole fucking newspaper? Especially because apparently everyone on social media now knows she is dating his son."

"She can recuse herself from the story," Janessa says, but for the first time she sounds uncertain.

"And you just turned my relationship with her into a public drama for everyone to gossip about. We live in a small town. It would have been big enough news on its own, but the editor dating the accused's son will feed the gossip mill for months."

"Max, the story hasn't run yet. Rhett called and asked me to confirm it this morning. Asked if I'd go on record. I told him I'd let him know later today. If you really want to, we can still stop the press. But Max, I've thought through it. What other options do we have? If we confront your dad, he's going to go apeshit and accuse us of being liars. Destroy all the evidence. No one has had the courage to stand up to him in all these years of documented blackmailing. If we don't do it, who will? I've thought about it. We don't have the finances to take him to court. But if we go to the media and they print it, a lot of things will happen and other people will get involved."

"He'll murder you, for starters," I say.

"Please," she says, and I can nearly hear her eyes roll. "First, if he tries to sue them for libel, I've already sent them the evidence. It will go to court. They'll have to do a whole discovery process for evidence. Which means he'll have to let them dig through all his business records. Uncle Maxwell definitely doesn't want that. And then, once his dirty laundry is aired and it circulates through the media, a bunch of those clients he's blackmailed will come forward."

"Or they won't because he's got dirt on them," I insist.

"His name will mean nothing anymore. People won't believe him or trust him. He'll be powerless to sink Lauren's career. If he tries to tank the newspaper, then people will think it's over the story. Accuse him of trying to conduct a cover up. Don't you see? It's brilliant."

"And what about Mom? Charlie? What will happen to them?"

"They have so much money saved up. They'll be fine."

"What if Charlie's involved in all this dirty stuff?" I say sadly, already knowing the answer.

"It's still illegal, Max. They are hurting people."

And as my heart sinks like a brick, I realize she's right.

She continues, "And whether or not the newspaper runs the story, I've already sent the pictures to the police. I looked it up, it's not illegal to send it to the paper. It's part of the First Amendment. But it does substantiate the claim by sending it to law enforcement."

"You're right. The police need to know and Dad would have figured out some way to blackmail or hurt us if we confronted him with all this." I sigh.

The only question is how do I navigate this with Lauren? Can we survive this upheaval, the public spotlight that is about to shine on both of us with my family in the pressure cooker to boot?

But even as I think it, I know how to fix it.

"I'm sorry, Max," Janessa says. "I think this is the right choice. It keeps him from slithering out of accountability with expensive lawyers and more blackmail. But if you tell me to back out, to ask them to pull it, I will."

"No," I say on an exhale. "You're right. If you're comfortable going on record, I'll support you."

When I hang up with Janessa, I open my texts and send two words to Lauren: "Run it."

And then I call Rhett.

Around 9 p.m., I get a text.

Lauren: I'm leaving the office.
Max: Will you come over?
Lauren: You sure you want me to?
Max: More sure than I've ever been in my life.
Lauren: Let me feed Lola and change clothes. I'll see you in a bit.

It's time to come clean with her about everything with my dad, and then we can brace for impact.

When Lauren knocks, Mags howls in greeting. I swing open the front door and take her in, dark circles under her eyes, blonde hair disheveled, wearing those leggings I love so much and a Nirvana t-shirt she must have snagged from my closet last time she was here.

I open the door wider and she comes inside. She turns to me as soon as I close the door.

"Max, I don't know what to say. What to do. This is all so . . . I don't know. So icky."

"It is," I agree. "Here, I'll get you some water, then let's sit and talk."

I make quick work of filling a glass and bringing it to her. When she sits down, legs stretched across my couch, Mags jumps up and lays on her feet.

"I'm sorry I didn't tell you about my dad," I say immediately. "For what it's worth, I thought this was going to be a private conversation between Janessa, Dad, and me. I had no idea Jan was going to take it to the media."

"I believe you," she says immediately. "I've had a lot of time to think about all of this today. I'm hurt you didn't tell me about what you found."

I start to apologize, but she cuts me off. "But I understand why you didn't. Between all of the parade activities and work, neither of us has had much down time. And, I'm glad I didn't know. No one can accuse me of hiding a story I didn't know about. One that another source reported. So, journalistically, it was the right call."

"And personally?" I ask.

"Personally, I hate that your dad put you in this position. That you have to make this kind of choice about the man who should have taken care of you. And I think what you and Janessa are doing is brave."

"But?" I ask.

She looks at me, eyes glassy. "But, I'm worried about the public spotlight this is going to place on us. Wonder if this means we should step back from each other. Take a break."

"That's exactly what my dad wants to happen with us, Lauren. And if we do that, he still wins. He may go down with the ship, but he'll be taking us with him. And I refuse to let that happen."

"Then what do we do?" her voice wavers.

I reach across the couch and pull her into me, spreading my legs so she can lay back against my chest while I wrap her up in my arms and hold her tight.

"I have to take a public stance. Tell the world it's true. And if someone tries to point the finger at us, I'll tell them you've recused yourself from the story. That we're together and this developing situation with my father has nothing to do with the relationship between you and me."

"You'd do that? For me?"

"Lauren, when are you going to learn that I'd do damn near anything for you?"

A sob escapes her—one born of exhaustion and too many feelings all at once. I know because I feel the exact same way. I squeeze her tighter and let her cry while all of my emotions run through me. Grateful that I'm still holding her, that I get to have her for as long as she wants me.

"You deserve better than this position your dad has put you in,

Max."

"And I'm getting much better than I deserve," I insist, kissing her temple.

"There is one piece of good news," she says. "I got our publisher's approval to make Rhett managing editor. I was going to push for it before this story to try to reclaim some of my personal time again, to finally start checking some things off that bucket list that I've always wanted to do. But this was as good a reason as any. The paper needs another boss, and I have to trust that someone else can take the wheel when I can't be the one to lead. I haven't told him yet. Waiting for this chaos to calm down a bit so it's a happy thing and not a 'you have to make this decision in the middle of a chaotic situation thing.'"

"That sounds like a real good choice there, birdie."

"Yeah, I think it is," she says. "It will be trial by fire for him. The story runs on the front page tomorrow."

"Yeah. I know."

"We'll weather this together," she says, then burrows into my chest, the wisps of her hair tickling my nose.

"Together," I agree. "I better go call Rhett and confirm everything so he has time to finalize the story for tomorrow. I'm gonna go to my bedroom to keep things separate. Make yourself at home. I'll be out in a bit and we can eat some dinner."

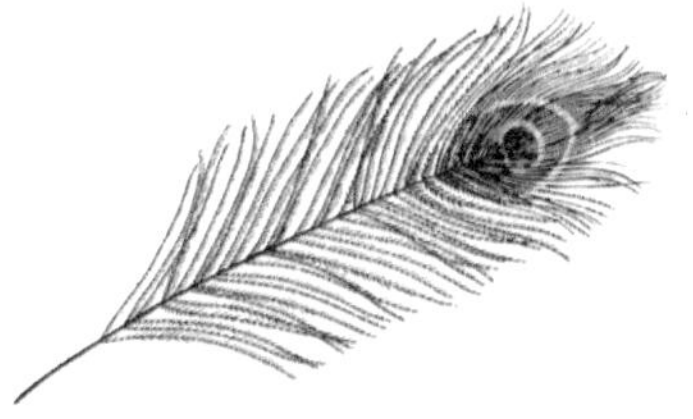

Chapter 48

LAUREN

February 24

The next day is every bit the shit storm we anticipated.

My phone blows up with text messages, only rivaled by the unending texts and calls Max receives. We decide to weather it together. I take the day off on what is arguably one of the biggest days ever at the office. I feel both guilty for not being there, and relieved to do what I need to: take care of my mental health and trust that Rhett can handle it.

And he does, like he was born to do it. Rhett's usually shy persona is put to the side as he addresses news stations head on, tells them that he's leading the piece on Maxwell Beaumont, Sr. while I take a short vacation. Insists on journalistic integrity.

I wince as I see that the social media views of the photo of Max and me kissing after the parade doubles, then triples the number of comments, shares, and likes. And then I delete my social media.

Max takes a week off work and spends today on and off calls with Janessa and his lawyer. He agreed to go on record about his dad. They both did. And they shared copies of the files. And, no surprise, his father's lawyer is pulling out all the stops to shut this down.

We stay at my house, just in case. Neither of us trusts Max's father. And Janessa stays with Gladys, the two of them baking pies while monitoring Gladys's security cameras. It's anxiety-inducing, but we make the most of our unplanned time together.

After a full day of tense conversations, Max turns to me and says, "Let's get out of here."

"I refuse to go to any public setting in this city. No bowling. No restaurants."

"I believe you said something about learning French and renting a cabin? I looked on AirBnb. How do you feel about Mountain Home, Arkansas?"

"I don't know if hiking and getting chased by bears again will help out with our attempt to lie low," I deadpan. "Plus, I feel bad running away and leaving Rhett with this dumpster fire. And what about your dad?"

"I was thinking more like hot tub time and Duolingo," he says. "But I see your point. Maybe something closer to home?"

"Hmmm. My aunt and uncle have a little lakehouse in Farmerville, about twenty minutes from here. It's not exactly AirBnb quality, but it's got vintage seventies charm. Plus, we could be back here easily if we're needed."

"I'll pack my bag and Mags's things," he says. "But that means I need to run to my apartment."

"What about Lola?" I ask, looking at my cat who is staring at me like she knows something is amiss.

"Bring her," he shrugs.

"What do you think about that, little lady?" I ask her.

She meows at me. Loudly.

"Yes," I say. "Let's do it."

The pitstop by Max's apartment is fast and furious. Both of us are on the lookout for his dad or a lawyer. But no one appears, and when we're on the road and headed to Farmerville, I finally feel like I can breathe.

We're at the lake in no time, the familiar setting of my childhood tucked away down a winding dirt road and through banks of pine trees.

When we open the screen door to go inside, it creaks, startling a racoon that skitters out from beneath the porch stairs. Mags goes nuts when she sees it, barking from her kennel in the car. Spider webs cling to corners, their prey wrapped up in buggy cocoons.

We step inside, greeted by the familiar yellow linoleum floors and wooden dining table with vintage wooden chairs.

"We may need to mop," I wince, noting the dust clinging to most surfaces. "And dust."

"But first, let's try out that porch swing," Max says, nodding to the screened in front porch that looks over the lake.

"Deal," I agree. We drop our bags, then go back outside to get Lola and Mags' kennels, opening them up and letting them explore the small house. Lola is going to have a blast chasing down all the creepy crawlies that are likely inside this place.

We walk out to the porch, taking a seat in the wide swing. I snuggle into Max's side while he slides his arm around my shoulders. Together, we extend and retract our legs, making the swing move. The late February air is cool this afternoon, and the perfect breeze filters in through the screen while the sun begins to set over the lake. It's easy to pretend that we can stay like this forever, that there's no crisis waiting for us when we return.

And so, tonight, I soak up the beauty around me and allow myself to pretend.

I wake up the next morning with my phone buzzing on the old nightstand next to the lakehouse bed. My instinct is to answer it while putting on my shoes and preparing to go into the office.

I'm halfway out of bed before I remember where I am: at a lakehouse. Taking a vacation. Sort of.

I pick up my phone, prepared to see the office number or Rhett's cell number. So I'm surprised to see Gladys Beaumont's name on my screen.

"Hello?" I answer cautiously. I haven't talked to her since the night of the Mardi Gras parade, but Janessa has kept us in the loop via text while she stays with her grandmother. Nothing too exciting to report thus far, which is the best case scenario.

"Hi Lauren, dear," she says cheerily. "How are you?"

"Um, I've been better."

"Yes, well, none of this chaos is your fault. I do hope you know that. This family drama has been a long time coming. And I am sorry that you were caught up in the whirlwind of it all."

"Thank you, Gladys. Are you alright? Janessa?"

"Oh honey, I own a funeral parlor. My job is literally burying bodies. My son finally getting called to the carpet on his terrible behavior feels rather light compared to death, don't you think?"

"Um," I hesitate, unsure of how to respond to that.

"And I'm so glad to hear that you and Max are taking a little vacation together. Janessa has kept me up to speed. But, my dear, I do need you and my grandson to come back into town for our final Fat Tuesday celebration and I'm almost certain Max has turned off his phone."

Max has definitely turned off his phone. But I'm not telling her that.

"And why do we need to be there? The parade is over."

"Yes, but Fat Tuesday is Mardi Gras. And, if you'll remember, it's the day we're presenting all the money we raised to our two nonprofits. I need you and Max there to present the checks."

"I thought we were lying low right now since the story about Mr. Beaumont ran in the paper?"

"Hmm. I think it's best if we don't let my son scare us into hiding any longer. A little birdie told me that his lawyer has told him to sit down and shut up. More of his clients are braving the storm and coming forward. The storm is growing, but the focus is shifting off the two of you."

"But Gladys, he's your son."

"He is. And I still love him. But I hate how he's divided this family. Pushed out Max and Janessa. I've tried my best to keep the peace, but there's only so much I can do. That man is stubborn and made shameful decisions. It's time for him to pay the piper. And there's nothing, even as his mother, that I can do about that."

A hand rubs my lower back, sliding beneath my t-shirt. Max's movements are slow and steady, reassuring. I turn to look behind me, admiring the rumpled man in twisted bed sheets.

"Let me talk to Max and I'll call you back," I say.

"Sounds good, dear."

I end the call and turn to face him fully. "Your grandmother wants us to come back to town for the Fat Tuesday celebration. Says the focus on your dad's scandal is shifting to the other people who are coming forward, people he's blackmailed."

I watch his face as I say the words, looking for a reaction. He frowns.

"Grandma thinks it's safe?"

"Yes. Your dad's lawyers have told him to lay low."

"What do you think?" he asks.

"I think we should go, even though I love this escape. We have been front and center of the krewe and not being there is more conspicuous than showing up. Plus, presenting these checks is fantastic PR, not only for the krewe, but for us as well."

"Let's do it, then."

"But Max, if you don't want to go, we don't have to."

He pulls me into him and I ease down onto the bed, laying my head on the pillow so we're eye to eye.

"I want to be there. My grandmother has always been my number one supporter. Even when it comes to matters with her own son. I'm not going to let her down now."

"Okay," I agree.

"Okay."

And then he leans in and kisses me.

Chapter 49

MAX

March 4

Fat Tuesday is a day of debauchery, a dedicated time to eat and drink all the things before Lent begins tomorrow on Ash Wednesday.

But right now, I just want to throw up. My lawyer called to tell me that my dad wants to meet in person. With legal counsel present, of course. I have every right to decline the invitation. But my mom followed up with her own call, pleading for me to do so.

And fuck if that didn't tug right at my guilt.

But first, we have some checks to present. So I plaster on a smile and reach for Lauren's hand. We meet the two groups receiving the donations at the Community Center hall. There's a step and repeat backdrop with the krewe's logo set up for photos.

Fortunately, it's a small affair: just the recipients, the krewe steering committee, us, and the cameras. Frank and Margie are there to accept one check on behalf of the nonprofit he set up to help kids who have to travel for health care needs. And the other goes to the Boys and Girls Club.

I'm glad we came back in town for this. It feels good, like putting a dent in the karmic balance my dad helped shift to the evil side. The scales of justice are starting to find some balance again.

When it's over and the recipients leave, my grandmother finds me and wraps me up in a tight hug. I told her earlier about Dad's request to meet. Talking to her about it in person was heartbreaking. Watching the way her expression falls when we talk about her son chips away at my own heart. I hate it. Hate that he put us both in this position, but grateful that we still have each other despite it all.

"Just remember, that no matter what he says to you, you still have a family. You have Janessa, me, and," she says, peeking around my shoulder to where Lauren is visiting with Amelia, "I think Lauren may be part of that family too."

I smile, lips closed. "I think you might be right about that, Grandma."

I give her a long hug, then walk over to Lauren and Amelia. We say our goodbyes to the rest of the steering committee and head out.

This day we should be celebrating feels solemn, but I know I need to talk to my dad to find some sort of closure.

"You sure you don't want me to go with you to meet with him?" Lauren asks.

"No. There is a long history between us. I appreciate your support, birdie. But this is something I have to do on my own."

She nods. "Call me after?"

"Of course," I say, placing a soft kiss on her lips.

We each get into our own cars and I drive over to my lawyer's office, stomach churning.

By the time I walk inside the law office, I feel like I've had five energy drinks. I'm so anxious my whole body aches from the way I've been tensed up. My lawyer, Tristan Galloway, stands up and greets me.

"We have them in a meeting room over here. Your mom is in there too," he says.

I nod, appreciating the heads up, and follow him back. I'm both surprised and not that my dad dragged her into this conversation. It's a smart move. I know he's heard my radio sign-off. He knows that she's a pawn to pull guilt and regret out of me.

I mentally fortify myself as Tristan opens the door to a wood-paneled room with a long board room table. Mom and Dad are sitting at the opposite end close to the window, their lawyer next to them. Mom looks terrible, her eyes puffy and red like she hasn't stopped crying in days. My heart tugs with the unexpected guilt.

Then I turn to my dad, and he looks like he's ready to flip the table or slam a fist into my face. Anger chases away my guilt. I walk past the chairs until I'm near them, then pull one out next to Mom and sit. Tristan sits beside me.

"My client has agreed to this exchange today," Tristan says. "With the understanding that legal counsel for both parties remain present for the duration of the conversation."

My dad's jaw flexes, but he nods.

He clears his throat. "Max, these past few days have been hell. I wish you would have come to talk to me about this before taking accusations to the media and destroying your mother's and my lives."

My hackles rise, but I stay silent, allowing him to fill the space and get out all his ire. He waits for a response, but when he gets none, he continues.

"Why did you do it, son?" It's the first time I hear a hint of sorrow.

"Do you really have to ask me that?"

"Your family has always had your back," he says, just the tiniest bits of emotion clinging to his words. "Any trouble you've gotten yourself into, I've always helped you out of it. And you threw me to the goddamn wolves."

"And by getting me out of trouble, do you mean threatening the livelihood of my girlfriend? Threatening the newspaper and her career? Because that sounds a helluva lot like destroying my life."

"I am trying to help you, Max. I knew she wouldn't risk the

newspaper. Nothing was going to come of it."

"Nothing except you scaring away the best thing that's ever happened to me, you mean."

"Max, that girl is only after your money," he says, as if he's talking to a toddler.

"Just because most of the relationships in your life are only after your money, doesn't mean the ones in mine are. I'm a thirty-four year old adult fully capable of making my own decisions. I choose her. Every single time I choose her. I choose her over money, over my career, over my own parents. I choose Lauren. And you have always chosen yourself. It's what got you into this mess. Your own choices and greed."

Dad grinds his teeth.

I sigh and turn to look at my mom, studying the lines in her forehead, remembering the way she'd bake my favorite snickerdoodles for me when I was a kid. My heart kicks in my chest as my voice softens. "For what it's worth Mom, I am sorry that you are mixed up in this. I love you. And if you ever want to try to pick up the pieces of our relationship, I'll be here."

I turn my attention back to my dad. "But we're done here, you and me. I won't tolerate the control and manipulation anymore. I've done my best to keep you out of my life, but hear me now. I'm done. Please don't contact me again."

I stand from the table and Tristan stands with me.

"You don't get to just walk out of here," my dad says, anger coloring his voice. "You are ruining me."

"You did that all by yourself," I say. I give one more glance to my mom. She smiles at me sadly. Then I turn and leave the room.

Once I'm back in my truck, I text Lauren.

Max: It's done. Can I come over?
Lauren: I'm at the office. Tonight?
Max: Everything okay?
Lauren: Yep, just sorting some things out.

Max: Sure. 6?

Lauren: Let's do 7. Grab a king cake before they all sell out today. *wink emoji*

Her response helps me relax. I drive back to my apartment, my mind slowly beginning to release decades of tension and trauma. It's time to begin fully owning my own life.

I pit stop at the best local bakery in town on my way home, picking up a raspberry cream cheese king cake, my last of the season. And I'm grateful, because this time Lauren and I get to share it.

Chapter 50

LAUREN

"Rhett, we want to offer you a position as managing editor of the newspaper," I say, failing to suppress a smile as I look across my desk at my right-hand man.

His mouth falls open. "Lauren, I don't know what to say."

"Say yes, please say yes," I plead and dramatically clasp my hands together.

He laughs. "Tell me what I'm agreeing to," he teases.

"Taking on some reporter assignment duties, managing deadlines and submissions. Helping me review big stories. Essentially getting a big pay raise to do everything you've been doing since January."

He glances down, and when he looks up again, a huge smile is spread across his face. "Yes. A hundred percent, yes."

I stand up and reach out to shake his hand. He clasps mine and we both grin.

His grin turns sheepish. "I'm not going to lie. The extra money sure will be nice with the baby on the way."

I freeze, my brain catching up to what he just said. "Amelia?" I ask with a gasp.

"Of course. Who else?"

"Rhett!" I cheer, then run around my desk and wrap him up in a hug. "You're going to be the best dad. Congratulations to you both."

"Aw thanks, boss."

I pull back and smirk. "Should you still call me boss if you're now also the boss?"

"There will only ever be one true boss around here. Don't forget it." He winks.

And all the pieces of my heart slide into place. This was the right decision. The one that allows me to enjoy my career and gives me time to start living my personal life outside of the office again.

When I pull into my driveway, I spy Max's truck already waiting on me. As soon as I park, he and Mags get out. He holds a big king cake box in his hands and has a wide grin on his face. And, I swear, he looks like he somehow grew younger since this morning.

I jog over to him, managing to keep my heels on, and throw my arms around his waist. He kisses the crown of my head. "Good to see you too, birdie. We have a lot to catch up on."

We enter through my front door and I turn the lights on. I take a moment to note all the new little additions that have found their way into my once plain home. A small collection of rocks from my cabin trip with Max. A framed, signed thank you card from the Krewe of Persici steering committee. A congratulations card from my staff on the refrigerator. Several strands of beads hang up on command hooks along the wall. One of my special queen throws, one of Max's king ones, and several from captains and other floats. Max's sweatshirt is thrown over the back of my couch.

Embracing life is livening up my space and it feels immensely satisfying. Better than climbing the career ladder, even.

Max walks up behind me and slides his hands around my waist, pulling me in tight to him. He leans down and kisses my cheek.

"So, I guess this means we finally get to have the talk," he says low and husky. My favorite voice. Saying my least favorite thing.

I spin in his arms and look at him, frowning. "What talk?"

He grins wickedly. "The girlfriend talk."

"Are you trying to tell me you have one, Max Beaumont?" I raise an eyebrow.

"I certainly hope I do," he says, bending to give me a quick kiss. "Especially considering the entire city of Ruston and beyond has seen us kissing. That social media post is a hot commodity."

I frown deeper. "Thanks to your dad."

"Which makes me love it even more. He tried to separate us, and instead it only made the world see how much I lo—care about you."

"Max! Were you going to say the 'L word?'"

"Depends."

"On?"

"If you're going to shove me away and tell me to get lost or not."

"Max, you idiot. I love you too and I am definitely your girlfriend."

A huge grin spreads across his face, lighting up all of his features, crinkling his eyes. And I get just a hint of what Max will look like as he grows older. I love it.

"Well, that's a relief, even though you just had to turn this into a competition and say it first."

I give him a little love slap on the chest and he chuckles, low and deep. "I love you too, birdie."

And my heart flutters, just like the endearment he's given me.

"Now, be a good girl and get your ass in the bedroom. Fat Tuesday is supposed to be about celebrating. I say we give into all the lust and gluttony of the day like a good King and Queen of Mardi Gras."

"But we're off duty," I protest.

"Hmmm," he growls. "I don't know about that. I wouldn't mind seeing you in your crown—and only your crown—tonight."

"Okay, but same rules apply to you, King Max."

"King of all the wild things," he says. I chuckle at the reference to the book I read at our first fundraising event.

Then he bends down and hoists me over one shoulder and carries me to the bedroom, giving me a slap on the ass for good measure. I squeal and reach down to spank him back. Just before we leave the living room, he reaches out his free hand and snags the king cake, bringing it with us.

Interlude

THE RUSTON DAILY LEADER

March 18

Twelve Come Forward in Maxwell Beaumont Case

By Rhett Hebert, Managing Editor

A dozen men and women have brought charges against Maxwell Beaumont, Sr., who has been accused of bribery, extortion, and blackmail.

A week ago, a source close to Beaumont presented *The Ruston Daily Leader* with evidence that Beaumont, Sr. had a list of clients with various personal leverages he was using against them to gain their business. The list was confirmed by his son, Max Beaumont, Jr. The alleged items varied and included illegal exchanges such as insider trading.

Due to the nature of the allegations on the list, and without confirmation that these accusations have occurred, *The Ruston Daily Leader* has turned the list over to law enforcement.

Since the article ran in the newspaper, a dozen of those on the list have come forward with accusations of extortion and blackmail against Beaumont, Sr.

"Maxwell Beaumont was using his connection with a local bank to threaten our small business loan," said Stephen Jackson. "We've been beholden to him for years, scared to act against him for fear more people would turn on us and our business would go under."

Jackson said that he knows of others who have been similarly extorted, but wants them to come forward on their own terms.

The Ruston Daily Leader reached out to Beaumont, Sr. for a statement, but he has yet to respond.

"When I discovered that my uncle was up to potentially illegal activities, I felt I had to do something," said Janessa Guiles. "Some people have criticized me for going to the media with the information, but I was scared that if I didn't, my uncle would figure out some way to cover it up. I also reported my information to local law enforcement."

As of this time, *The Ruston Daily Leader* has shared all of the information we have received on this allegation with law enforcement. This story is still developing.

Interlude

KREWE OF PERSICI SOCIAL MEDIA POST

Thank you for your support of Ruston's very first Mardi Gras event this year! With your help we were able to donate more than $10,000 to two local nonprofits that support the needs of children. We look forward to celebrating with you again next year.

And remember, let the good times roll!

[Pictured: King's float in Downtown Ruston]

Chapter 51

LAUREN

Six Weeks Later

I was worried about accusations of biased reporting after my relationship with Max went semi-viral. But letting Rhett take the lead and recusing myself was the right move. Even now, six weeks later, someone will occasionally bring the whole mess up to me. I just say "no comment" and change the subject.

The silver lining in all of this is that Rhett was able to prove himself as managing editor not only to me, but to the entire staff and our publisher. That, and my ability to finally take years of accrued vacation time—which Leslie pushed me to do. Repeatedly.

Still, training Rhett as managing editor has taken time. I do a lot at the office. So much so that I underestimated how much time it would take to train him. He's a fast learner though, and I'm slowly relinquishing some of the reins.

Max has been patient as I put in the extra hours to train Rhett, knowing that it will pay off for both of us in the long run. Max is the first boyfriend I've ever had who was willing to support me in what I need in my relationship and my job.

And Max has been in demand more than ever, both at his job and with media interview requests, since this whole story broke with his dad. But he always makes time for me. For us.

Which is why I'm not surprised that he has some sort of surprise date planned for us tonight. He told me to bring my leggings, a t-shirt, and work out shoes and to keep an open mind. The weather has warmed up since Easter, and I'm half expecting some sort of surprise hiking trip. Which would be fine. Fun even. I just wish I were prepared with a suitcase.

When he pulls up in his truck and tells me to get in, I know that I'm willing to go anywhere with this man—even if it means facing down a bear again. But when I open the door to his truck and look around, I don't see Mags. Something local then. He'd never leave her behind.

"So what am I in for tonight?" I ask.

"You'll see," he teases. When we pull up to the dance studio where Amara taught us how to waltz a couple of months ago, I look to him for an answer.

He shrugs. "Learning other dances was on your bucket list."

My jaw drops. "You're serious? Dare I ask what style of dance?"

"You dare not."

I laugh and follow him in.

We enter the studio to find a new instructor named Leonore. And it turns out that she is here to teach us to salsa. I'm not sure whether to celebrate or run out the door.

"It's all in the hips," she insists as she follows us onto the dance floor.

And, just like waltzing, we are a hot mess at first. We step on each other's feet. And when Leonore grabs Max's hips and yells, "No like this!" I can't help it, I burst out laughing. They both frown at me. Somehow we stumble through it. And when Leonore demands we return in a week, we're both too scared to tell her no.

"That was really thoughtful," I tell Max as we leave the dance studio.

"I think it was a disaster," he insists.

"But we laughed."

"Correction, you laughed. I had my hips aggressively swiveled by a short, demanding woman."

"I thought you liked to be bossed around a bit."

"Only by you, birdie," he says, voice dipping low.

"Hmmm," I purr, leaning into him. "And yet, you agreed to do it again."

"Only because if I didn't, I think Leonore would stalk me and drag me back into the studio until my hips swivel appropriately."

I burst out laughing, stomach aching with the feeling.

When I look at Max, he's staring at me in wonder.

"What?" I say, feeling embarrassed.

"Nothing. It's just. You're beautiful, Lauren. So beautiful. And sometimes I can't believe you're mine."

"Well, now you really are embarrassing me," I demure.

"I mean it. Hey everyone!" Max shouts to the empty road lit only by street lights. "Lauren Landau is my girlfriend and I love her!"

I cackle and try to shush him. "She's so sexy!" he yells again.

"Stop it, you terror!"

He quiets and looks at me, gaze heated. Then he leans in. "And she's mine. All mine."

He dips down, lips finding mine in a lazy, searing kiss.

Epilogue

MAX

January 6, Epiphany
Nearly One Year Later

I wait anxiously inside the shared cabin living room. I've been hiking solo all day while Lauren sits on the screened-in porch with her laptop and writes like her life depends on it.

And maybe it does. Because this is her ultimate bucket list item: writing a book. And I'm doing my best to give her the space to do so.

But I miss her. I've gotten spoiled over the last few months since Lauren invited me to move in with her. And while I miss some parts of my bachelor pad, sharing a space with Lauren has been the best thing that's ever happened to me.

Even Mags and Lola have become fast friends. It turns out that as soon as Mags acknowledged that Lola was the boss, all power dynamics were settled. I know the feeling, pup. Lauren is my North Star, and I'll never stop being grateful that Mardi Gras brought us together.

We get to spend nearly all our down time together now. Well, except when she's darting off for romance book club with Janessa and the girls. Even Leslie and my grandmother have joined them. The whole experience, with Lauren growing close to the two other women

I love most in the world, makes her feel even more like family.

Which is why I'm currently pacing, wearing through the cabin's living room rug, looking at the clock. She has made it a point to close her laptop at 5 p.m. every day so we can have time together. And, right now, it's 4:50 p.m.

My phone buzzes with a text from Janessa. It's a link to a news story. I tap it and read the headline: Beaumont convicted of fraud and blackmail charges. I quickly scroll through the story, stomach lurching as I read the details. While his sentencing hasn't happened yet, it seems like Dad serving jail time is inevitable. This is only one of the many cases that has been brought against him since that story ran.

My already tense nerves tighten, though there's some relief there too. Maybe now Mom can finally begin to live her own life for the first time in decades. And, fortunately, my brother Charles wasn't involved in any of the scandalous dealings. I wonder if either of them will reach out to me?

I send a quick text back to Janessa, thanking her for sending the article to me and promising to catch up with her about it after we get back from our trip. She hearts the message, then I tuck my phone away in my pocket.

Mags barks at me, mad that I won't stand still. Finally, the porch door creaks open and Lauren emerges from her writing den. She looks tired, but happy, the way she does most of the time these days.

Since Rhett took over as managing editor, Lauren has finally started taking rotating weekends off and planning vacations, crossing things off her now-expanded bucket list. And we've been spending all our extra time together. Bowling. Dance lessons. Hanging out with her nieces and nephew so Leslie and Adam can take some much-needed date nights.

Anything that sounds fun? We go for it.

For about six weeks at the end of the year, Lauren was back on her old work grind after Amelia had the baby and Rhett took paternity leave. Baby Margaret Kathryn Hebert was born on the first day of autumn, which couldn't have been more perfect.

But even without Rhett there for those weeks, Lauren has trusted more of her team and diversified her workload, giving other staff members the chance to grow and earn promotions.

I'm so damn proud of her.

I take a step closer to her, feeling jittery.

"Why are you acting weird?" she asks, scanning me for some clue as to the source of my nerves.

"I'm not acting weird. I just miss you, birdie."

"Yeah, I don't believe you. What's behind your back?"

"Oh, this?" I say, pulling out the object in question: a slice of king cake on a plate. "Happy Epiphany. It's the first day of the Mardi Gras season. Thought I'd get you a slice of king cake to commemorate our first meeting a year ago."

She laughs and extends her hands to accept the plate. "Ah yes, our Mardi Gras meet-cute. Who would have known then what kind of chaos we were destined for?"

"With all those books you read, you should have known a start like that was destined for a whirlwind romance."

She picks up the piece of cake and takes a bite. "Delicious."

"Just chew carefully," I say. "You might have the piece with the baby in it."

She rolls her eyes and pokes around dramatically. "I think it's all clear," she says, then freezes. "Wait, what is that? A platinum baby?" She unearths the item and holds it up.

I drop to one knee, and I swear, even in this January weather, I'm sweating through my shirt. She gasps, then looks down at me.

"Max," she says, emotion building in her throat. "Is this?"

"Lauren," I say, voice shaking. "My queen, my birdie, my everything. You're mine. I'm yours. There's no one else for me. Will you be my wife?"

She bursts into tears. I've never seen her cry, not like this, and it takes me completely by surprise. I stand up and scoop her into my arms, carrying her to the couch. I sit down and cradle her, Lola and Mags jumping up on either side of us.

"Hey birdie. It's okay. You can say no. I mean, I wouldn't love it, but I love you and we can take all the time you need to warm up to the idea."

"It's not that," she says laughing and crying at the same time. "It's just. Max. I'm so surprised. I never thought I'd have this, any of this. Not the writing time. The perfect partner. Love. Yes, I'll marry you, you goof. Yes, of course. It's just—"

My heart freezes in my chest, waiting for the but.

"Well the ring is covered in cinnamon and frosting and sliding it onto my finger might be impossible."

I laugh in joy and relief, scooting her over to the couch cushion. I take the ring from her and run it under the sink water until it's clean, then return to the couch. I sit down, take her left ring finger, and slide the ring home. The marquis diamond catches the sun filtering through the cabin window.

The sight of my ring on her finger tugs at my heart, squeezes my chest. I swallow down the emotion threatening to choke me. I need to keep it together for this next part.

I reach into my pocket and pull out a piece of paper. I clear my throat, give her a wicked grin, and then I begin to read. "And oh, how she throbbed for him," I say in my sexiest, sultriest voice. "Alexis leaned in and nipped him on the neck. Caden growled, 'That's right. You're mine. My wife.'"

"You're so bad," Lauren giggles, immediately recognizing the lines from one of her most recent reads. "How do you even find these passages?"

"Well, I learned that there is this highlight feature on your e-reader . . ."

"You didn't!"

"I did."

"I feel betrayed," she says dramatically.

"Hey, a guy's gotta get practice in somehow. How else will I narrate your audiobook?"

"Okay, that's fair. I guess I'll allow it. But next time, I get to pick what you read to me." Her tone turns heated.

"Deal. But I get narrator's choice on performance style."

I lean in and kiss her, then pull her to straddle my lap. She holds up her hand and admires the diamond there.

"I'm so happy," she says, emotion clouding her voice.

"It's everything you've always deserved. Everything we've both deserved."

She holds my jaw in her hands, searches my face, then leans down and kisses me.

Acknowledgments

I wrote this book after an epic career change that allowed me to finally step out of a multi-year shame storm. There were many people who were there for me during that painful life transition, and this book exists because they loved me and reminded me of who I truly am. To that end, I'm grateful for my husband, Mark, who was there every step of the way. And the real life Aunt Lar Lar, Laura Dawson, who, along with my editing partner in crime, Dani Galliaro, and my sister, Martha Claire Lepore, were the first to catch me when I fell and prop me back up on my feet again, stronger than ever before. They encouraged me to write the damn book I wanted to write without guardrails. I just want to hug you all forever and ever.

A huge thank you to Kirsten, my everyday Marco Polo pal, who quite literally forced me to turn this Mardi Gras thing from a short story into a novel. And she was right, dammit. Mardi Gras did need its own book. Thank you for listening to hours of me work through the plot holes and suggesting things when I got stuck. You're the best, Kitten. With all my love, Biscuit.

To the Madams. Each and every one of you was a part of this book's success. You are always the first to support me, and ready to march into a fight (or issue curses and spells) on my behalf. Becka, Chandler, Jacqui, Jenn, Kelsey, Kira, Lindsey, Liz, Margo, Nat, Sarah,

Vinsci: y'all are my favorite bushes.

My beta readers for this book were fire. Thank you to Liz for teaching me all the right words for all the dancing things, as well as offering critical feedback on bowling—both in how the game works and its correlation with sex. I still laugh about it. Also you were right about the Nerds Gummy Clusters. Kirsten and Jackie, who came in hot with the unhinged commentary and kept me laughing. And Amanda, Chandler, Gwen, Lucy, Stephanie, and Tammy. I'm grateful!

Dani, you have been the friend, co-worker, and editor I never knew how much I needed. Thank you for wollerin' around with me in the sad and triumphant and helping build this book into something special. You're "perfect."

Chandler, you've been the best PA. Thanks for helping launch this baby out into the world. I owe you a king cake. Delaine, for always yelling the loudest about my books, thanks for shoving them into the hands of unsuspecting victims.

As always, I'm grateful to The Bookery in Cincinnati, for always putting my books on their shelves and talking about them to every customer who walks through the door. What a joy to have such a wonderful independent bookstore partner!

To my coworkers, who embraced me immediately, and taught me all the ways of gray cats, I hit the jackpot with y'all!

To my readers who have been with me from the very beginning, and those who took a chance on me when you saw me with my little table at a book event, or hit download on your e-reader, or picked up one of novels inside a book store: You're the reason I can keep doing this!

And finally, for all of my family who yell for me the loudest, especially my mom, mother-in-law, sisters, and children. I'm lucky to have all of you in my village.

This book healed my little workaholic soul. And I hope you found a little bit of lagniappe in it too!

About the Author

Jessica Booth writes small town, steamy Southern romance novels with loveable pets and book boyfriends that will make you swoon (even if they make you cry a little along the way). She has published four books and a novella.

Although she grew up in Louisiana, she now resides in Ohio with her husband, four kids, and a couple of hounds. They love to spend their time exploring parks, visiting indie bookstores, or outside digging up worms and transforming piles of sticks into castles.

Follow Jessica online:
www.jessicaboothauthor.com
www.instagram.com/jessicaboothauthor
www.tiktok.com/readbelievelove